# A Day Late

## Foothills #3

### Carrie Thorne

Published by Thorny Books

Carrie Thorne

https://carriethorne.com/

# Also by Carrie Thorne

## A Demon Hunter Romance

Six
Wildest
Changed
Echo
Fury (TBD)

## Foothills

All the Days After
The Next Day
A Day Late
A New Day
About Yesterday
280 Days (2025)
Day Dreaming (2026)
Again Tomorrow (TBD)
Days of Summer (TBD)

## A Beachside Romance Series

Chasing Forever
Running Home
Hiding Away

## Standalones

The Christmas Bet: A Double Feature Christmas Standalone.

Enjoy free books, first looks,
review team access,
and occasional hellos from Carrie?

**Let's do this: carriethorne.com/newsletter**

*This one's for my friends out there who have
stayed in a relationship longer than they should have,
no matter the reason for staying or finally leaving.
Been there, done that, bought the t-shirt. ;)*

# 1

## A-R-R-O-G-A-N-T

"Let's go, our flight leaves in an hour." Ryder's exasperated tone percolated up the stairs and stabbed straight into the crunchy center of her amygdala. Typical. Now it was her fault they were running behind. She'd been ready for two hours.

"I'll meet you in the car," Claire hollered as she shoved her spare phone charger in her purse and flew down the stairs of the hollow townhouse.

*Almost on vacation*, she reminded herself. Glad she'd gripped the banister, her boots skidded on the Saltillo tile at the foot of the stairs as she hooked a sliding U, flicked off the hall light on her way by, and entered the dry heat of the garage before he could comment on her tardiness.

The last few weeks—okay, months—had barreled by while she'd been immersed in a delirium of studying and long hours of clinicals. Ryder had been more than patient while she finished grad school. And he hadn't complained about her tendency to crash after a long day, home for a rare meal, and burning the midnight oil, night after night. In an equitable exchange, she'd shown understanding while he built a name for himself at one of the west coast's top marketing firms.

That had always been their plan. First date conversation: *I'm at a critical point in my career*, he'd said. *That's ok, I have another two years of veterinary training ahead*, she'd responded. Careers first, then each other. Once things were settled, they'd find the house with the white picket fence, get a dog, and pop out a couple of kids.

She'd turned thirty last week. Where had her twenties gone? Baby number one was supposed to be at least a year old by now.

Ryder hoisted her suitcase off the ground and tossed it in the back of the SUV. "Why did you pack so much? Foothills may be in the middle of nowhere, but the house has every-thing you could possibly need." He shot her a look with those famous heartbreaker baby blues. Infamous anyway. His dark eyebrows scowled so fiercely that she felt about as small as the toy poodle she'd neutered last week.

She resisted the urge to rip her suitcase out of his grip and take care of things herself. Help wasn't exactly appreciated when it was paired with criticism. Instead, she hopped into the passenger seat before he caught her rolling her eyes. "The forecast calls for lower-than-average temperatures and prob-able snow, so I had to buy enough winter clothes and boots for the trip, as I didn't own any, and I wasn't sure how many layers I would need. And I want to be prepared for anything. I'm not the bimbo that shows up in heels for hiking, nor the dowdy one in hiking boots at a cocktail party. I thought you liked Foothills."

Ryder clicked the button to close the rear door and started the car as he slid into the driver's seat. "When did I say that?"

*Grrr.* They rarely saw each other enough to have human conversations lately, but at least she had the decency to re-member the important ones. "A few weeks ago, when we booked the trip. I thought you wanted to move back home? You mentioned commuting to Seattle like your mom, and I was going to open my own clinic."

"Hell, no. Dr. Mallory prefers to be the bigshot fish dominating the small pond of Foothills. I suppose if you have your heart set on Washington, I could probably commute between Seattle and Phoenix. We'd see less of each other, but I'm only at the office in Phoenix one or two days a week as it is." Flying through the yellow light as he pulled out of their cookie-cutter neighborhood, he veered around a stopped bus, revealing the Phoenix airport in the distance.

Claire clutched the door handle to avoid crashing her skull into the window as he took the next corner. Whether they were running late or ahead of schedule, he'd still drive recklessly, as rules apparently didn't apply to handsome marketing consultants. Yet he maintained a clean driving record. Unlike her. Police seemed to take one look at her and decide she deserved every penny of the ticket. No idea why; she looked perfectly kind and innocent, or so she thought. Quirky, maybe, but she could pull off normal like the best of them. Almost.

As much as she loved his sleek Cayenne, it was a little unnecessary in arid Phoenix. They'd intended to drive it up to the mountains to go skiing, but they were well into winter and this was the first time they were leaving the city together.

"On the way home, let's spend a day or two in Seattle and check out the area," he suggested as he wove between cars, inches from knocking off the rear bumper of a turning sedan.

Compromise. Relationships were about give and take. Wasn't that what her mother was always telling her? Seattle was at least better than Phoenix. Despite growing up in the desert metropolis, she had no desire to stay there indefinitely.

There weren't many places she could treat both horses and dogs, but she couldn't decide between them and had spent way too much extra time in school to treat animals of all shapes and sizes. Except reptiles. Her toes curled in, and her gag reflex threatened the safety of her breakfast at the prospect of examining a python.

She could look at the rural areas outside Seattle for work. Reverse commuting. It was a thing, right? Although, more drive time for her and flight time for him would add a new level of strain to the relationship. What about when they had kids?

Her suitcase crashed and rolled across the back of the SUV as he rounded the last corner into the long-term parking lot. She envisioned the gooey mess if her toiletries busted open and soaked into her clothes, or worse, into the "gown" she'd packed for the terrifying "gala." She'd suspected his family was loaded, but that costly addition to her wardrobe had sealed it.

As soon as he shifted into park, Claire grabbed her purse and stuffed in her sweatshirt for the plane. She snatched her aforementioned-overloaded suitcase out of the back and was on the move, knowing Ryder would catch up with his long legs and impatient gait. It was a toasty seventy-two degrees now, but highs in the Cascade Foothills today looked to be in the mid-twenties.

"Think we could go ice skating?" she asked as she speed-walked to keep pace with Ryder, who passed her before they even reached the sidewalk. The pace beyond what the wobbly wheels could handle, her suitcase rocked and bounced behind her like a seabass fighting for its life. In preparation for the trip, she'd invested in the tall, lace-up Sorrel boots she'd drooled over for ages, but sadly had never had an excuse to invest in. But now her feet were roasting.

He grunted, not glancing back. "I suppose so. They usually set up a skating rink downtown. It's not Minnesota; there aren't many frozen lakes, so it's a pretty pathetic rink. There are better ones closer to civilization, where Grady played hockey, but those are indoors and don't make good tourist stops."

*Rinky-dink rink.* She snorted, sadly keeping the witty joke to herself, knowing few appreciated her infantile humor, Ryder not among them. At least she entertained herself. "Didn't you play hockey, too?"

"I participated for the requisite season. I mean, we both got roped into more extra-curriculars than we had time for thanks to Patricia's big dreams for her conversationally well-rounded children. But hockey was Grady's thing. Matched his temper." He paused mid-stride, but she wasn't paying attention and crashed into him. Grabbing her shoulders, he steadied her against him. Easing back, his expression softened. "I'm sorry I'm so irritable today. I haven't been home in years. My family drives me crazy. Well, Haley's alright, but she won't be able to make it home this time."

Up on her tiptoes, she pressed her lips to his and pulled back. "Thanks for taking me home to meet your family. I've been so distracted lately; I should have seen how much this was stressing you out."

He let out a long sigh, then took her hand and stared at their joined knuckles. "I may dread seeing my family, but I'm glad you and I will get time together."

Past the hullabaloo of the busy airport, they walked straight to the express line. Thanks to his job, he was frequently on the road and weaved through the airport with shocking familiarity. The security guards practically called him by name. Actually, they *did* call him by name. Yikes. Claire didn't even remember the last time she'd flown anywhere.

After the easiest trip through airport security that she'd ever experienced as they cruised through the express lane, inspiring jealous looks from those left in the line like engorged cows waiting to be milked, their pace finally eased when they neared the gate. "Is anyone picking us up from SeaTac?"

Accustomed to traveling for business, he didn't bother with cozy sweats like so many of the others they passed in the terminal. Dressed in designer jeans, button-up top and leather shoes, he would look out of place if they were to fly coach.

Not that he would ever stoop so low. "No. I booked a rental so we can have our own car."

"Oh. Ok. Are they planning anything special tonight to welcome you home?" For all his hesitation, she knew he wasn't *estranged* from his family. He called his mother every Monday after work. As a renowned neurosurgeon, his mother must be interesting, and his stepfather owned a logging company which dominated half the Cascades. The conversation shouldn't be dull at least.

Needless to say, Claire was more than a little nervous about meeting his wealthy family. They came from such different backgrounds. Different presents, really. Her parents and brothers lived in the Phoenix area and saw each other often, at least once a month, for family dinners.

"We'll be there for their annual winter gala, but otherwise, no."

"First-class passengers to Seattle are welcome to begin boarding at this time," a soothing voice announced over the loudspeaker as they approached the gate. She followed Ryder down the ramp and settled into their front-row seats.

Maybe she ought to travel with him more often. This first-class thing was pretty great. Free drinks served before they even took off—although her stomach was too nervous to consider imbibing—easy access to the bathroom, and plenty of legroom. Cuddled up in the plush leather seat, she watched the flight attendants gossiping as they secured for takeoff.

As the plane taxied down the runway, Ryder linked his hand with hers. Land whizzed by outside, the engine stirring a deep rumbling as they accelerated. Looking past Ryder, she watched as they overcame gravity and rose above the city.

"You know, if you like the Seattle area, we could look for houses on the water. My mother would be able to find us the best private schools, for when the day comes. What do you think?" He kissed the back of her hand with their fingers still joined.

"Sure, let's look into it." Things were already looking up. No work, no school, only quality time together, and maybe indulge in that sex thing they used to enjoy. Neither had even been interested in eons, with how hectic things had been. "Think we could find something with a large enough lot so we can have dogs, and maybe even chickens? We could board horses. I don't need a cow."

Ryder downed the last of his whiskey with a gulp, grimacing as the large swallow worked its way down. "A cow? Chickens? Did you grow up with farm animals in Phoenix?"

Easing her hand away, Claire snagged the crossword puzzle out of the seatback pocket. "No."

"We could get a dog. There are excellent breeders in the area."

"Sure." She moved her attention to the crossword. *Full of oneself*, eight letters, starts with A. Ha, got that one. A-R-R-O-G-A-N-T.

"You're catching on." Grady grinned at Sophie, skating backward in front of her as she slid along the ice.

When Foothills' annual rink had been set up, Tattling Pippa had let it slip that Grady had played hockey since he was old enough to put on skates. Having played regularly until moving home to Foothills two years ago, Grady spent as many winter lunch breaks as he could manage on the ice.

Sophie's arms flailed, but Grady gently reminded her to look ahead rather than at her feet. Her fiancé was working nights as the newest member of the Foothills Police Department and hadn't gotten around to taking her out. Thus, Sophie had strong-armed Grady into being her skating instructor. Not that he minded.

Despite his heart shattering when Sophie chose Asher over him, Grady and Sophie had become good friends. Not that he hadn't been a dick about it in the beginning. And, okay, shattered was probably too strong of a word.

Sophie was gorgeous, intelligent, and funny, but the spark she shared with Asher told Grady everything he needed to know. If it hadn't been for Asher showing up when he did, she probably would have settled for him. Time and again, he'd been the guy women had considered settling for, yet he never seemed to make that final cut.

Asher and he had been roommates, until a few weeks ago, and had quickly learned the joy of messing with each other. Just for fun. Grady reached for Sophie's hand and slid to a stop. He pulled his phone from his pocket and plastered a friendly peck on her cheek, the mountains gleaming in the freezing sun behind them. Smiling for the camera, her nose scrunched at his obvious Asher-focused-taunt. He snapped the selfie and sent it to Asher, who was sleeping off last night's shift at home.

Freya waved from the side as she removed her skates, done for the day. "Give him a break. At least skip the kiss."

His phone buzzed with a response from Asher. A flip-off emoji. Huh, he hadn't seen that one before. Smirking, he hollered to Freya, "You didn't tell him you were coming with us, did you? I'm trying to make him jealous so he'll dream about me necking with his woman."

Sophie rolled her eyes. "I don't think he has any jealousy issues, but Freya has been trying to drag me out all winter, and he knows she wouldn't miss my wobbly ankles and inevitable wipeouts."

A familiar sensation fluttered in his chest as Sophie read the text that buzzed in on her phone. No doubt about who sent the text and the gist of it, based on the heat flaming over her cheeks. Asher may not have jealousy issues, but Grady did. At least, not about Sophie anymore, but... yeah, he was so far off-track from where he had envisioned himself at this point in life.

He'd accepted that Sophie wasn't the one for him. All his friends were deliriously happily in love, and happily-ever-after hadn't been on any of their radars. Well, Pippa had been planning to marry Lincoln since kindergarten, but Asher had been the epitome of irresponsible bachelor, until Sophie had entered his life. Zane and Freya had been set on keeping things casual, until they accidentally eloped last summer.

Not that he wanted to avoid his friends. They were awesome. Seriously, they'd changed his life in such a good way. A year ago? He was a festering jackass. Since he'd been roped into the crew, having an almost foreign, unyielding support? Incredible. His infamous temper was almost nonexistent these days.

Dammit. He was handsome, articulate, financially stable, and, pretentious as it may sound, he was good at *everything*. Further supporting the egomaniac he'd been raised to be, he knew he had poetic, ocean blue eyes, untamable surfer blond hair that people paid a fortune for—that he came by naturally—and a great body, if he said so himself.

Still, it wasn't enough. In an effort to build flawless human beings out of her offspring, his mother had enrolled her children in every extracurricular activity under the sun. Hockey, football, baseball, riding, martial arts, piano, debate. He'd hated debate, so why had he gone with lawyer?

Sophie dropped his hand and motioned to the exit. "I need to head out. You coming over Saturday?"

"Yeah, sounds great." Grady blinked away the pity-party-for-one that was hammering in his thick skull. "That reminds me. My parent's annual gala is on the twentieth. Patricia said I could invite a few guests. Apparently, now that I am thirty and a successful attorney, I'm allowed to have an opinion. I wasn't planning to torture you guys with it, but now that it's approaching, I think I'd enjoy seeing Asher and Zane suffering with me in penguin suits. You guys in?" He skated to the side and told Freya and Sophie the details of the annual bore-fest, in which his mother and stepfather got dolled up in their fanciest attire and invited their snootiest friends for a fancy-ass party so she could show off her accomplishments.

Freya grinned, her eyes twinkling. "Love it. We'll be there. Zane will hate it, but I'll wear something slinky and he'll give in. Asher won't be pleased, but he'll go. Pippa will be on board, of course."

As he escorted Sophie to the exit, although she was much more capable on skates than she'd been an hour ago, she asked. "Are you heading back to work?"

He glanced at his watch. "My cases are wrapped up for the week, so I'm going to run a few drills, then I'll head over to Black Op."

They paused, their mirrored expressions drooping into pity, as tended to happen when he accidentally let himself look lonely. Watching his two very taken, very committed friends walk away, he skated to the side to grab a puck and stick to burn off... whatever the hell was rotting his soul.

Grady dribbled a few quick plays, letting the adrenaline surge as the thrill of the game flooded him. Players skating full speed at him to take the puck, checking them as he passed. A Mallory never got into fights, unless it was in the spirit of the game, then it was not only permitted, but encouraged. Naturally, he'd taken to hockey like a salmon to the stream. Feet moving, eyes on the goal, he ran a one-man scrimmage. Skates scraping the hard surface under his feet, that crisp smell of the ice bringing him into the moment, he almost forgot where he was.

Until he saw her.

# 2

## F-O-R-T-U-I-T-O-U-S

An icy blast of wind blew Claire's hair into her face. Blinded, choking, she coughed the *I've-been-traveling*, limp brown locks out of her mouth. Not auburn or chestnut or even chocolate, just brown. Not wavy or straight, more of an awkward mix that required a plethora of products and tempering that she rarely bothered with.

Now that she'd directed her pitiful mop to blow with the wind, she inhaled deeply to get a feel for the local air. Frozen moisture invaded painfully into her nares, her first whiff of the Pacific Northwest threatening to freeze her turbinates. Most animals that were adapted to the cold wouldn't have this issue, but humans were tool makers. Did REI sell nose warmers? She'd seen pictures of icicles that had grown into beards and pictured the same happening to her nasal mucosa.

Frigid air pierced her pores. She pulled her coat tighter, wondering how ridiculous she would look if she hid her face and waited for the wind to stop. A balmy thirty degrees Fahrenheit in Seattle today, according to their pilot anyway, but her app told her it would be a good ten degrees colder in the Cascade Foothills... where they would be. She trotted to catch up to Ryder.

Had she been thinking, she'd have her gloves on already. Rooky mistake. She was due for a new adventure, but did it have to be so painful?

Her fingers were frozen to the handle of her suitcase as she dragged it behind her. To think, she'd worried the wool sweater and down coat would be excessive. Even her toes were numb despite her insulated boots. Good thing his family didn't live in Minnesota. She didn't even want to think about what sub-zero temperatures might feel like. And that whole wind-chill thing? She was beginning to understand what that meant.

As usual, Ryder hadn't skimped. The rental car was toasty and waiting for them. A sleek red sportscar that screamed, *Look at me.* Ryder slid into the driver's seat to rev the engine while she packed away her suitcase and closed the trunk.

She jumped into the passenger seat and reached across to Ryder's hand to warm the icicles she used to call fingers. He'd been smart and had worn gloves on the walk to the rental car. "Shit, your hand is freezing." He winced and pulled his hand away. "Here," he offered as he turned on her seat heater. "Sit on your hands for a bit. You'll warm up in no time."

A winch seemed to pull tighter and tighter over Claire's head the closer they got to Foothills. What if his family didn't like her? Although she could maintain polite and normal and presentable for a short time, she could be a bit offbeat. Not everyone appreciated her humor.

Not that she felt inferior, but, dammit, she'd grown up calculating the grocery bill as they shopped. They weren't poor, exactly, and things hadn't been so tight that they hadn't been able to go on family trips, but they were careful. Her dad worked as a plumber since before she was born. Once her mom finished grad school to get her promotion at the state, things were more comfortable. However, they wouldn't ever have dreamed of hiring "staff" like Ryder had grown up with.

They would stay in the guest wing. Wing. Huh. She'd never been in a house with "wings." He didn't think they had much staff these days, just a cook, housekeeper, cleaning staff, landscaper, and stablemaster. Yes, stablemaster. Claire had seen plenty of stables in her training, but to imagine his family had a regular *stablemaster*... that really increased the intimidation factor.

Ryder hated to ride, but his family had always kept horses. Apparently, all the Mallory family had ridden competitively when they were younger. From the moment they booked the trip, Claire hinted that he ought to take her out on a trail ride. When hinting got her nowhere, she resorted to begging. The night before they'd left, Ryder finally agreed it might be fun.

Claire got to choose one activity each year. Her mother would have preferred ballet, but she was not nearly coordinated enough for any sort of formal dance. Anything pertaining to horses had been Claire's favorite.

"Hey, Claire, I should have mentioned something sooner. I have a phone meeting in half an hour, and we won't make it to the house in time. Do you want to roam the shops while I make the call from the car?" He shot her a winning smile. That smile had won her over when they'd started seeing each other.

Well, they never formally traversed the dating stage of a relationship. Neither of their schedules allowed for that. Roommates-with-benefits was as good of a place to start as any. Regardless, he knew it was a lady-killer smile and used it often, so it wasn't nearly as effective as it had been at the start.

She guessed that's how it went. After enough time with a person, the mystery waned. Her parents certainly had no mystery left in their relationship. Hell, the whole family knew about her father's bowel habits. Too many over-sharers in the Dabney family. Still, her parents loved each other. Plenty of nagging and griping, the occasional raised voice, and plenty of details she didn't want to know about, yet somehow did.

"Sure. Let's head to that skating rink you mentioned, then you can join me as soon as the meeting's over and teach me some fancy moves." Claire grinned, imagining her inner figure skater coming to life.

He shrugged. "Maybe."

"I thought you reserved vacation time for the whole trip?" As much as she'd known he couldn't disconnect, she'd been foolishly optimistic. With a protracted breath, she closed her eyes and awaited the inevitable response. Was she alone in believing that this trip was the last hope they had for making this work? Or was Ryder worried, too, realizing that this should be easier? At the rate things were going, she was beginning to realize that he wasn't grasping the gravity of the trip.

"I did. I am. But, if I get this contract sealed, I might land that promotion and the flexibility to live anywhere." Again, that ridiculous grin with deep dimples, designed to charm the pants off many a woman before she came around. And capped it off with that twinkle in his eye that said he really meant it.

The tight band around her skull constricted tighter. Resisting the urge to rub her temples, refusing to play the martyr, she watched out the window as evidence of civilization came into view. Farmhouses. Sheep, goats, horses, and cows. Ryder had put her name on the rental agreement for the car, so while he was tucked away in meetings, she could sneak away to see the sights.

Foothills proper was as adorable as she had imagined. Livelier and more three dimensional than compared to the internet street-view tour she'd played with last night, it buzzed with humanity. They drove passed a classically old-fashioned hardware store, a casual diner, a hole-in-the-wall pub, a surprisingly high-end clothing boutique, and a hopping brewhouse with an inviting year-round outdoor dining setup. She turned her head away, so Ryder didn't see her laughing at her own joke. *Hopping* brewhouse. Ha. She was hilarious.

He hooked the next right and pulled into the skating rink. Two women were chatting as they climbed into their car and pulled away. The lot was otherwise empty aside from a black SUV. Ahead, in front of a wedding-style windowed tent that must hold the skating rink, a blue shanty was decked out with signs for ice skate rentals, family night promos, and lunch date specials. Adorable.

Ryder paused heavily as he shifted out of gear. "I shouldn't be more than thirty minutes. Why don't you go rent some gear, and I'll meet you out there?"

Nodding with a blatantly phony smile, Claire eased out of the car. She shouldn't judge; he was trying. And his job meant the world to him. She'd been too busy for him for months. Her mother would tell her she should give him time to catch up.

Claire pulled on her knit cap and inhaled a crisp breath of air before heading into the shanty. As jolly as Santa, but not nearly so jellied, the cashier passed across scuffed white skates that looked serviceable, albeit not as glamorous as she had pictured. With a shrug and a smile, Claire accepted the well-loved skates. Glamor wasn't her thing, anyway.

The scent of ice, fresh from the freezer, teased at her nose as she strolled inside. Whizzing past, back and forth on the ice like a devil chased at his heels, the hockey player didn't seem to notice he was going to have to share soon.

If all went well, he wouldn't laugh at her too much when she inevitably biffed it.

Out of the corner of his eye, he saw a gorgeous brunette, sleek hair tucked adorably into a knit cap, cautiously stepping out onto the ice. Grinding to a halt, Grady ceased his drills. Quitting time anyway.

Great legs, long and athletic in dark denim, were about the only thing not encased in puffball, as she was so heavily bundled with a parka and thick gloves. The instant her skate hit the ice, she braced herself against the wall. Warily, she pulled her other foot onto the ice.

And that was it.

Feet slipping chaotically forward and back, threatening splits or a backward spill, she lurched and latched tighter onto the side. She gripped the half-wall that surrounded the rink, her feet oscillating between wiggling and slipping underneath her as she tried to get her balance.

Sensing disaster ready to strike, he scooped the puck onto his stick, wincing as she seemed to debate attempting to venture away from her safety net.

As she dared to loosen her grip on the wall, her feet flew out from under her, and she crashed and fell flat on her ass.

He flicked the puck into his hand and skated toward her. "You ok?"

Cheeks rosy, either from the cold or embarrassment, she chortled with a rich belly laugh and shook her head in delight. "Peachy keen. My butt's numb, but I remain unharmed. Slippery stuff, isn't it?"

Grady laughed right along with her, immediately enchanted by her self-effacing humor. "That it is. Need a hand?" he offered as he set the hockey stick and puck on the lip of the half-wall.

Wiggling her legs, setting her thickly gloved hands on the ice, she scrunched her face in complex calculation. "Actually, yes. Thanks." She slid her gloves off and tossed them over the wall, pitching her coat after them.

Apparently feeling more agile without the bulk, she extended her hands up to him. Awfully trusting in response to an overly helpful hockey player on an empty rink. Her nails were trimmed short, but not chewed to the nubs like Sophie's. Her sweater was a rough wool, practical but trendy.

He reached for her hands, and for the first time, she looked at him—like, right at him. Into him. Dancing with amusement and shock, the prettiest set of hazel eyes he'd ever seen locked onto his and sent an arrow straight into his soul. Yeah, that's right, he said soul. His buddies would mock him to no end if they heard it, but he didn't care. All those stupid sonnets and love songs and romantic nonsense his friends had spouted all blossomed in his head like a victory garden on steroids.

Tongue tied, he linked his hands with hers. As electric as her gaze, their interlocked fingers sent shocks rocketing through him, fingertips to toes to the tips of his hair. Straight into the aforementioned soul. The sensation wasn't painful like touching an electric fence, but equally exhilarating as the hum vibrated over his skin.

Bracing his skates to support them both, Grady deftly pulled her to her feet. As her skates wobbled, she almost biffed it again. Catching her before she could slip, he held her close to keep her steady.

Okay, maybe he was an ass, but the complete faith she granted him, her body pressed tight against his... damn, it had been way too long since he'd even remotely been this close with a woman that wasn't off the market.

Shit. She probably was. They were always taken. He'd developed a complex about it. Or did he aim for women that were unavailable, or didn't want him back?

Clinging to his shoulders with an iron grip, she redirected her gaze from her wobbly skates and looked up at him again. Eyes locked onto his, she worked her rosy, plump lower lip between her teeth. That spectacular zing shot through him again—and he suspected her too, as she was suddenly off balance again. Feet wavering, she shrieked and giggled with a throaty laugh as she attempted to steady herself.

He wrapped his arm around her waist, knowing she was going to fall again at the rate she was going. Before he could lock his grip, her feet slid out from under her and pulled them both down to the ice. With a thud against the ice that jarred his already unsteady brain, he landed on his back... with her sprawled on top of him.

She managed to apologize, but it was barely comprehensible through her hysterical laughter.

Lying on the freezing ground, a gorgeous stranger clinging to him with impressively strong and wiry limbs, Grady found himself lost in hysterics right along with her, his own belly laugh unfamiliar and... altering. She tried to pull herself off of him, but slipped and narrowly missed jabbing her knee into his groin. He reached out to block her knee and found his hand clutched around her thigh.

"Sorry," she managed as she calmed her giggle fit. She rolled off him and dropped flat on her back at his side, their feet still entangled.

Grady turned his head and grinned over at her. "I may be going out on a limb here, but is this your first time on the ice?"

Again, there went the rich, honest giggle. "Yes. Again, I'm so, so sorry. I had visions of gracefully spinning pirouettes around the rink. Not sure why, as I can't manage a pirouette on land. I hope I haven't chipped my ischial tuberosity." She winced as she pushed herself up to a sitting position and gazed wistfully around the rink, those mysterious eyes-of-many-colors sparkling in amusement.

He sat up on his elbows and watched, fascinated, as she seemed totally at ease with her awkwardness. Gorgeous, good sense of humor, intelligent, witty... hell, she was absolutely taken. That's the way this worked. He was interested. She was unavailable.

And for the first time in documented history, his infamous eloquence failed him. Okay, probably not the first time, but between his mother and his high school guidance counselor, he'd been forced into studying law because it would be cruel to deprive the world of his silver tongue. And now, the most appealing woman he'd ever seen had her legs wrapped around him, and he was utterly speechless. "So... what brings you to Foothills?" he inquired, terrified to move, lest she stop touching him.

At his question, she scowled. "It's... complicated."

Great. Complicated. It always was. Why couldn't he be a woman's complication for once?

On that note, he untangled their limbs and skates and stood up. She checked her hands and feet on the slick surface, debating how to stand up. He extended his hand and coached her through it. "Let's try this again."

She took his hands, and that electric shock zapped through him again, no less stirring. As he pulled her to stand, he wrapped both arms securely around her waist. Fuck, she fit against him like she was built to stand and hug him all day.

And he was officially a sap.

Her feet wiggled, and she looked about to crash again.

"Easy there. Lock your ankles and hold your feet still. Don't move yet."

That laugh resonated over him. "I'm trying. Okay. Ankles locked. I'm pretending these are heels instead of skates, if you think that might help?" She was staring at her feet as if commanding them to obey.

"I guess I couldn't say if that strategy works, as I've never worn heels." He grinned with the corner of his mouth, hoping to hear that laugh again.

She didn't disappoint. With a delicious giggle, she held tighter, so the reaction wouldn't destabilize her precarious posture. Still looking down at their feet, she giggled again. "I think you would have to special order high heels to fit those big feet in."

All the air rushed from his lungs... and the blood rushed south, and his chest vibrated with a desperately horny laugh. "Wow. You went there, didn't you?"

A snorty chortle chirped from her lips as she wiggled against him, clinging and risking taking them both crashing to the ground again. "Dammit, you know what I mean."

"I hope so."

Calming herself enough to look him in the eye, she chewed that lip again. "Well, you didn't drop me and skate away in horror, so that's a plus. Not everyone appreciates my dopey humor."

"My gloves are big too, if you were wondering." He winked.

"Good thing we don't know each other, or I suspect you'd never let me live this down." She grinned, flushed as she calmed the giggle fit.

"Yeah, good thing," he murmured, an ache brewing deep in his belly. "Anyway, it's a good ten feet back to the wall. Or do you think you're up to trying a lap?"

"I'm sure you don't have time to—"

"I've got time." Shit, he probably sounded as desperate as he was. One lap. And he could cling to remembering the thrill of her in his arms for the rest of eternity. Or convince her to ditch that complication. He really was an ass. A pathetically sentimental ass.

"Okay. What do I do?"

"You haven't fallen again, right?"

"That's because you're holding onto me."

"You're still on your feet because you're not worrying about falling."

"Hmm. Distraction. I like it."

Gliding backward, holding her tight against him, he pulled her along.

"Ooo," she squeaked, full grin in place. "I'm skating."

"Getting there," he crooned. He felt like he was encouraging a young foal on its first steps. "Now, we're going to move a few inches. Look up at me." Dumb idea. What color were those eyes? Brown or green or gray? Hazel didn't quite capture it.

Her smile faltered, her lip tugged between her teeth again as she watched him, humor fading.

"See? It's easier if you look up and don't think about what you're doing. It's like sex, natural and exhilarating once you get the rhythm."

That full-bodied, rolling laugh warmed him to the core. Distracted, she didn't seem to notice they were nearly halfway around the lap. He grinned and gestured to their feet with his eyes, holding her tight so she wouldn't slip when she looked down.

"Hey, I'm really skating," she beamed. Her feet wobbled a little, but she brought her eyes back to his and steadied herself again.

As they relaxed and she seemed to catch on, he loosened his grip and moved to her side. At the loss of stability, he could sense her impending panic. "Define complicated."

Her back straightened and her gaze shifted to the far wall of the rink. At least she wasn't thinking about falling. "Complicated isn't the right word, I guess. I'm in one of those weird transitional moments in life, and I'm not sure I'm on the right track. It's like I can see light at the end of the tunnel, but did I turn down the right tunnel?"

"That's profound. I'm in a similar jam myself. I assumed forty would be the midlife crisis birthday, but turning thirty is kicking my ass. And I can't help but berate myself for still feeling like a stupid kid when I was supposed to be a grownup by now." Her hand relaxed in his and they synchronously glided around the rink.

"Exactly. By my thirtieth birthday, I was supposed to be married with at least one kid and established in my career. The career thing is fine. I mean, I started a little later than I'd planned, but I'm there. It's the other parts that aren't going according to schedule."

"I've got a friend that has had her life mapped out since she was in elementary school and hasn't strayed from it yet. I don't know how she keeps it all rolling. Life is riddled with complications."

"You might be right. I suppose it's not too late to take a different tunnel."

"Or even take the scenic route."

They neared the exit. She began to pull away, but he didn't want it to end. Now or ever. He wasn't waiting around until it was too late this time. "I know you're probably just in town visiting, but while you're here, if you want to—"

"I can't. I..." she interrupted as she made for the exit. Steadier now, she stepped off the ice. "I'm such a jerk. I shouldn't have... I'm with someone." The wave of guilt wafting off her was palpable.

"Of course. I didn't... I mean... You're gorgeous and funny, and I did want to ask you out, but I get it. I hope everything works out for you." And, as usual, he was too late.

"Thanks for the rescue." Her lusciously pink lips turned up in a half smile, her eyebrows pulled together in consternation. She glanced back to the ice like she wanted to say something else, but wouldn't. "Bye."

Grady watched as the woman of his dreams walked away on wobbly legs. Out of his reach, as usual. Story of his life.

# 3

## L-E-A-P-O-F-F-A-I-T-H

Claire tucked her coat under her arm, running a minimum hundred-point-four degrees after her skating lesson. As she neared the impractical car, she found Ryder still parked, engine running to stay warm, phone to his ear, hand gesturing madly, engrossed in a heated debate. She knew she hadn't been gone long enough, but she couldn't stay at the rink any longer. With every second spent with her skating partner, she felt herself ripping apart at the seams.

Although she had completely humiliated herself, she'd had a great time doing so. She couldn't remember the last time she'd laughed so hard. Hell, her abs already ached and would for days.

She rolled her eyes at herself. Always greener pastures, right? She had a foundation with Ryder. If this week went well, and they made up for the last few months of the widening crevasse that had grown between them, she'd be glad she stuck with him. Ryder was everything she wanted: smart, handsome, successful. When they'd met, she could swear he had a sense of humor and had been doting. Hadn't he?

It was natural to have crushes on attractive men, despite being in a long-term relationship, right? Her mom was certain that Ryder was planning to pop the question on the trip. That would be great. Next step. He probably had the ring in his suitcase. He'd want to make a big fuss with flowers and champagne, down on one knee.

Lucky thing she wouldn't have to see her sexy hockey player again. She'd avoid the skating rink, and she'd be gone soon. No harm, no foul. A good reminder that life wasn't a romance novel.

She tossed her coat in the backseat, grabbed her book, and hopped in the passenger seat next to Ryder. Only a minute or two passed before she realized she was holding her book upside down. Right about the time she saw her handsome stranger walking out to the shiny black Forerunner parked a few spaces away in the otherwise empty lot.

Grateful the windows of the rental car were tinted, she watched as he tossed his skates into the back. Rather violently, actually. After slamming the driver's door behind him, he ran a hand through his unruly blond hair before smacking his forehead into the steering wheel.

A loopy grin took over her expression. She couldn't help but feel chills, fabulous jitters of excitement, that he was as thrown by their meeting as she was.

"What happened to the swimsuit theme I'd submitted? He's approaching this all wrong." Ryder's voice edged at her raw nerves.

Now or never. Fate was a nasty bitch, and she refused to ruin something magical for a chance at rekindling what was a terrible relationship to begin with.

Remember the old Claire? The one who didn't accept a B-minus in Anatomy and Physiology, sophomore year of college? The Claire who socked Jimmy Porter in the nose when he grabbed her ass at junior prom? Or the Claire that aced her first round of clinicals despite the flu, a sprained ankle, and a broken wrist, all in one semester?

Claire Dabney let nothing get in the way of what she wanted. She rotated away from Ryder and opened the car door. Ready to throw out the book and chase him down, she looked around and realized he was gone.

The thundering in her chest lurched, the adrenaline hammering over her like the August summer sun on her paint-chipped sedan. She released the door handle and lowered back into her seat. Overthinking bit her in the ass. Nothing new there.

Maybe fate was telling her something after all. Appreciate what you've got, as anything as miraculous as you think you may have experienced—when you're tired and burned out—is fleeting and will fizzle out as fast as a meteor in the sky. Despite her best efforts to muster a poker face, the disappointment was just too deep, and her face drooped like a candle set too close to a fire, her tear ducts leaking hot acid.

Think about something else. Anything. Hip replacement, neutering, gangrenous splinters...

Not working.

She opened her book.

Ryder's meeting didn't last too much longer, thank goodness. Within ten minutes of glaring at her stupid romance novel with the stupid happy couple that traveled through time to find each other, Ryder was scheduling a follow-up call for tomorrow and hanging up. Fiction. The book was a trivial piece of fiction that provided a nice distraction on the flight up. Nothing more. People didn't find that sort of connection. Why did people read this tripe?

"Have a good time?" Ryder asked her as he drove out of the parking lot.

Scrunching her eyebrows together, Claire considered her response. "I'm a terrible skater."

"I could have told you that." Chuckling, Ryder drove through the rest of the lovely little town toward the mountains. Really lovely. But she suspected it would be nothing more than the annual visits to the sweet little town at a maximum, even if they moved to Seattle.

She blinked back the acid in her eyes and responded in her clearest voice. "Hey, I'd never skated before. You never know, maybe I was gifted at it but had never had the chance to find out." Not likely, but worth dreaming.

"Babe, you can barely dance." There were those irritating dimples.

"I'm not that bad of a dancer. I'm agile and graceful. Hey, I can reduce an equine rectal prolapse with my eyes closed. How many people do you know who can say that?" Claire found her smile, flashing him a shit-eating grin. Apparently, making him uncomfortable was a great way to improve her mood.

Flying around an icy looking corner, he turned off the main road onto a pristinely smooth driveway. "I don't know what that is, but it sounds disgusting. Please don't say anything like that in front of my parents."

Claire ignored the comment and looked around. How could he not love Foothills? The long driveway was flanked with massive evergreen trees, branches hanging low, and heavily frosted, winterized maples created a mystical canopy overhead.

Then the house came into view. *Holy shit, Claire, you're in way over your head.* Her eyes gaped open, and her tongue grew thick and dry and a little itchy, like she'd been chewing on alfalfa all afternoon. This was not the northwest ranch she'd imagined when he described his logging mogul stepfather and his mother's fondness for horses.

Painted immaculately snow white with black trim and a black roof, the house stood grandly over the massive estate. Even the entrance was intimidating. Topiary-trimmed hedges flanked a solid black wooden door, and the doorstep was wide enough to fit her entire family. Ryder parked the flashy car and hopped out. Claire followed along behind, remaining as unobtrusive as possible. "Shouldn't we get the bags?" she whispered behind him.

"I'll get them later. Let's head inside. I need a drink."

Before they reached the front door, it swung wide open. An ancient woman with thick gray hair pulled back in a neat ponytail, dressed in black jeans and a purple cable-knit sweater, greeted them. Claire hoped this was his mother, but wasn't optimistic at this point. And she looked nothing like him. "Ryder, it's about time. Your flight landed hours ago."

"Hattie. It's good to see you." He smiled and accepted the woman's warm hug.

"Aren't you going to introduce me to our guest?" Hattie smiled widely and peered around Ryder to get a good look at Claire.

With a deep breath, pasting on her friendliest expression, Claire bravely stepped forward. This woman was approachable and clearly *not* his mother. "Hi. I'm Claire."

Before she knew what hit her, rather than taking her offered hand for a casual greeting, the woman dragged her into in a firm embrace. "Welcome, Claire. I'm glad Ryder found you. You're just the sweetest thing, aren't you? Come on in, let's get you settled. You must be worn out after a long day of traveling." The woman rattled away, not leaving room for awkward silence as Claire struggled to catch her balance. "I'm Hattie. Most would consider me the housekeeper, but I'm a woman-of-all-trades. I keep things running around here and am your point of contact for anything you might need or want. Mostly, I keep these boys in line." She winked at Claire behind Ryder's back. She pulled back and squeezed Claire's hand, face scrunched in an eager grin as she guided Claire into the house.

"Thank you, Hattie. I'd love to freshen up."

Inside, Claire's intimidation fired right back up again at the sight of the imposing foyer. Expansive white tile floor covered the area, looking remarkably similar to the ice she'd biffed it on earlier. Beyond the foyer, a stately parlor with white carpeting and white sofas and white pillows and white blankets overlooked the mountains through a mammoth wall of invisibly clean windows. That window was the real gem of the house, the one appeal she'd found so far. With its inspiring view of the snowcapped Cascades, she felt like an eagle catching an updraft, soaring from peak to peak. Despite the roaring fire inside the grand fireplace, and the stack of white and cream-colored knit blankets rolled and artfully displayed in a basket under the sofa table, the room remained cold and unwelcoming.

Hattie led them up the stairs on the left and down a long, wide hallway until they reached the suite on the end. "This is the blue room. Make yourself at home. Dinner is in an hour." Hattie squeezed her hand again, as if sensing her complete lack of ease, and left her alone with Ryder.

Ryder went straight for one of the facing leather chairs in the sitting room and plopped his feet onto the wagon-wheel coffee table in the middle, groaning and looking markedly unrelaxed as he settled in for a long vacation. Off to the right, there was a robin's egg blue wall with a shaggy cow picture hanging in the center, and through a set of French doors on the left, was a bedroom that could be featured in a magazine. Expensive-looking tree-stump side-tables surrounded the rustic iron bedframe, and a blue and white railroad striped duvet capped off the designer look.

Claire turned toward Ryder, hoping they could sit and veg before meeting his parents. Her limbs were tingling with too many nerves to even attempt the feat at the moment. If they were half as intimidating as the house, she'd never fit in. In the time she'd taken to scope out their suite, he'd poured himself a glass of whiskey and was back in his chair. "Hey, Claire. Why don't you go freshen up a bit, get changed, and we'll head down for dinner? Sounds like Patricia will be home from work soon."

"I guess I don't normally 'dress for dinner.' Is this a formal thing?" She cringed, imagining having to *dress for dinner* each night that she was here. Despite her over-packed suitcase, she hadn't exactly planned for multiple outfit changes each day.

He rolled his eyes and chuckled. Stupid dimples again. "No. Washingtonians don't 'dress for dinner' as a general rule. Your butt's wet from the ice."

"Oh. Ok." Ribs heavy from exhaustion, Claire headed into the bathroom to freshen up, as directed. By the time she got back, she found Ryder rolling in with their suitcases. Whether or not this was a dressy affair, she felt she ought to step it up a bit. She pulled on a black plaid skirt over cable-knit tights, adding knee-high boots and a rose-colored sweater. Close enough.

As she walked out of the bedroom, Ryder's dimples softened. "Hey. Thanks again for doing this."

"What?"

"Coming up to meet my family. It's been way too long since I've been home."

"Of course."

He reached out and took her hands, pulling her against him. Bracing one hand on each of her cheeks, he kissed her slow and easy. "It's been a long haul for us both. I don't know what I was thinking, bringing you here for our first real vacation and not having wrapped up the vodka campaign first. Next time, let's go someplace we can relax and be ourselves."

Nodding sadly, she feigned a smile, wishing she could remember what that meant. Had she ever seen Ryder *relax*?

G rady dashed up the left stairs to the guest suites and let himself in the first door on the right. Not his childhood bedroom, as that had been converted into a craft room years ago. Not that anyone around here crafted, so the room was largely an experiment in dust collecting. If dust were allowed in this house.

Now that he was an adult, he was to stay in one of the larger guest quarters. If he ever found a wife, it would be more suiting. So said his mother.

He was assigned to the green room. And it was very green. Olive green area rug, lime green modern art on the wall, forest green sheets, drab green towels. It was rather tempting to call the army to see if they wanted any ideas for a new camo design, although some of these shades did not exist in nature. Some would call it on-trend. He called it nauseating.

Not that he was complaining. He was glad to have a roof over his head. After their rental house burned down a few weeks ago, Asher moved in with Sophie. Not much had been Asher's anyway, as he'd already been transitioning to Sophie's bit by bit. Grady, however, had been forced to start over, down to the socks and shampoo.

From the soot-covered shell of a house, not much had been salvageable. Most of his belongings had been so saturated with smoke, they would never have come clean, anyway. Right away, he'd been forced to reinvest in personal essentials. The rest, furniture and other odds-and-ends, could wait until he found his own place.

It had been four exceedingly long weeks at his mother and stepfather's house. His own father had passed away before he was old enough to remember. Theoretically, Patricia was a romantic, as she'd kept his name, not changing when she married his half-sister Haley's father, nor when she married Bill. But Grady knew it was because she liked the sound of Dr. Mallory, or, more importantly, it was the name she was already published under. Either way, as much as Patricia drove him nuts, she usually meant well and took pride in her children.

She'd married her second husband before Grady had even learned to walk. He'd been decent. And had given Grady and Ryder a sister, who had immediately steadied things. But when Grady was in high school, they divorced, and Haley moved with her dad to California. Husband number three wasn't so bad, but by the time Bill Stellan came around, Grady had been nearly grown. So, the monstrosity of a house wasn't exactly *home*.

Since he'd left for college, immediately after graduating from high school, right on schedule as expected, he visited as infrequently as possible. Somehow, he'd forgotten how pretentious they were. He'd grown up with Hattie, initially their au pair, and now the woman-of-all-trades, he supposed, but the rest of the staff were all new.

After staying at Black Op for as long as humanly possible, Grady hoped to hell he was late for dinner, but Hattie had waved at him on her way out and announced that he had half an hour to unwind before dinner. More, he was hoping to forget the woman who had broken his heart in less than half an hour's time. He pulled a fresh pair of jeans from his underwhelming closet and changed out of his wet-butt jeans—thanks to his mystery woman—and into a dry pair. Not much to choose from, he snagged a fresh shirt as well. Thanks to the fire, he had about a week's worth of clothes to his name, and would need to shop again when the season changed.

Why was he so messed up about a woman he hardly knew? Well, she was among many that he felt something for that was already spoken for. But there was something different about her.

*Knock it off. You're just in a self-pitying jag because your life sucks right now.*

His mother would no doubt prefer he changed into nice slacks, and possibly a button-up, rather than the t-shirt and jeans. At some point, she'd figure out he didn't care for her suggestions.

Burned out from the long day, he stretched out on the sage green couch, plopping feet up on the spruce green throw pillow. Why did he enjoy the act so much, knowing his mother would cringe if she caught him tarnishing the satin with his bare feet? *Ha*, he answered his own question. Speak of the devil. He heard a rapid knock at the door.

Impatient, as always, she didn't wait for his response. Quick as a frog's tongue, he pulled his feet from the pillow before he was caught. Not worth the argument while he was stuck under her roof.

Must be a clinic day; her unnatural platinum hair graced the tops of her shoulders and she was decked out in unwrinkled black slacks and a red silk top, impressive considering the ten-hour day and two-hour commute. She looked almost approachable on surgery days, her hair slicked back and face devoid of makeup, truly stunning without the fuss, but she didn't seem to realize it. Those days were becoming fewer and farther between as she considered retirement.

"Grady, I am so disappointed in you." She gracefully lowered herself onto the opposite end of the couch and smoothed her already-flawless hair.

"Sorry." No idea what he'd done this time.

"Bill tells me you turned down Joseph Mathers' divorce case, spent the afternoon on the ice, and then were off to your little beer hobby." Yeah, that would disappoint her alright.

Grady ran a hand through his hair, messing it up even more than its usual disarray. "It's up to me which cases I take, which I refuse, and my reasons for making those decisions. You wouldn't operate unless you were confident in all aspects of the approach and potential outcomes."

She sighed, the creases in her forehead almost visible. Botox must be wearing off. "You're a capable attorney. I know you would have handled his divorce authentically and successfully."

Grady rose to his feet and made for the exit. After the day he'd had, he really wasn't in the mood for another of her lectures. If one didn't stand up to one's own mother by the time he reached his thirtieth year, when would he? He hesitated in the doorway. "I certainly could have, but it's my decision. I don't know where you get your gossip, but it's none of your business how I spend my day."

The man had been caught cheating on his wife. With his business partner. In the middle of his office. With the door wide open. And he expected to walk away with everything.

This is the shit Grady didn't want to take on when he studied law. Yet, it seemed to be the type of case that landed on his doorstep most often, thanks to his parents and their uppity friends. When they'd paid for him to go to law school, they must have envisioned all the power they could accumulate by having his expertise and influence. And he knew she had visions of politics in his future.

Environmental law might have been cool, but any tree-hugging wouldn't have reflected well on Bill Stellan's timber empire. Tax law might have been interesting, but there wouldn't be exciting cases in this small town. He'd considered prosecution, but he also didn't want to risk putting an innocent behind bars.

"Wait, Grady?" Without a stray hair or catch in her step, she moved like a fucking jaguar to catch him before he was out of sight.

In anticipation of a cherry-on-top addition to her disappointment, he raised an eyebrow and paused at the top of the stairs.

"Don't forget our family dinner tonight. Ryder's home and has brought his fiancée."

"Engaged? When did that happen?"

"When I spoke with him last week and told him how wonderful it would be if I could announce his engagement at the gala. As luck would have it, he'd just proposed."

Uh-huh. Rather coincidental timing. And now his brother had yet another leg up on him. Engaged, with perfect timing for Patricia to claim her latest mother-of-the-year prize and renewed bragging rights. After they'd both graduated and started working, with no anticipated milestones to tick off, she must have run out of boasts.

Grady was not looking forward to meeting the fiancée. Like all the others, she was likely as much a showpiece for Ryder's career as Patricia's children were for her social status. Ryder wouldn't care, as long as she gave a decent blowjob.

Grady shook his head and tried to clear the image. He still was haunted by the memory of Ryder getting some from Grady's ex-girlfriend in the stables. Having no interest in horses, Ryder had apparently made good use of the stables over the years for other mounting purposes. Neither had seemed to care that Grady had been due home from college at any moment.

# 4

## S-T-U-P-E-F-I-E-D

Claire hung behind Ryder as he strode down the hall toward the dining room. In an effort to make up for her solo ice-skating venture—as far as he knew anyway—Ryder promised he'd take her horseback riding tomorrow and spend the next day exploring the area, maybe even a little hiking, if the weather cooperated. Hopefully, they could spend as many day trips away from this haunted mansion as possible.

Before today, she hadn't seen him in a week. His toothbrush had migrated about the bathroom, plus the ebb and flow of the laundry pile, so she knew he was coming home each night. Not that she had been much more available.

As she'd already learned to expect in the cavernous mansion, the dining room was ostentatious. If the ceilings weren't so high, she'd feel claustrophobic thanks to the ominous crystal chandelier that hung precariously overhead. In earthquake territory. It was the sort that came crashing down in thriller movies, crushing the villain because the hero was too honorable to kill him directly. She shivered at the thought and averted her gaze.

From what must be the kitchen, a slim, graceful woman in expensive-looking slacks and a silk top glided toward her.

"You must be Claire. I'm Patricia." Not Pat or Patty, but Patricia. Her presentation matched the house, down to the platinum hair.

Claire shook a sturdy, firm hand. Brain surgeon, she reminded herself. As soon as Patricia released her, Claire stuffed her hands in her pockets to hide her fidget. She painted a polite smile across her face and remembered all those manners her parents had drilled into her. Not that the Dabney house was formal, but her parents insisted she at least know how to behave. Claire made a mental note to call home later with profuse thanks.

"Thank you so much for having me. You have a beautiful home." It didn't matter what the home looked like, you always compliment it to your host or hostess. She may be awkward, but she knew how to fit in. Sort of. Pay a respectful compliment or keep your trap shut.

Patricia waved her hand and rolled her eyes nonchalantly. "Aren't you sweet." Oh boy. Condescension, here we come. Why did everyone always call her sweet? Annoying, really.

Behind her, the raspy bass of a former smoker clearing his throat caught her attention. "Claire. Bill Stellan. Welcome to Foothills."

She turned to see Ryder's stepdad. He looked a little more human than his wife. More relaxed, she supposed. With crinkled eyes and weathered skin, he still embodied the forester he'd begun his career as. No longer out in the field, his belly and cheeks were rounded from a more sedentary lifestyle.

She followed along and sat in her assigned seat next to Ryder. Surprisingly, the family all sat at one end of the colossal table. Must be so they didn't need to holler across the huge table to ask for the salt.

Claire was just lowering her napkin to her lap when *he* walked in. Her skating partner. The hockey player. The one that got away.

*Dammit, don't think like that.*

Luck, fate, Aphrodite, whoever was currently messing with her life, was pissing her off. Things with Ryder were complicated enough.

Part in panic and part in crushing exhilaration, her heart fluttered wildly in her chest like a stampeding herd of bison. Not that she'd ever heard bison stampede in real life. Dressed in casual jeans slung low on his narrow hips, a fitted black t-shirt, bare feet, and surfer blond hair tousled playfully, he sauntered in like an actor on the cover of a magazine trying to show his bad-boy side. He was clearly the black sheep of the Mallory family. Damned if it didn't make her like him even more.

Biting her lip, she tried to hide her response. To suppress the massive grin of joy that her hormones were thrusting out in all directions, declaring that everything was going to be okay.

The second he saw her, the air rushed out of the room like she was being sucked into the vacuum of space. Might be less painful, at least, inevitably imploding at the force of the extreme pressure change.

His gaze rested on her for a moment. His Adam's apple bobbed in his throat.

Good. He was as miserable and thrilled as she was. Maybe that frivolous romance novel hadn't been wrong after all? At least she didn't have to travel back to the ancient Highlands to find him.

Hopefully, no one noticed their matching flushed cheeks, or would at least assume it was because of the blazing, oversized fireplace. At least she wasn't freezing in the winter weather anymore, but the man was dangerous to her health, inducing premature hot flashes.

He sat in his assigned seat across the table, flicked his napkin as he lowered it to his lap, and leaned back in his chair, adopting a poker face and pretending he was completely at ease. In the blink of an eye, she ceased to exist, moment gone.

Like her presence didn't cause every nerve in his body to fire at once, urging him to take her hand and run for the hills together.

*O*f all the...

Fuck.

It was her. First woman he'd asked out in months. First woman to ever make him yearn so deeply he ached down into his soul. That made him even think that word, *soul*.

After being teased too many times, he'd stopped letting the corny side show. But he was a romantic at heart. Only Zane even had a cluc, exchanging romance novels with him like a horny book club.

Neither a Mallory nor an impassioned lawyer should stoop so low as to express deep feelings, particularly with regards to concepts as nebulous and personal as romance. Accustomed to masking any sort of meaningful emotions, as he'd silently refused to ignore them anyway, he hid it well.

As usual, he'd more than missed his opportunity. Fate was downright kicking him in the balls this time. Was he a serial killer in a past life?

Sitting across from him, she held her shoulders primly high in the oversized dining chair. Perfect manners, dressed in a delicate sweater... she was not what he had pictured for Ryder. Brains and a quirky sense of humor. She didn't match his brother at all. But she was the forever-type of partner, not to mention fucking gorgeous with silky brown hair, mysterious eyes, and lush lips that... there was no way his brother was going to be stupid enough to give her up.

Patricia cleared her throat. "Grady, aren't you going to introduce yourself to our guest? This is Claire." Her prominent blue eyes bugged and her head tilted toward Claire meaningfully as she admonished her adult son for his boorish behavior.

"Hi Claire," he managed to say without rasping. Here he sat, physically aching with jealousy, and he didn't even know her name until this moment.

Equally uncomfortable, Claire smiled, but her pouty lower lip tucked between her teeth. "Hello, Grady."

Conversation bounced around the table, dull and polite. His parents were skilled in the art of conversation. Although they would fit in better in the heart of Seattle, or more appropriately, somewhere East Coast, he suspected they enjoyed being the upper crust of their confined society.

Claire seemed to take the entire awful dinner in stride. Ryder poured her a huge glass of red wine, which she politely took a small sip of with a grimace, then abandoned. Grady glanced away when she caught him observing her distaste, biting his tongue to mask his amusement.

She smiled as she chewed the tiniest bite of Brussels sprouts he'd ever seen. Her face pinched as she fought a strong gag reflex while she swallowed the repulsive excuse for a vegetable.

Patricia tried to talk about surgery, knowing Claire would also have surgical interest, but she couldn't seem to help repeatedly redirecting the conversation back to how brain surgery was so much more complex than setting a fracture.

Bill attempted to bring the conversation back to a more universal topic, but seemed to make things that much more uncomfortable. "So, Claire. I hear you work with large and small animals. You'd be in high demand around here."

At this, she perked up. She wiped a nonexistent drip of beurre blanc sauce from the side of her mouth. "I saw dozens of large-scale farms on the drive in. What a great place to practice veterinary medicine."

Bill beamed, proud of his hometown. "The Kittridge place down the road just went on the market. You two should take a look."

Patricia's eyes lit up like a matched pair of blue moons.

No one had mentioned the Kittridge place to Grady. Closer to his parents than he was comfortable with, but he really liked the house and the land. More of a homey-ranch style and less of the out-of-place-sterility that this place exuded.

Ryder swallowed the bite of salmon down what must have been a suddenly dry throat before responding, as evidenced by his huge eyes and coughing choke. "We're not moving to Foothills. Or any small town. No offense, but the life's not for me." Silence tunneled around the table as everyone stopped chewing midway through their current bite, aside from Ryder, who chased his bold statement with a swig of his wine to dislodge the salmon.

Grady looked across the table to Claire. Her eyebrows were raised in false support of her fiancé, and she was working her bottom lip in her teeth again.

Grady shifted his focus to Ryder. "Not big enough pockets in Foothills?" Smug asshole. What did Claire see in him?

"Grady. Not at the table." Of course. One must always use excellent manners at the dinner table. "Six months of living with that troublemaker, Asher, spending your free time at the brewery with that other one, and you've developed the manners of a sailor." She tsked her disappointment. As usual.

"Mother—"

"I know," she huffed, then folded and refolded her napkin. "I'm still upset that pretty Sophie chose him over you."

Grady cringed, hating how adeptly his mother sniffed out gossip. "That's not how it happened—" It totally was. "—They're great together and are two of my best friends."

"Well." She nodded, taking a definitive sip of wine, the red expertly paired with the meal. "Did you ever call Miss Perry like I suggested? She's so well-traveled and is already transforming the high school foreign language department. And Haley and she were always so close. Imagine, if you and she married, then maybe Haley would come visit more often."

"No, I didn't ask her out. And you could fly down to visit Haley, and not expect her to be the one to reach out."

"Don't think I didn't hear how Trace passed you over for that... that football player after Haley moved away. But from what I hear, she's looking to settle down."

Tongue firmly embedded between his teeth, Grady shoved back from the table. "I think I'll pass on dessert," he said as he pushed away from the table, grabbing his plate and backing away toward the kitchen. "Seahawks kickoff in ten if anyone is interested." He may have abhorrent manners, according to his mother, but he knew at least his stepdad would enjoy a good football game.

# 5

## I-M-P-A-L-E-D

"**U**nnecessary roughness? Are you kidding?" Bill's raspy voice echoed down the hall.

Claire heard the expletives pouring out of the entertainment room from the top of the stairs off the kitchen. She'd only gotten lost a few times in her search for football and an escape from pretension. Straight after dinner, Ryder went upstairs to "wrap up the meeting" from earlier. She had no idea what that meant, but she wasn't surprised. She'd tossed her sweater in their bedroom before heading downstairs for the game. Not wanting to risk another fiery blush at her proximity to Grady, she opted for the lighter weight white cotton t-shirt.

From the arched doorway to the entertainment room, Claire took in the scene. It was quite a setup. A pair of over-stuffed black leather sofas faced each other around a large, tiled coffee table, and two plush recliners were aimed at the TV screen. Bill looked like a king on his throne, his feet up and empty beer glass clutched tight in his hand as he stretched out on a recliner. Opposite the entrance, a slick bar with a variety of liquors and fancy snacks stepped up the man-cave aspect. Between her and the bar, behind the recliners, there was a billiard table with the cues and balls prearranged for play whenever the mood may strike. Plank walnut lined the floors and walls, with forest green accents on the lights and décor.

She paused when she allowed her gaze to land on Grady before anyone realized she was here. His arms were in the air as he swore at the referees through the screen. That hair seemed to be eternally unruly, and now it was downright wild.

At the commercial break, Bill turned and saw Claire hesitating in the doorway. "Come on in, girlie. Ryder's not a football fan, but hopefully he's brought someone home who enjoys the finer things in life?" He chuckled merrily as he gestured to the sitting area. Thankfully, he didn't seem to be the sexist sort to hang a *No Girls Allowed* sign on entering the man-cave. Her brothers had tried that once. *Once.*

Grateful for the welcome, Claire took a few steps into the room. "I'd love to join you. I'm more of an Arizona fan, but I'll settle for the Seahawks, since the Fire knocked us out of the playoffs."

Grady hopped up from the couch and foolishly attempted to flatten his hair before giving up and shoving his hands in his pockets. "Can I get you a beer?" he offered, making his way to the bar.

"Top me off?" Bill asked as he held his empty glass in the air. "We're big Fire fans too, so you're in poor company. Grady, you ever talk to Finn anymore? I know your mother made it clear she's got something against him—lord knows why, but he's a hell of a player."

"Not in a while."

Claire walked over to Bill and took his glass. "I can get it."

Grady moved with the elegance of his mother, but in a masculine way. Smoother, like he could finesse his way through anything. He took Bill's glass from her hand and motioned to the barstools for her to sit while he fixed their drinks. "You're on vacation, I'll get it. What's your poison?"

With the ease of a seasoned bartender, although she doubted that he'd worked his way through school as she had, he filled Bill's glass from a built-in tap and made a quick delivery while she looked at the options behind the bar. They must entertain a lot. Hopefully they didn't drink these alone.

"I'll try that IPA."

"Excellent choice." He carefully poured the glass and passed it down the bar to her.

Still seated on her stool, she took a sip and turned toward him. "This is good. Is it local?"

He rested his palms on the bar in front of her, and she could feel the heat radiating off him as if he were inches away, rather than the maximum distance the bar would allow. Her eyes locked onto his corded arms. That spectacular muscle tone that took more than just a few days a week at the gym, working arms that didn't take to idleness. Not the arms she'd expect for the lawyer-son of a wealthy family. She almost drooled, but luckily, she was able to manage her secretions.

"As local as it gets. I, uh, I'm co-owner of a craft brewery. This one's pretty hoppy."

"I like a beer that bites me back." She grinned over the mouth of the glass at him.

He shook his head in disbelief and grinned at her. "How did you end up with my brother? He hates football. Not big on beer. Nor animals, for that matter." Pausing, his eyes met hers and she felt that same liquid heat pooling deep in her belly that he seemed to fuel every time he met her gaze. "Or being out on the ice."

Blushing, she sighed, trying to shake the thrill that shot through her veins. In that impulsive moment, she'd been ready to chase him down and ask him to be her complication. How would tonight have been different if she hadn't hesitated? Regardless, she wasn't sure what to do with this second chance. Things were likely to get really awkward, really quickly. Already rapidly migrating in that direction.

"In the way people usually meet. At a party. Some friends set us up. Our apartment leases were about up, and we were both busy with school and work, so we sort of moved in together and started dating on the same day."

"Love at first sight then."

Her gaze landed on his long fingers, rapidly tapping against the bar to the tune of *The Terminator*'s iconic theme song. He was an utter mystery, and the complete opposite of his brother. The air in the room was getting thicker and heavier by the moment, filling her lungs with confusion and arousal.

If only he knew just how much she knew what that phrase meant to her now. She'd have laughed her ass off at anyone who had declared that they had experienced love at first sight. Well, that may be the predicament she found herself in now... and it was a hell of a lot more painful than it was rumored to be. Well, Cupid did fire an arrow, delivering a sharp, bloody, excruciating blow as you realized you were a goner. It might be that other L-word, but she'd felt that when she'd met Ryder.

It was an entirely unique sensation she floated on right now.

Her throat swelled as she tried to finish the conversation, really *not* wanting to talk about her relationship with Ryder at the moment, and absolutely not with Grady. "Well, we hit it off right away. I'm sure you know how charming Ryder is."

Grady raised his eyebrows and let out a slow-burning exhale. "Yeah. I'm familiar with his appeal."

Claire wasn't sure what that was all about, but clearly the brothers didn't get along. She'd been with Ryder for two entire years, and he rarely talked about his brother.

Avoiding the inevitable awkwardness if she pursued that line of questioning, she took her beer and found a spot on the couch in time for the second quarter. Grady safely sat across from her, stealing glances whenever she'd holler at the screen. Or when she'd attempted to study him. Her cheeks would flame and the heat from the stolen look would lick through her veins, both a warning and a temptation. By the time Bill started snoring as the game neared the final minutes, Claire realized she'd lost track of the game entirely, her mind a muddled tangle of confusion.

"Hey Babe, are you in here?" Ryder came whistling around the corner, a mysterious smile pasted onto his face.

Claire cringed, immediately shifting her attention to the game. The moniker, the tone, the look. Would it have bothered her twenty-four hours ago? "Yeah. Two minutes left in the fourth quarter."

Ryder sat next to her on the couch and slipped his hand into hers.

The game suddenly aggravating, she flailed her hands in the air and shouted at the TV, "What? Offsides? What game are the refs watching?"

He cleared his throat and said, "I didn't realize you were so passionate about football."

Claire shrugged. "I didn't get to watch much the last few seasons. Too busy."

Ryder shifted his hand to her thigh, his fingers edging along the bottom of her skirt.

Grady stood abruptly and stalked out of the room without a backward glance.

"**A**re you ok?" Ryder's hair stood on end, crackling from the static electricity of pulling his sweater over his head and setting it neatly on the top of his suitcase. Intolerant of the disarray, he smoothed the unruly spikes that didn't dare flip back out of place.

"Fine." She was fine. Totally fine. After dropping her skirt, tights, and t-shirt on the floor by the bed, she crawled into the cool Egyptian cotton sheets and flicked off her bra, forgetting she'd still had it on.

Sliding the rest of his clothes off and stacking the folded discards atop the dresser, Ryder slipped into bed next to her. Reaching his hand over, he grazed smooth fingertips over her abdomen. "You seem distracted."

She flipped to her side, and his hand pulled away to avoid getting squished. Lungs heavy with pent-up carbon dioxide, she couldn't squeeze another drop of air in until she let it all out in a sustained huff. She *was* distracted. And irritable. Realizing your life was not quite where you hoped it would be by this time, turned completely upside down realizing you'd turned down a wrong path, tended to do that to a person. "It's been a long couple of months. Hard to decompress."

Ryder rolled onto his back and rubbed his hands over his face. Tan and muscled, his arms were toned from hours at the gym each week. Instead of meeting her on breaks. "For both of us. I'm sorry I've been so distant lately."

Watching his familiar movements, her head swimming on the cloud-like pillow, Claire responded softly, "Me too."

"I was hoping this trip would help us reconnect and figure out where we're going." Ryder's chest rose and fell with deliberate breaths.

"Yeah. That's what I'd been hoping."

"I have a video meeting in the morning. They're thinking of giving the lead on the vodka campaign to Menard with the timeline moving up, so I won't be able to join you on the horses like I'd hoped. If I nail this meeting, I'll be able to buy a little schedule freedom for us, and maybe I can take you out for a nice dinner? There's an authentic Italian place on the edge of town. We can visit, just the two of us, without my pretentious mother, my self-absorbed stepfather, and certainly without my hopeless brother. And we'll see where we're at."

With a shrug and that damn lip creeping into her teeth, Claire nodded. "Okay. Maybe I can catch the stablemaster to show me around in the morning."

Ryder flipped to his side to face her and flashed his sexy dimples and smoldering eyes. He reached under the sheet and grazed the back of his hand along the curve of her breast.

With a sharp intake of breath, Claire rotated out of his reach. A few days ago, she was desperate for his touch. Had gone too long without it. "I'm really tired. It's been a long day."

"Okay. Goodnight, Claire." Turned away, she couldn't see if her resistance had doused that smolder... or if he was as relieved as she was.

Maybe if her brain would relax a bit, she could catch a few hours of sleep. Claire rolled onto her abdomen and glared out the open curtains at the sliver of silver moon, faint and distorted under the thin layer of clouds. A few long blinks. Maybe she'd fall asleep soon.

Anytime now. Cold air seemed to freeze the life and energy from the muscles and the brain, so sleep ought to be setting in anytime. Soon.

Fuck it. She knew why she wasn't sleeping. Why Ryder's hand felt like it didn't belong on her body. Maybe it wouldn't have a few days ago either, as the distance between them had multiplied logarithmically these past few months, and they became ships passing in the night rather than lovers. She knew what she had to do. Dinner alone would be a good time to do it.

As her blinks grew longer, it was Grady that filled the preamble of her dreams. Similar eyes, but the passion behind his, the intensity with which he seemed to view everything, melted her insides to molten lava. Similar chiseled jaw, but Grady's lack of dimples charmed her. The fiercely flexing mastication muscle in his jaw told of all the heavy thoughts he didn't share. Never quite assimilating to his environment, his hair was always on end as if he struggled to find his balance on uneven terrain.

# 6

## M-O-U-N-T-U-P

Breakfast was not a formal affair at Mallory Mansion. Ooh, she'd better be careful she didn't say that out loud. Pretentious as the house was, it might come across as disrespectful.

Hattie was in the kitchen scrambling eggs on the stovetop. "Good morning, Claire. Did you sleep well?"

"I slept great, thanks, Hattie. This looks amazing." She cringed, afraid to find out she'd made a faux pas and breakfast was DIY in Mallory Mansion.

Generously, Hattie nodded to the cupboard above the dishwasher and said, "Grab yourself a plate. I expect Grady will be down at any moment, so I'm making his favorite. There's plenty here, but if you would like something else, I'll be happy to make it for you." Hattie stirred the eggs and added cheese and cracked pepper as they spoke.

Claire helped herself to some coffee. "I would love some of those eggs. If you're sure that you have enough." She parked herself at the breakfast bar to visit with Hattie.

"For you, anything. Now, I'll warn you, I'm not much of a chef. Karl makes lunch and dinner, so I pitch in on breakfast for those who get up early enough, otherwise I think these kids would have lived off sugary cereal growing up, if that. Too busy to stop to eat, but far too active to start the day without a good breakfast. Now, you sit yourself down and tell me all about why you became a veterinarian." Hattie added another slice of sourdough to the toaster for Claire.

Tingling ran down her spine as she felt Grady coming up behind her. Dammit. Hours since she'd met him, and she could already sense when those aromatically testosterone-laden pheromones got within ten yards of her.

Grady poured himself a steaming cup of black coffee and parked himself next to her at the breakfast bar. "Smells amazing, Hattie."

He nudged Claire's knee with his. "You're up early. Aside from Hattie and me, no one else wakes before dawn on weekends."

"Nasty habit, I know. I was hoping to check out the horses this morning, maybe see the routine." She took a sip of the piping hot liquid that warmed her throat, but the heat she felt sitting next to Grady was much further south.

Grady raised his coffee in salute. "Our stablemaster is home with the flu. We have a high schooler that assists her, but he's caught the same flu. So, you are stuck with me this morning." Despite his attempt at humor, she swam in the warm, tropical ocean of his eyes, rather unamused and finding herself in deeper water all the time. Oh boy, he was triggering corny thoughts and cornier descriptions. "Ryder texted me a few minutes ago to ask if I'd take you for a ride."

Claire choked on her coffee, straining to block the vision that invoked. Far too vivid after her dreamful night. "Great. Thanks."

Out of the corner of her eye, she could see Hattie plating their food and trying to remain inconspicuous. Wordlessly, Hattie slid their plates across the breakfast bar and disappeared from the room before either could take much notice. The steamy, gooey eggs warmed her tummy and promised to keep her cozy for the rest of the day. She glimpsed Grady blushing at something he was clearly quite amused by. Likely caught up in the same mounting imagery that she was.

"What do you think?" Grady asked as Claire followed him into the stables, not having a clue what to say. His tongue was completely tied around her, nervous about things he *knew* he did well.

The chill in the air was suffocating. It didn't matter how thick your coat was in this weather, it seeped into your bones. Claire pulled her jacket tighter around her. Phoenix was a far cry from Washington in winter, especially in the higher elevations like this.

Grady watched as Claire took in her surroundings. She was like a kid in a candy store. The barns were impressive. Although his mother didn't ride much these days, she still enjoyed keeping attractive stables and fine horses.

Claire seemed pleased with what she saw. "This is a great setup. We didn't have land or money for a horse of my own, so I borrowed at our local stables. This is the type of place I dreamed about."

On seeing the stable with new eyes, he appreciated the grandeur of it. Having left the design to professionals, his mother, fortunately, hadn't had a hand in its construction. There was room for a dozen horses, but they didn't keep nearly that many these days.

Without a horse of her own, or even easy access or funds, it must have been a major undertaking for her parents. "What made you interested in horses?"

She walked up to Daisy, laughing with that enchanting laugh of hers. A curious horse, Daisy stuck her head out of the stall, looking for a little loving from her visitor. "What kid didn't want to grow up to be a cowgirl? Besides, I fully blame my mother. I showed a slight interest right around my birthday one year, and my mom bought me this horse encyclopedia. By the time I was nine, I knew the inside and outside of every breed of horse."

"And so it began." From his coat pocket, he pulled out a handful of carrots to give to the horses. Claire held her hand out, and he passed some to her, careful to avoid the potential electrocution if they connected again.

She held her palm out flat, leaving Daisy to nibble the snack. "Weird as it may sound, I think cows might be even more interesting. What strange creatures. Multiple compartments to their stomachs, sleeping aligned with the poles. They seem so dull, but they've got such heavy emotion in their eyes."

She was so passionate about so many things. It was incredible. Refreshing. Just being around her made the world a little more colorful.

Grady hung back, not letting himself get closer. He was getting sucked in too deep already. "What does Ryder think about your fascination with cows?"

Daisy poked her head out for one last pat before Claire broke away and moved to check in the other stalls. Without answering his question, she took a deep breath before turning back toward him. "Show me the routine."

His fault. Touchy subject. Following along as he tossed breakfast to each of the horses, helping to haul and tidy as they went, Claire examined each horse while they worked. The routine seemed to help soothe her, the tension she'd sported all morning fading.

He was just giving Misty a nose rub and a carrot when Claire broke the silence. "I guess I don't know what you do for a living. I mean, you said you were part owner in a craft brewery, but I thought you were a lawyer."

"Ryder doesn't say much about his family, does he?"

And that lip was back in her teeth. His poor brain went right in the gutter, imagining running his tongue along the imprint she'd made. That pouty lower lip was absolutely worth biting. Sucking on. Hell, he could spend all morning writing an entire opening argument about those lips.

*Stop it. Ryder's, remember?*

*As if that ever mattered to Ryder.*

*It should have. Don't stoop to his level.*

Shit. Childish arguments spun his head until his vision blurred. He needed to get a life. Quickly. He bit his own lip to silence his rambling brain. Contagious, apparently.

"No. Well, maybe. We've both been so busy that we haven't talked much lately." She shrugged and grabbed another carrot and brought it to Caesar in the next stall.

Lately? "Claire, I've been a lawyer since you met my brother, and we started the brewery last summer." He stood and watched as she avoided eye contact.

"Okay. So, that's a no. He doesn't talk about his family much." Neatly avoiding further questioning, she crossed the barn and perused the office and tack room.

He let it slide.

"Take me for a ride?" Hands folded behind her back, she asked sweetly, the corner of her mouth quirked up as she realized her innuendo. Again.

Ha. He saw through it already. That charming face she pasted on seemed designed to get her way, without a person realizing that she'd gotten away with murder.

Hell, yeah, he wanted to say *yes*. Her tempting lips were in full pout, driving his imagination straight to the gutter. He stepped closer, so they were toe-to-toe, the air between them sucking him closer like gravity was simply doing its thing, and he was the fool to ignore it. "Look, my libido's running on overdrive already. Don't push me." Brushing past her, bristling with unbridled sexual frustration, he escaped into the tack room to grab his favorite saddle and, well, hide.

From the middle of the stables, her husky, mischievous laugh reverberated across the cavernous room and somehow made everything okay. At his honesty, she could have taken that so badly and stormed into the house, declaring to her fiancé that his brother was a lecher and a jerk.

Claire watched as Grady saddled the horses with the ease of experience. He'd taken Misty and left her to take "old reliable." "He knows the trails better than I do," he'd commented. Her favorite horse growing up had been so experienced at competition, and she so fresh and nervous, that he'd run the barrel races without any input from her.

They mounted up and headed out into the freezing morning. In the dense fog, the rising sun cast an eerie glow on the ice-tipped greenery surrounding them. Sadly, the mountains were hidden behind layers of mist and clouds.

The first few hundred yards, the trail had been too narrow for them to ride side by side, but it widened now, and they walked through a field, its crunchy grass compressed under the weight of the thick frost. "Do you always ride Western? I saw several English saddles in the tack room," she asked.

Their legs a few feet away, the proximity to him even warmer than that radiating off Caesar, she tried not to imagine climbing onto Misty with him and stealing some of his body heat. Or burying her nose in that neck and seeing if he smelled as temptingly rugged as he looked.

"Usually. Makes a lot more sense on the trails. But I do enjoy jumping."

"I've always wondered at that. It seems like such an awkward use for a horse, jumping over poles on a prancing mare."

"Ever been to the UK? Tons of old stone fences. I couldn't say that's the reason, but it would be a real short ride if you had to turn around every time you came upon an obstacle."

"Fair point. I hadn't thought of that."

"Caesar thinks that's a bunch of nonsense, don't you pal?" He reached across and patted Caesar's neck affectionately. She tried to not wish it were her thigh.

"Do you normally live with your parents?" Not exactly the question a thirty-year-old attorney-slash-brewer wanted to hear from a woman, not even his brother's girlfriend. She couldn't help it. He just didn't fit in with the pretentious extravagance of the home.

He cringed at the question. "Hell no. Sorry, that sounded harsh. No, this is not my first choice of residence. My rental house burned down a few weeks ago. It was crash with my parents or couch surf with friends. While my friends offered their places, they're all still in the honeymoon phase of their relationships, and I wasn't looking to be a third wheel."

"I'm so sorry. Did you lose much?" She quickly amended, "I mean, of course you lost a lot. What did you lose that was important to you?" Foot in mouth, as usual, she pushed more than she should. *Way to go, Claire.*

At the fork in the trail, he turned onto the less beaten path. "Nothing much. I salvaged some old photo albums, but they smell so terrible, I'm not sure they are ever going to be worth looking at again. Anything valuable was here, anyway. Patricia doesn't trust me with heirlooms. She'd prefer I get married first and entrust my wife to care for them." Despite his nonchalance, his tone was gloomy.

Leather creaked under her as the saddle shifted with the sharp incline of the trail. "You don't sound like you lost nothing important." She raised an eyebrow at him. Her mouth quirked up in challenge.

With a laugh, he shook his head. "I lost nothing that's not replaceable. It just shook me is all."

"I can't imagine. Sounds awful."

Like something out of Middle Earth, she felt like she was venturing into an enchanted, dangerous land as the mist grew thicker rather than dissipating with the elevation change. Somehow, she could feel the mountains more than see them, sense the air thinning as she struggled to keep up with her body's oxygen demand. Although, that might just be her heart racing as she struggled to reign in her imagination. Grady had an excellent seat and maintained an effortless posture that showed off his lean build, even through the heavy coat.

*Oh boy, Claire. You've been cooped up too long.*

"I'd been living with my friend, Asher. It was mostly my stuff in the house, so he was settled within a day with his girlfriend. Actually, fiancée now. Damn, everyone's getting engaged or married these days. Anyway, the fire wasn't much of a loss for him. I could have crashed on my couch at the office as my partner suggested, but I don't want to spend any more time there than I already have to."

The fog condensed around them until she couldn't see past Grady. Good thing he'd given her Caesar; she could hardly make out the trail. Caesar seemed confident in their trajectory, almost as comfortable as Grady, both in their natural habitat.

"You don't like being a lawyer?" The trail narrowed, and Grady was in front of her again. His style on a horse was incredible, totally natural and relaxed, and his silent commands to Misty were impeccable. At her question, his posture stiffened.

"It's a foolish thing, to go all the way through law school, only to realize you really don't like it."

"If you could go back and do it again, what would you do?"

Grady took another small path on the left and stopped in a small clearing. "I have absolutely no idea. I like the brewhouse, but it's so new, I can't be sure yet that I can make a career of it. And I can't let down my clients. There aren't many legal resources around here. Most of all, I can't abandon Lincoln."

"Partner?"

"Yeah. He loves the job."

Claire pulled up next to him, getting close enough that her leg pressed up against his. Caesar didn't mind. He leaned in, clearly enjoying a little snuggle time with Misty. "If you can't quit, what can you do to make it more tolerable?"

He looked over at her, his cheeks pink from the chill wind of the morning, flushed with warmth and life in stark contrast to the January day. "Not attending to my parents' snooty friends and their little indiscretions, but I don't hear the end of it when I refuse to take their cases. Only taking on cases that don't require going to court. I fucking hate standing before a judge. I do that enough at home."

"I can see that," Claire muttered, then realized she'd pretty much vocalized her distaste for his mother. "I mean—"

"Nope. Too late. You said it, you can't take it back."

"But I—"

"And I like you even better now." He grinned.

More hooked than ever, Claire's gaze fell to his very kissable lips. He looked as miserable as she was. Maybe more so, as she was at least passionate about her career choice. Eyes straying down from that incredible mouth, she envisioned crawling onto his lap, unzipping that coat, and wrapping her arms around his waist. Caesar snorted and shifted his feet in place to keep pace with Misty.

"Anyway, this is one of my favorite spots. Not that you can tell with all the fog, but the view is spectacular. We should head back. I'm sure Ryder has plans for the two of you for today."

Claire didn't argue as she let him pass and lead the way back. Yeah, fun plans alright. Even if she decided to stay with him, which was becoming less appealing by the minute, he would always choose his career over her. As immersed as she'd been in preparing for her career, she did not envision a career-centric life after graduation. "Sure," she murmured. She just had to get through until dinner tonight, when she could end things and move on to the next phase of her life.

They took the long way back; he didn't say as much, but she felt it. Caesar too, as he kept trying to veer off in a different direction, cold and ready for a treat back at the stables. Both remained quiet for a while, knowing it was a downright stupid idea to continue on the emotional path they'd been riding. But neither of the humans in the group was in any rush to return to the house and the future that awaited them.

G rady threw his legs over, dismounted, and landed on the ground with a thud. He offered to take care of the horses and saddles so Claire could go in and warm up. She didn't complain once, despite her desert-acclimated metabolism, but the rapid chattering of her teeth over the last half mile had him worrying for the health of her dentition.

And he needed space. The more time he spent with her, the more time he wanted to spend with her. Each minute made the next that much more painful. What would his mother say when he skipped Claire and Ryder's wedding? No way he could attend and come out whole.

Stubborn, Claire insisted on staying and helping. "Foothills is a gorgeous place. A far cry from Phoenix."

Polite conversation. Yes, much safer than letting his imagination wander, wondering *what if.* "I spent a few days in Phoenix a few years back. Like I was on Mars or something, bleak. I can understand the appeal though. It was sunny every day that I was there."

And silence. Superficial was safer, but tougher when he was so preoccupied with her every movement. Caesar leaned into her as she brushed his coat after removing the saddle. It was a heavy saddle, and she'd pulled it off the tall stallion and returned it to the tack room without breaking a sweat. Important in her line of work, he supposed.

"I bet you're a great vet," he commented as she cooed to Caesar, the massive horse nuzzling, relishing in the praise.

"It's not easy to convince a horse to take their medicine, so it takes a little TLC sometimes." She led Caesar back to his stall and locked it behind her. Clearly craving a little more attention, the horse put his head out and nudged her for a little more of that sweet-talk. The horse sighed longingly. Grady did too. Claire rewarded Caesar with a chin rub.

Unable to resist, Grady walked over and stood next to her, with the excuse of bringing Caesar another carrot. They stood inches away. It may as well be miles for all the difference it made. She was still his brother's fiancée. Which he told himself no less than every five minutes, because every four minutes, his imagination wandered, considering how soft that skin really was, how those lush lips might feel against his.

Still, the electricity between them crackled and zapped like a broken power line, ripped apart in a storm. Inches away, he couldn't resist the magnetic pull. He shoved his hands in his pockets and closed his eyes, needing to convince himself to back away.

After one last pat for Caesar, Claire turned abruptly. She must not have realized just how close she was standing, and pressed her hands on his chest to steady herself instead of smacking into him.

Her lips parted slightly, inviting, and she leaned a fraction of an inch closer.

Desperate for one taste before accepting the loss of eternity with Claire, taking one last risk, consequences be damned, he leaned in, closing the distance before either had a chance to hesitate. Chest rising and falling in rhythm with his, her gaze trained on his mouth, she waited.

A reminder that he shouldn't have needed, her phone buzzed in her pocket. He parked his tongue in his teeth and stepped back.

Claire jerked back and bit that lip he had almost gotten a taste of. Her eyes-of-many-colors were heavy with regret—that it had nearly happened or had been interrupted, he couldn't be sure. And he hated that he'd put her in the position of having to decide.

Caesar nudged him and snorted a reprimand in his ear.

*I know, old boy. I know. Just once.*

Claire glared at her phone as she read the screen. "Dammit," she muttered under her breath. "Sorry. Ryder's done with his meeting."

Grady tried not to jump for joy at her displeasure in hearing from Ryder, not actually wanting her to be unhappy, but still...

"Grady, I—" She trailed off and backed away, not leaving him a clue about what she wanted to say.

He was hoping for, *I'm leaving Ryder, because you're the only one for me*, but he suspected it was *Don't get any ideas, you jerk*.

"It's ok. I... yeah. Go join your fiancé."

Her head whipped around and she glared at him. "Fiancé?"

"Yeah. Congratulations, by the way." He tried to sound genuine, but it was really tough when he'd been within a breath of kissing her.

She let out a feral growl, stomped her foot, and stormed out of the stables. Huh. Something was definitely afoot at the Circle K.

7

# C-A-R-P-E-D-I-E-M

*Fiancé? Engaged? Ryder, you've hit an all-time low.* It was all about image, and something told her he'd started telling people they were engaged to get a leg up on some gig.

Claire pulled her coat tighter around her. Not that she was cold. Actually, her body temperature must have risen a solid five degrees after the near-kiss with Grady. But angry chills ran down her spine, thanks to Ryder.

One stupid trip. That's all she'd planned to re-kindle whatever spark that had existed between them. Within a day, that spark had been stomped on and she couldn't even remember what it looked like.

It was painfully clear that they were over. They'd been a convenient match, but they didn't have a damn thing in common.

Yeah, she was lusting after Grady, big time, but there was something more. Convenience and lust had driven her to hook up with Ryder. When lust fizzled, what remained? What if this was just lust with Grady? She'd dump her boyfriend... fiancé, apparently, and be left with the same drab fizzle as the dust settled?

No, something told her it was more than just lust. Sure, her nipples perked up and her ovaries danced in elation at the wallop of testosterone when he walked into a room. But there was something else.

Practically: She'd already invested two long years with Ryder, and her frontal lobe was settling on staying the course. Biologically: Her uterus declared either Mallory would make beautiful babies. Orgasmically: Many, many parts of her were hooting and hollering for her to give Grady a chance.

Hell, on the flight up, she'd debated calling it quits with Ryder after they'd butted heads on every detail along the way. Then, he'd been sweet and swapped spots with her so she could have the window seat and see the Cascades and Seattle as they landed. He'd even held her hand for no reason, but she couldn't help but feel the affection was his way of making an effort, rather than simply craving the connection.

Tonight. No problem. A romantic dinner for two. And then? Was it really ever okay to have *The Talk* on a trip to meet his family? If she talked to him now, she wouldn't feel comfortable staying any longer, not that she was comfortable staying now, but it would get super awkward. And she wouldn't get to see more of those gorgeous horses.

Or Grady. But, if she waited and had the talk when they got back home, she'd have to spend a miserable vacation being ignored by Ryder, subtly criticized by his crazy parents, and heartbroken with every minute she couldn't do anything about Grady.

No, she was an honest person. She wasn't going to wait around on this one. Maybe she could stay at a hotel in town and meet with local vet clinics. Who knows, maybe she'd find a job here? And find an excuse to explore where things went with Grady?

Impressed with her own problem solving in sixty-seconds-or-less, Claire nodded in satisfaction.

Dump Ryder. Why wait until dinner?

Explore this beautiful town.

Find her dream job.

Seduce her nearly brother-in-law.

She swung open the door and strolled inside. Nothing was better than a good plan.

In the mudroom, she kicked off her boots and hung her jacket on the tidy hook. Despite Ryder's comments on her over packing, she couldn't have spared much. Layers were key. Plus, she needed work boots *and* cute boots *and* sexy dress shoes.

Claire hiked up her oversized wool socks that had loosened when she tugged off her work boots and made for the kitchen to grab another cup of coffee before she dumped Ryder. That term always sounded so crass. Before she declared her intention to discontinue their relationship.

Patricia's voice twittered from the kitchen, stalling Claire in her tracks. Ducking back out of sight, she pinned herself to the wall between the kitchen and the mudroom. She couldn't handle the woman right now.

"You won't miss the gala?" Did Patricia always use that snooty tone, or was it just for show? "Wonderful. Ryder is engaged, so I want everyone to meet Claire... She's stunning, just wait until you meet her... She's a veterinarian. A little rough around the edges, as one would expect for someone in her line of work and from a modest background, but she's quite lovely... Don't repeat that yet, I'm hoping to announce it at the gala and turn it into an impromptu engagement party."

Huh. Take offense? Or focus on the possible compliment wedged in there? Claire pondered which to choose. She searched for a subtle exit. Nope, she had to wait it out here until Patricia left—hopefully out the other door. Go back out to the stables and risk jumping Grady? Or chance Patricia catching her eavesdropping? Rock and a hard place.

A giggle rattled her throat as she visualized being stuck between Grady's hard place and a... well, anything, as long as one side was Grady… *dammit, Claire. A few more hours. Then a reasonable amount of time so you don't look like a slut.*

Pinned against the wall, she went with eavesdropping. Safest choice all around.

She leapt out of her socks when the mudroom door opened and Grady came strolling in. He hopped on one foot to pull up his loose wool sock before he saw Claire. Her heart thunked peculiarly in her chest when she felt his eyes on her. His look, pinched and angry when he'd entered, softened, and his breathing shallowed.

Nope, she was not alone in this crush. Was it a crush when both parties were crushing? She supposed that was the appropriate term when both of their hearts were shattering into teeny-tiny, itty-bitty little pieces.

Patricia's shrilly delighted voice brought her back to the present. "I'm sure your daughter will be disappointed there will be one fewer Mallory on the market… No, nothing from Grady yet… No, I'm sure he likes girls. I'm open either way, but he has terrible luck…"

Grady rolled his eyes and was about to stalk into the kitchen. Claire smacked him in the gut as he tried to walk past her. Okay, so *gut* was the wrong word. Injured her hand on the rock-hard abs was more accurate. The sensation was beyond tempting. She wanted to flatten her palm and explore a bit. She really didn't need to feel just how built he was; it really didn't help her personal hell-bubble she was stuck in until she could sort this whole mess out.

Instead, she moved her finger to her lips to shush him and pushed him back.

He took position against the wall next to her and whispered in her ear, "Hear anything good?"

As close as possible so they wouldn't be heard, and so she could enjoy the lingering scent of frost and horses and leather on his skin, she whispered back, "I wasn't trying to listen in, but I heard her gossiping about me so I waited, and, honestly, hid, and if she saw me *now*, it would be really awkward. So I'm stuck here until the right moment when I can pretend that I just walked in."

He nodded in understanding and listened with her. Although there was plenty of wall to hide behind, he stayed shoulder to shoulder.

"I don't know what to do about Grady. I had hoped he would mellow out by this age, but he can't seem to settle. Maybe he's too much like his father. He is cursed with his temper and his stubbornness both."

Groaning inwardly, Grady thumped the back of his head against the wall. This conversation wouldn't be any more flattering for him than it had been for her. She leaned into him and patted his arm companionably. With his opposite hand, he reached over and held her hand over his arm. Warmth tingled through her at the connection. She glanced up, noting that his eyes had closed in a melodramatic grimace as he listened to his mother gripe about his inadequacies.

Hattie came around the corner. Claire jumped out of her skin at the surprise. As did Hattie. Claire and Grady both shushed her before she inadvertently gave away their position. A good sport, Hattie waved her hand playfully and turned back to the kitchen.

A cacophony filled the kitchen as Hattie decided now was a good time to grind coffee and reorganize the pots and pans.

"I'm sorry Mariah, I'll have to call you back... Hattie, what are you doing? I was on the phone."

Innocently, Hattie's syrupy-sweet voice echoed across the room. "I apologize. I'm just so nervous about the gala that I can't seem to think straight. Do you have a final guest list for me to review?"

"Of course." And Patricia dashed out the opposite door.

*Nice save, Hattie.* "The coast is clear," they heard her announce from the kitchen after a few moments. Hattie went straight for Grady as Claire went to pour some coffee.

Holding his face in her hands, Hattie shook her head meaningfully. "Don't you listen to a word of that nonsense. You're an amazing man with a good heart. You'll find your way."

Grady looked to be holding up ok, but at Hattie's attention, he exhaled a pained sigh. Claire moved to the coffee pot and poured them each an afternoon mug. A smile settling on his lips, he accepted. Impatience weighing on her, Claire let her fingers brush over his at the exchange, then headed upstairs. She was out of steam and knew she wouldn't be able to resist the urge to wrap her arms around him much longer. So, naturally, she ran away before she did anything stupid.

G rady watched as Claire escaped up the stairs. Lucky. He hadn't caught as much of the conversation as Claire had, but it sounded like his mother really liked Claire. Well, as much as Patricia liked anyone that wasn't herself.

Oddly, he was glad. He couldn't have waited silently in the wings if she had insulted Claire. But, as usual, he was the disappointment in his mother's eyes. Actually, he was glad he had eavesdropped this time. He'd always wondered *why*. Ryder and Haley had endured their share of "constructive criticism" over the years, but he'd always taken the brunt of it. Now he realized why. He was the spitting image of his father, Patricia's worst decision and most resented regret.

Hattie shook her finger at him, then grabbed a washrag from the sink and started cleaning up the latest kitchen mess. "Don't you waste another minute dwelling on that baloney. Now, tell me. How are the horses today? You took Claire for a nice long trek on our beautiful trails. You were gone most of the day and must be starving."

He clutched the coffee Claire had brought him and pulled up a barstool. Hattie had been more of a mother to him than

Patricia. Having already raised four of her own children that had grown, she'd shared her momliness with Haley, Ryder, and him. Where his mother lacked it, Hattie made up for it in spades. "We had some protein bars on the ride. I still can't believe they sold Lil. With just the three horses, I wonder if Patricia's planning to phase them out, now that she doesn't ride much anymore?"

Nodding knowingly, Hattie agreed. "I suspect you're the only one that takes any joy in them anymore. Patricia hasn't ridden in years. Too busy." She paused in wiping down the countertops, letting her grip on the washrag loosen. "And what about you? How are you enjoying your work these days?"

Grady didn't answer, instead staring into his cup for the answer to what felt like a rhetorical question.

"You are too brain-washed by your mother. I'm proud of all that you have accomplished. But it's time to do what makes you happy. For you. And no one else."

He shrugged, but continued to stare into his untouched coffee. He was wound up enough and didn't need the caffeine right now.

"And what about Claire?" Old know-it-all eyed him with that gypsy stare that pierced right into his soul. She was downright spooky sometimes.

"What about Claire?" he asked, knowing she'd see right through him.

"You have one week to found out. Are you going to do anything about her?"

"She's Ryder's fiancée. There's nothing to do." His stomach churned, outraged at himself, knowing he wouldn't speak up. The thought of coffee made his gut rebel. That love at first sight business was a load of bullshit. It was just his typical reaction to an off-limits, appealing woman.

"Is she? It's up to you to act in time."

He shook his head. "It's already too late."

The insults may have been more tolerable. He rose from the barstool and tried to escape the kitchen before she responded. But she knew him too well. "Sometimes, a woman wants a man to fight for her. Makes her know just how important she is to him."

"Sounds a little sexist."

"And a man wants a woman to fight for him, too."

# 8

## E-N-M-I-T-Y

"Ryder?" Claire searched the blue suite. Where was he? The bed was neatly made, the bathroom tidy, the pillows properly fluffed in the sitting area.

Ryder's official it's-not-going-well tone bounced down the hall. Poking her head in, she found him pacing in front of a sturdy wooden desk with his laptop open and papers scattered across the desk and floor. Huh, library. Cool. There had to be perks to living in a colossal home. The walls were lined with books from floor to ceiling, although mostly decorative from the look of things.

If this were her library? She'd add some sink-into furniture, maybe a cozy chair in front of the fire, another in place of the desk so she could look out the window and watch the snow fall. If it would ever snow. The forecast teased at it. But since they'd landed, not a single flake.

"I've got this. They're not backing out now... I'll come up with something... Great. Keep me posted." He ran his hand through his mussed hair. Even his button-up was wrinkled.

Ryder hung up the phone and turned to her. His eyebrows scrunched as he took in her appearance. She glanced down and could see why he looked a little stunned. Her socks were floppingly loose at her toes again, mud splatters decorated her jeans from cleaning out horse stalls, and her t-shirt was sticking to her skin after being squished under her heavy sweater and coat all day.

"Hey, Claire. I hope Grady took you for a decent ride." *Oh, it was more than decent.* "I'll owe him big time, but it's freezing out there. You must be a solid ice cube." Eyes soft, connected with hers, he rounded the desk and took her hands in his, pulling her closer as he sat on the edge of the desk. He tapped the tip of her Rudolf nose.

"Cold, but beautiful."

"It was a great town to grow up in," he conceded.

*Don't make this any harder.*

He pushed on. "Seriously, I hope my brother was good company. He can be a little rough around the edges."

*Funny, that's just what your mother said about me.* "What is it with you two? You never talk about him, and, quite frankly, he didn't have much to say about you either."

"We haven't talked much in years, so there isn't much to say I guess."

"He's your brother. That doesn't bother you?"

"I suppose it does. He's still pissy about... a fight we got in."

"Were you friends before that fight?"

"Claire. I know what you're getting at. You can't fix this."

"No. But you can. Just talk to him." Claire pictured Grady's cringe as his mother raked him over the coals this afternoon, after upbraiding him at dinner the night before. She knew their father was out of the picture, and they hardly saw their sister. How could Ryder be okay with staying at odds with him?

"Fine. I'll talk to him."

"Before we go home."

"I will." He teased his hands through his dark hair, the typical preciseness of his style wavering. "I promise. You had an okay day?"

"I had a great time, really. I can't believe you don't want to move back here."

"Look, I'm not cut out for small town life. But while we're here, we could look into a place in the suburbs? Meet halfway in the middle? How does that sound?"

She nodded weakly and let out a heavy sigh, resolving to get it over with sooner than later. "Ryder, do you ever think that we—"

Grady appeared in the doorway. "Hey." He tightened his hand in his hair and leaned against the doorjamb.

Ryder flashed him a dark glare. "Hey."

"I don't know about you guys, but I can't handle another family dinner. Thought I'd head to Ahab's with some friends. You in?"

Shoulders relaxing, Ryder said, "God yes. I haven't been in ages." He glanced to Claire, opened and closed his mouth wordlessly, then laced his fingers with hers. "Actually, I was going to take Claire to the Italian place."

Claire freed her hand. "We can go tomorrow, that's okay. You guys never get to hang out." Glutton for punishment, that's what she was.

"Great." Grady's expression didn't lighten, but his gaze moved back and forth between Claire and Ryder, sensing the heaviness of the unfinished conversation. "If you want to carpool, we can head out around six?"

Claire nodded like an addled bobble-head. That uncertainty in his tone was enough to make her want to wrap her arms around him and try to rebuild the tower of self-confidence she could see had so freshly crumbled.

Pausing and taking Claire's hand, Ryder gently tugged. "Sound good?"

She nodded. Her stomach churned with the oddest sensation that she was cheating on both of them. What the hell had she gotten herself into?

As Grady backed out of the room, Claire turned to Ryder. "I was hoping we could talk. Do you have a minute?"

"Yeah. I've been wanting to talk to you, too." Ryder's phone buzzed.

The moment she went to open her mouth, it buzzed again.

"Babe, I'm so sorry, but I have to take this." He glared at the phone, hesitating. "No, I'm sorry. You're more important. What did you want to talk to me about?"

His phone quit ringing, but started right back up again. She could see him fighting it, but even if he ignored it, his attention was already diverted.

"Later. It's fine." She offered a weak smile and shrugged, backing out of the room.

A wave of relief smoothed the tension from his body, and he answered the phone.

Making her way back to the blue suite, Claire crashed on the sofa and pulled out her phone. She opened her contacts and hovered over her mother's number.

Nope. That conversation was... too premature. What if this creepy house had ears?

Instead, she pulled up details on Ahab's. The website required that she confirm her age over twenty-one, then took her to a quirky page filled with cartoony sailors overlying pictures of people laughing over drinks in a tavern atmosphere. Okay, nothing fancy. Thank goodness.

Claire flipped open her suitcase and pulled out a pair of distressed jeans and a casual white button-up. Realizing she hadn't gone out in months, she found her mascara was pretty near dried out, but she made it work, adding a subtle sweep of eyeliner. No point in lipstick, as she knew she'd chew it off anyway.

And then she curled up with a book.

And played Solitaire on her phone.

Then charged her phone while she touched up her makeup and tried on all her sweaters one by one, then had to straighten her hair thanks to the frizz after trying on the sweaters, landing back on the button-up, but this time she rolled the sleeves up.

Finally, a knock at the door. Leaping off the sofa, then slowing her pace so she didn't look as lonely-desperate as she felt, she eased open the door.

Fresh in athletic-fit faded jeans and a simple Black Op Brewing Company t-shirt that hugged every drool-worthy line on the man, Grady stepped back and shoved his hands in his pockets. He scuffed his hiking boot on the floor before making eye contact. "Ready?" he asked.

"Sure. Um, have you seen Ryder?"

He shook his head. "I figured he was with you."

Fury tensing through her spine, Claire brushed past him and down the hall to Ryder's makeshift office. She could hear his frustrated tone as she neared the library.

She popped her head in and found him pacing and rubbing his hand over his face. He caught sight of her, Grady appearing behind her seconds later. Hand covering the receiver, Ryder whispered, "This isn't going great. Grady, would you mind if Claire rode over with you and I'll meet you guys there?"

Claire pasted on what she hoped was an understanding expression, but she might have overdone the smile. She clicked the door closed behind her, turned and crashed smack-dab into Grady.

Unflinching, he caught her, his hands gripped her waist to steady them both. Eyes wide, she could have caught her breath from the crash, but couldn't seem to re-center when his hands were on her.

He froze, looking down, as if equally moved by the connection that could quickly, easily, and lustily turn into—as the Brits called it, or so she learned on TV—a snog.

Heart thundering in her chest, Claire wanted to move in. Wanted to trace the angle of his jaw and indulge in that kiss that almost happened this morning.

Like he'd been caught with his hand in the cookie jar, Grady jerked away and stared at his hands, as if they were completely foreign.

"Sorry," Claire murmured.

"Yeah, um..." Grady stepped back. "Ready to go?"

She nodded stupidly.

"Okay. I'll just, um, meet you by the front door in five?"

Again, her head bobbled like she was a complete ninny. She didn't even know what a ninny was, exactly, but it sounded neither attractive nor worldly.

Decked out in her new favorite boots, plus a scarf that matched her new coat, she trotted down the stairs. Patiently waiting by the front door, Grady stood with his hands in his pockets. Not playing with his phone or calling or texting or tapping his foot. Just waiting.

Despite her better judgment, Claire approached and stopped just out of arm's reach, knowing better than to exist within touching distance. She really, really needed to have that chat with Ryder.

"Ready?" he asked.

Again with the nodding, she halted her bobbing head and answered, "Yes."

She followed him out to the car and climbed into the passenger seat of his SUV. Buckling, she shivered as he fired up the engine.

Claire reached for the seat heater at the same moment Grady did, their fingers connecting and setting off blazing hot fireworks. This was getting ridiculous.

"Sorry," he muttered.

She settled back into her seat, the heat already radiating beneath her, and folded her arms over her chest.

"Claire?" he asked, the breathy tone sending tingles from her finest capillaries to her deepest veins.

Okay, she needed to get a grip. Wasn't that what Ryder... and her parents, brothers, friends... anyone who knew her well, said on a regular basis? She ran with her imagination far too often. "Yes?"

"I... never mind."

"Okay." Why couldn't she just say it? *Grady, I don't love your brother. But you do something to me. Do you believe in love at first sight? Because I don't. Didn't. But I may have been mistaken. Kiss me and let's see if I'm right.* Nope. She absolutely did not have the courage for that.

They said nothing for the rest of the drive into town. *Awkward* didn't quite capture the vibe. Nothing could measure the humming, unspoken words on both of their lips, nor the zapping electricity that threatened to blast the SUV to shreds.

Claire tucked her hands in her lap and visually explored as they approached downtown. Well, *down* wasn't quite the word. Foothills was perched atop the world, settled between rows of midnight blue mountains that faded to black as the sun set. The amber streetlights countered the onset of night, and the glowing shop windows welcomed visitors to stay awhile. The local population might not be much, but Foothills was clearly a hub for tourists, residents of the smaller neighboring towns, and anyone wanting to hide from the big box stores and breathe some fresh air.

Grady's phone chirped, and he answered over Bluetooth. "What's up?"

Zane's name popped up on the screen. "Hey, where you at?"

"Turning into Ahab's in about thirty seconds."

"I'm picking up Freya and realized I forgot my wallet at work. Mind grabbing it and we'll meet you at dinner?"

He glanced to Claire, brow scrunched as if he truly felt guilty about disrupting her evening, and whispered, "That okay?"

Utterly glowing at his unrehearsed thoughtfulness, she answered, "Of course."

Back to Zane, he said, "Sure thing."

After ending the call, he said, "It'll be a quick stop. Promise."

"I've been hoping to get the chance to see your brewery."

They passed a quirky bar with a flashy, anchor-shaped *Ahab's* sign, but Grady drove past. Happily settled on the main drag about a block down and over, stood Black Op Brewing Company. The building merged industrial with alpine design, the trendy appeal confirmed by groups of beanie-topped friends chatting it up around firepits on the patio.

"This is the place?" she asked, tempted to smack herself on the head at her stupid question.

"This is it."

"Why aren't we going here instead?"

"Zane and I have been spending most of our waking hours here as things take off, not that it's a chore, but it's nice to get away and unwind now and again. Besides, Ahab's is a tradition; we go every few months." Grady drove past and turned down the next alley.

"Do you brew here onsite?"

"Zane's the brewer, I do... whatever Zane doesn't like to do." He parked in a tucked-away spot in the alley. "Come on, I'll show you around. We're early as it is." He led the way in a back door.

Inside, Claire's brain tied into curious knots, too many questions struck her at once as another dimension stacked onto the interesting man. Grady motioned her to enter first, and already the crowd was vibrating with enthusiasm. Gigantic stainless-steel brewing tanks stood behind reclaimed floor-to-ceiling warehouse windows. The plank floors looked to have been laid centuries ago, but the solid wood beams and steel girders, copper tables, and savory scents were modern.

Pausing at the door to the kitchen, Grady said, "We mostly serve light fare, but for those looking for something casual, it's a great dinner spot. Zane built most of the menu, but we sell some meats, cheeses, and baked goods from other local restaurants, and they're starting to pick up our beers." His lips raised to an easy smile.

"Smells amazing." Her lip tucked between her teeth, she closed her eyes and imagined taking a bite of whatever cheesy-savory goodness she'd caught the scent of.

When she opened her eyes, she found his gaze locked onto her lips, his breath coming shallow. Clearing his throat, he pointed to the bar. "Most of our sales actually come from sixpacks and kegs. Although our growlers are gaining popularity."

"Uh-huh," she murmured, unsure if she'd responded out loud or not.

"Offices are up the stairs," he said over the hum of the crowd, following close behind as they wove between tables.

In front of her, a guy tipped back in his chair and crashed to the floor.

Grady wrapped his hand around her middle and pulled her out of the collision zone—and tight against him. The shrouded groan in his voice as she pressed snugly against him sent a seismic wave over her skin. A desperate whimper vibrating in her throat, she froze, terrified to move and lose the connection.

From the floor, the uncoordinated guy cackled as his feet waved in the air before nodding an apology and rolling to a stand, grabbing his coat off the ground while his friends teased him.

Grady's hand splayed over her abdomen. With her ass pressed up against his groin, she melted into a long, satisfied snuggle and leaned into him. But, like a wave of ice water crashing over her, she remembered she hadn't had that talk with Ryder yet. Damn morals. "Thanks," she said, then made for the stairs as soon as the coast was clear.

Grady reached around and unlatched the employees-only chain, then followed her up the stairs. Immediately, she was drawn to the massive tanks and complex system and wandered to the balcony to scope out the setup. Grady disappeared into an office, and she turned to check out the rest of the upstairs.

While he rummaged in what must be Zane's desk, Claire wandered into the other office. There was a huge painting behind his desk, oversized, giving her the sensation of coasting like a hawk on an updraft over a white-topped mountain. A collage of assorted photos hung artfully on the opposite wall. Her favorite, the largest and anchor of the collection, was of Grady laughing, completely carefree, with a group of friends in front of the brewhouse. Opening day.

Grady appeared, stuffing a wallet into his coat pocket.

Still grinning at the photograph, Claire waved him over. Pointing, she asked, "Where is this cheerful guy?"

He shifted his weight on his feet and tugged at his surfer-blond hair. "Stepped away from the office for the moment."

She nudged him in the tummy. "Actually, I see a glimpse of him tonight. You're happy here."

"It's a good business; Zane has great vision. But this other guy? You caught him at a strange time. He's got a lot going on right now. And living with Patricia doesn't help."

"Nor does having Ryder visit. As he hardly talks about you, and I don't think you two have said more than five words to each other since we got in, I'm guessing there's a story there."

"One or two." His voice was clipped, clearly no keener to talk about it than Ryder was.

"I was surprised he took you up on the dinner invitation tonight."

"I didn't know you guys had dinner plans already, and I didn't want you to have to choke down more Brussels sprouts and red wine."

Blushing, she grinned. "I appreciate that."

"Besides, I figured I'd better try."

In the corner of the collage, she landed on a photo of him, maybe in high school, with Ryder and a girl a few years younger. "Is this Haley?"

"You haven't met her yet?"

"Our place is pretty sparse, as neither of us has had much time to decorate. Thus, Ryder doesn't keep family pictures around, but I haven't put any up either. As this is the first time I have met his mother, stepfather, and brother, I suppose I shouldn't be surprised I didn't recognize his half-sister." All three grinned adorably in the photo, thick as thieves with a shared conspiratorial mischief, as if they were about to unveil a sneaky prank. "What happened between you two?"

Grady cringed, his jaw ticking rapidly.

"Sorry," she said, quickly retracting her question. "Not my business."

He gripped his hand in his hair and said, "No, if it's anyone's business, it's yours. He, uh, there was this woman I was seeing... Actually, on second thought, maybe you should ask him."

"Okay." She shoved her hands in her pockets before she palmed that jaw to calm the clench. How hard he worked to keep a lid on the temper gutted her, and she sensed how rarely he was able to let loose. Not in the stiff Mallory household anyway. She wandered out of the office and leaned against the iron rail that overlooked the brewing tanks. Hair brushing over her shoulder as she looked back, she found him leaned against the doorway, watching, the temper fade to sad. "How did a lawyer end up co-owner of a craft brewery?"

The corner of his lips quirked up as he strolled to her side and leaned against the rail. Those ocean eyes lit up, his smile coming easy. "Too easy. Zane got out of the Navy last year. A bit of a mess, with no idea what he wanted to do. Anyway, he experimented with brewing as a hobby. Amazing stuff, professional quality. He'd invested a lot of time and energy into it, but hadn't had any intention of doing anything with the skill. One night at Ahab's, I hinted that he had an incredible talent and that this area needed a decent microbrew. A week later, he called me up and asked if I could offer some legal advice. As we were going through the details, I, uh, sort of offered to invest a huge chunk of my savings and go in as a full partner."

"I'm guessing he was on board?"

"To say the least. He's the artist, no interest in the business end of things. I don't mind that stuff, especially when it interests me, so here we are." Full grin, he turned toward her, his eyes drifting down, catching her gnawing on her lower lip as she tried to not grin back like a sap-happy groupie.

Grady stepped back and stuffed his hands in his pockets.

Claire did the same. "We should get going."

"Yeah." He locked the office doors and flicked off the upstairs lights. "Claire?"

"Yes?" she asked, a desperation in her voice. Dammit, she needed to get better at hiding her reactions.

"Ryder and I don't talk much because of an old girlfriend. As much as I'd love to piss him off and give him a taste of his own medicine, that's not me."

Falling, dropping like a fiery ball of lead in her stomach... or an organ slightly superior and lateral, wrenched and threatened acute arrest. She bit her lips together and nodded, unable to find anything to say that wouldn't make it worse.

Nodding, she followed him down the stairs. Rather than heading out the back, he motioned to the front door. Outside, the patio heaters and firepits kept the vicinity comfortable, but the moment they crossed the iron gate, the chill night sent a billion nanoscopic icepicks into her skin.

As the noise of the brewhouse quieted behind them, he nodded. "Ahab's is probably packed. Easier to stay parked here and... well, I guess Ryder will take you home after."

She nodded.

The walk was short and... not so sweet. Grady didn't say a word. Claire couldn't find a single word in the entire English language, or Latin for that matter, that wouldn't make them both sink deeper into aching misery.

Inside, the heat and the commotion of the crowd knocked her backward into Grady. His hand laced around her middle to steady her, as he had at Black Op. Stiffening, both pulled away. Grady stuffed his hands back in his pockets, but leaned in close so she could hear him over the roar of the crowd. Cheek to cheek, he said, "Ahab's is quirky, the food's decent, and it's a Foothills original."

Leaning in, letting the rough growth of his weekend beard brush her cheek, she asked, "Why the whaler's theme?"

"Clever marketing tactic."

"Ryder would never come up with something this off-the-wall."

At his brother's name, Grady pulled away and his smile faded. Claire followed him through the crowd.

Two couples were already seated at a row of pushed-to-gether high-top tables in the back. Grady pulled out a stool for Claire, then sat down next to her. "This is Claire, Ryder's fiancée."

They introduced themselves, friendly but curious looks on every face. Asher was shockingly handsome, and Sophie a good match for him. Pippa was vibrantly bubbly, and her husband Lincoln was gracious, offering Claire a pint first thing. Asher raised his glass. "Are you surviving Patricia so far? I have yet to win her favor, but I can't say that I've tried."

A mountain of appetizers appeared on the table, and Claire waited an appropriate moment for the others to dig in, then scooped a variety on her plate, grabbing for the jalapeno poppers at the same time as Sophie. She flashed her a wink, and Sophie passed the platter closer so they could share.

Claire sat up straight in her stool and devoured a bite of popper, considering how to respond. "I honestly haven't had much interaction with her, aside from light conversation over dinner."

Eyebrow raised, Asher said, "You can be honest. As she thinks Zane and I have corrupted Grady beyond repair, I treat her with the same respect that she treats me."

Grady groaned and glared into his beer. "We got to overhear Patricia's latest rant about my inadequacies as a potential mate for some lucky woman. But she did seem to compliment Claire behind her back."

"I believe the words were, 'rough around the edges,' but otherwise I seem to have passed inspection so far. But I haven't exactly let her see my quirks."

Grady leaned his knee against hers. "Quirky is a good thing."

Across the table, Sophie scrunched her eyebrows suspiciously at his remark.

Claire blushed, but didn't get to respond. A pair of hands grasped her shoulders. Ryder leaned down and plastered a kiss on her temple. "She is quirky. But lovably so."

After dropping onto the stool next to her, Ryder linked his fingers with hers and stole the last buffalo wing from her plate. Scowling, she stuffed in the last bite of popper and looked to the center of the table for more, but the wings had disappeared faster than the poppers.

Grady grabbed the last two from his plate and slid them on hers, wiped his fingertips on his napkin, and disappeared into his shell.

A few minutes later, another tray appeared, quickly followed by Zane, tall, broad, and starkly handsome as he was in the pictures at Black Op, and possessively holding hands with a fairy-amazon woman that shared an adoring grin before taking a seat against the wall.

Grady made the introductions, then fell markedly quiet. Ryder settled in against her, friendly and easygoing as he nailed a sweet kiss on her cheek. Where was the good-boyfriend side of him *yesterday?*

Sipping the whiskey he'd ordered, skipping on the shared pitcher, Ryder leaned forward to talk over her and asked Grady, "Two business partners, huh? Patricia said the beer was a hobby."

"Patricia thinks a lot of things," Grady muttered, punctuating the sarcasm with a swig of his beer.

Lincoln swallowed and shook his head. "And here I thought all you Mallorys would appreciate that Grady's a workaholic. I thought that was a family trait."

Ryder snorted. "That's Patricia's thing. As soon as I've got a solid foundation, I'm setting my own hours."

*I'll believe that when I see it.* Claire closed her eyes so no one could see the eye-roll.

With Grady scowling into his glass, Ryder surfing the arrogant wave, Lincoln and Zane puffing up to defend their mutual business partner, and Claire slumping down in her stool, Freya dinged her spoon against her glass and said, "Okay. Okay, moving along. Claire, I'm dragging you out later this week and we'll hang out?"

Claire lit up and nodded vigorously. Safely away from both Mallory brothers? Brilliant plan. "That would be great. This is my first vacation in years."

"You get to choose then. I'll send you some ideas. Hiking or something touristy... or relaxing. Think it over." Freya seemed to read her mind, knowing Claire was having the least relaxing vacation in history.

On either side of her, neither Mallory seemed to notice, and looked ready to throttle each other.

Freya powered on. "First, I think we all need to chill out. Let's play a game or something."

Pippa wiggled in her seat and grinned mischievously. "How about Never Have I Ever again? Grady and I kicked all of your asses last time. And now we have new blood to make it interesting."

Asher's lips quirked into an amused grin. "Let's flip it this time, whoever is the most *experienced* wins."

Under his breath, Ryder laughed and said, "Nah, I think Claire might tie the innocence duo."

*And that's not helpful.* Claire parked her tongue between her teeth and counted to five. No luck. She went for ten.

Grady leaned forward and clenched his fingers in his hair as he shook his head. "Please god no."

Sophie objected with a hair-shifting headshake. "I think we're getting too old for—"

Pippa ignored her completely. "I've never had a one-night stand."

Sliding off his stool, Ryder raised a finger with the other adventurous folks and said, "Sorry, I need a quick pit stop. I'll hurry, I don't want to miss Grady's admission that he is truly Mr. Perfect."

Grady raised a middle finger to flip him off before burying his head in his hands. He stayed quiet until it got to his turn, not a finger raised. Well, aside from the middle one. That one he put back down once Ryder was out of sight. "Pass," he muttered.

Claire's hand reached under the table and rested on his knee, her soothing whisper against his ear bordering on torture. "You okay?"

Completely at her mercy, he glanced her way. Her hazel eyes were downright melty, her pouty lip turned down just for him. He gave her a soft nod and sat up taller on his stool.

Eyebrows pulled together knowingly, a sparkle in her deep blues, Freya smiled to herself. Witchy sometimes, and knowing she saw right through him, Grady subtly shook his head. *Later*, he mouthed silently. No doubt, she wasn't going to let him off the hook until she'd heard the full story.

Ryder reappeared, plopped down on his stool, tugged Claire against him, and spread his hand over her thigh. Posture stiffening, she forced a smile and released her hand from Grady.

"Did I miss it?" Ryder asked.

Pippa smiled. "Grady was trying to pass, but we know he's got lots of Nevers. Come on Grady, don't let me down."

"Mr. Goody-Two-Shoes? Of course he does. Come on Grady. See if you can out-never Claire. You got her on the speeding tickets. What about getting less than an A-minus? Or killing off a few of those brain cells in college? Sex anywhere other than a practical mattress?"

"Fuck off," he muttered under his breath. "I think you've been spending too much time partying to impress your skeezy clients."

"Hey, I figured by now you would have figured out that playing it straight not nearly as fun."

"Fine." He sat up in his seat, gaze locked onto Ryder. "I've never fucked anyone else's girlfriend." And this is why his mother wasn't wrong in her rant about his temper. And why he didn't play competitive... anything anymore. The entire table fell quiet, the awkward pall as thick as this morning's fog.

Claire stiffened next to him, then her eyes lit up as she blurted out, "I've never had an orgasm."

The entire table stared, mouths gaping wide open. Ryder's mouth scrunched into a *what-the-fuck-are-you-talking-about* that looked painfully natural. How did she end up with an asshole that didn't get her humor? Quirky, yeah, but wicked.

"Just messing around." She laughed, patting the side of Grady's leg before pulling her hand back away. "Okay, I've never been off the continent."

Shit, Ryder's turn. Grady was tempted to make an emergency escape, but, dammit, these were *his* friends. "I've never been kicked out of a bar."

Grady clenched his jaw and tried to calm down before he got them both kicked out. Tempted to raise his middle finger, he downed a swig of his beer and held out his thumb. It had been Ryder's fault, so the finger really should go to him.

The challenges bounced around again, his friends doing their best to ease the tension. Well, most of them. Asher wasn't so subtle. "I've never kissed anyone's ass to sell them anything."

The corner of Grady's lips turned up as Asher nudged him under the table. Claire bit her lips together and stared at the ceiling with a discreet smile.

Grady kept it tame for the next few rounds, feeding Asher and Freya easy points to end the game as quickly as possible. He was too wiped from the long day out in the cold anyway. Maybe tonight hadn't been the best night to hang out. He was ready to crash and sleep for the next week and a half... until Claire was out of his life.

She wasn't any perkier. As the night wore on, she slouched in her chair and faded from the conversation.

Wide awake and raring to go, Ryder hopped up from his stool and rubbed a hand on Claire's shoulder. "I see some old friends. Let me introduce you around?"

Claire shook her head. "Not this time."

While Ryder spent the next hour chatting it up, Claire's eyes fluttered shut, and she slumped against Grady's side. Against his better judgment, he breathed her in, her hair soft against his rough growth of beard, her scent filled with lavender and leather and absolutely not the tropical flower he'd pictured for Ryder.

Grady gulped his water and groaned, "You know what? I think we need some new games. Doesn't matter how we play it, I always get my ass kicked."

Asher's eyes darted back and forth between Grady and Claire. "Yeah, you do lose too much."

Sophie pointed behind him. "Looks like Ryder's racking up another round at billiards. You should take Claire home."

Eyes heavy, Claire lifted her head and turned to discover that Ryder showed no signs of slowing, then rotated back on her stool. "I'm sorry, Grady, do you mind? I can't seem to keep my eyes open."

*As you wish,* he thought, patting himself on the back for not saying it out loud. His feelings were already pretty damn obvious. "Sure," he said instead, his voice full of gravel.

# 9

## W-H-O-O-P-S-A-D-A-I-S-Y

"I swear, I didn't even know you were interested." Trace Perry covered her mouth, her delighted shock brightening her naturally brilliant demeanor.

"Not even a little? Haley moved away. But you kept coming over to hang out, so I thought *you* were interested. Yeah, we were friends enough, but I wasn't subtle." Grady took a bite of his smoked salmon with gruyere over spring greens, smiling through full cheeks.

She set down the chunk of pretzel she'd been about to bite and shook her head. "No way. I was so pathetically lonely, I figured you thought I didn't have anywhere else to go."

"Come on, you were hot. Still are." He took a slow sip of his beer, a coffee stout, and Zane's latest creation.

"Well, thank you." A soft pink blush heated her cheeks, but her grin didn't show a hint of bashful. Comfortable with her porcelain skin showing every emotion, Trace was the first to admit when she was embarrassed. "But seriously. You were this force of nature. Good at *everything*. Captain of the football team as a junior, balancing that with the competitive hockey league you did year-round. The rodeos, golf, swimming, debate. Dated the entire cheerleading team. A freckled, unathletic freshman that was absolutely *not* in the popular crowd? I thought you asked me to homecoming as a pity date."

"So you went with Finn Halseth instead."

Seconds later, Zoe Halseth appeared to refill their waters. "Hey Trace. Mom wanted me to pass along a thanks for the pastries you dropped by. I was so relieved she ate something."

Grady mirrored the melty regret in Zoe's eyes. "How is she doing?"

"Not good." Zoe set down the water pitcher as her hand started to shake. "Evan and I are picking up the weight around here so Dad can go to her chemo infusions with her."

Trace rested her hand on Zoe's. "Please. Anything I can do to help, don't hesitate."

Zoe wiped away a bead of moisture from her eyelashes and nodded. "Absolutely." She picked up the water and forced a smile. "Finn should be home to visit after the postseason is done. I'm sure he'll look you up when he gets here."

Blushing, Trace chugged her refilled water.

Zoe winced. "Grady. I'm sure he'll be glad to see you, too."

Grady smiled as he took a slow sip of beer. *Rub it in*.

As Zoe backed away, she said, "Oh, I heard Ryder is in town. Say 'Hi' for me?"

His eyebrows quirked together. "Sure thing." Interesting.

Trace set down her empty water glass and sighed, biting her smile as Zoe disappeared. "That adds a measure of awkward."

"Well, you chose Finn over me once before." He flashed her a wink and leaned back in his chair.

"It is good to see you, Grady. I wasn't sure this was a setup until Patricia told me how busy you've been at work as the successful attorney who is going to be mayor in a few years."

His turn to wince. He rubbed a hand over his mouth. "Mayor? Oh, she is a wonder."

"She's a proud mama."

"Mama is far too maternal of a word for Patricia."

"Fair point. But she thinks the world of you." Trace nudged his foot as a foggy pall threatened to wash over him. "Grady, I've always thought the world of you, too." She caught his attempt to argue and powered on, "but Finn was it for me back then."

"He was a lonely puppy with no friends, and you were a softie. But as he turned out to be a good friend of mine, too, no hard feelings."

"Why did you ask me out? Today, I mean. Aside from Patricia working on this since I got home." She ripped off a bite of pretzel and dunked in cheese soup. "I'm glad you did, but..."

He picked up his beer and set it back down, knowing she was right without even hearing the end of her trailed-off thought. "I haven't been out much since I finished law school and, shit, I needed an excuse to get out of the house. An evening with Trace? As a date or as friends, it sounded like a good distraction."

"No way. You always have one in your sights. You're telling me you didn't have a single woman on your radar until your mother insisted you call me?"

"Not a single one." The corner of his mouth quirked up, hoping she didn't catch how he drew out the word *single*.

She chewed another morsel of cheesy pretzel and considered, grinning as her eyes laid on his ticking jaw. "There's more to this story. Spill."

"Spill? I'm not Haley. Not out to be spilling any feelings, here." His tone was harsh, but he couldn't help but grin. Yeah, probably a good thing neither seemed to be making any moves toward hooking up tonight. Hot as she was, the idea of kissing her? Like a sister or something.

"Hmm. Patricia told me Ryder is in town with his adorable fiancée, the veterinarian that is a little quirky, but very down-to-earth, and she thinks we'll get along great."

"You two would get along great. Claire and Ryder are out to dinner at the Italian place. This is her meet-the-future-in-laws trip. Patricia is thrilled to get to announce their engagement at her annual gala."

"You said Claire and Ryder. Not Ryder and Claire."

"Shit, Trace. You're a bloodhound." He leaned back in his chair and shook his head, chuckling under his breath.

"You fell for your future sister-in-law."

Stiffening, checking that no one was listening in, Grady shushed her. "Have not."

"No? Tell me about her and your entirely platonic feelings for each other."

Grady gulped the last of his beer and stared at the receding foam pooling at the bottom. "No."

"Is she nice?"

"Yeah."

"Is she pretty?"

"Yes. As are you."

"What was she wearing when she left for dinner?"

"Trace," he warned.

She raised an eyebrow, and the corner of her mouth quirked up like she'd been caught by a sneaky fisherman, as Haley's always was when she knew she was right.

"Fine. A black cable-knit sweaterdress with boots that go over her knees."

"Tights or no?"

"None. And yes, her legs are long and toned and shapely and... I'm in such deep shit."

"Wow, you've got it bad."

He lowered his elbows to the table and rubbed his hand over his mouth. "I am aware. Can you see why I called you?"

"You were hoping lightning would strike and release you from the spell?"

"Yeah."

"Grady?"

"Yeah?"

"Does she feel the same?"

He flashed back to the near-kiss in the stables. Then when that guy at Black Op crashed in front of her; she'd leaned into him, her pulse racing as fast as his, and not because of the near-miss. Her hand on his thigh last night at Ahab's to comfort him. "I don't know. If she does, and doesn't end things with Ryder?"

Mouth as parched as the Sonoran Desert thanks to the dry red wine that Ryder had insisted would complement her mushroom ravioli, Claire gulped her water as she glanced around the lovely restaurant. Dim lighting, tables spaced far enough apart for romantic privacy, decent acoustics. Ryder's uninterrupted attention. It was time. Past time.

"I heard a rumor that we were engaged." Her lip throbbed from where she'd worked it all afternoon, worrying about how to start this dreaded conversation. Her knee vibrated at rapid speed, restless as she'd hid in their suite all day to avoid running into anyone. One more spark with Grady and she would probably ignite.

Ryder winced, his brow heavy with guilt. "About that. Patricia was nagging me about how I'm too old to be still playing the field, and why can't I settle down like my perfect little sister. Preferably that I get moving *now*, so she can announce it at the gala. And, well, I panicked and told her we were already engaged. I'm so sorry, I forgot to mention it."

After meeting Patricia, she could absolutely understand where that little fib came from. "You could have at least warned me." Break-ups sucked. Especially when he'd inevitably ask for a reason, and she really didn't want to tell him the full details. At least, not the reason for her poor timing.

"I figured Grady would be grateful I took some of the pressure off him. Patricia was beaming when we left, as he's out with Trace. She's an old friend and gorgeous redhead. Perfect for him."

Desperate for a distraction, Claire gulped down her desiccant-infused wine. As the last of the moisture in her mouth sapped away, she picked up her water glass and pouted when she discovered she'd already finished it off. This was going great. Like the skating rink. Too late. A sign. *Sure, what sort of sign is this vague? Stop fantasizing about your fiancé's brother and go with the safe, no-brainer relationship in front of you?*

When the server appeared with their dinners, Ryder waited for her to take the first bite, then eased back into conversation. "Grady had the hots for her in high school, but, as usual, he hesitated and she hooked up with another guy."

"How long have they been seeing each other?"

"I have no idea. Grady and I don't exactly sit and talk about relationships. But it's Grady, he's always got someone on the line."

"Player, huh?" She chewed the mushroom ravioli until it degraded to a nauseating paste. Not daring to swallow, she kept chewing for fear she might choke on it.

"Makes me—before I met you—look like a saint. Seriously. Name a single woman in town, and he's either slept with her or tried."

"Oh." Pressure welled behind her eyes. Was she getting Grave's disease? Blinking, she tried to equalize before scheduling the thyroidectomy.

And she folded. Cat got her tongue. Ryder wasn't so bad. At least she knew him.

Why had she let herself get so worked up about a guy she didn't even know? One that, from the sounds of things, was adept at flashing a few winks and dampening some panties.

*Holy shit, Claire, get a grip.* Nerve lost, appetite toast, Claire couldn't work up the courage to dump him tonight.

When they got back to the blue suite that night, they crawled quietly into bed. Ryder leaned in and kissed her goodnight. Lips soft against hers, he moved in to take it further.

Pulling away, still suffering from the world's worst cases of cottonmouth and ocular pressure, Claire closed her eyes and forced a smile. "I've got a migraine."

Confused, or so it felt from the stiff rollover, Ryder shut off the lamp. Voice crackling as he spoke under the brightening glow of the moon, he said, "Claire?"

"Yeah?"

After a long inhale, staring up at the ceiling on the opposite side of the bed, Ryder finally spoke. "I'm sorry things don't seem to be getting any easier. Let's just get through this trip and take some time when we get home. Now's not the time to be making any big decisions."

Hair tangling against the pillow as she nodded, Claire murmured, "You're right. I can't think straight right now."

Hours later, eyes still wide open, Claire stared up at the ceiling. Ryder snored softly beside her, peacefully in dreamland. Midnight. One. Two.

Regret was a terrible sleep-depriver. She should have just ended it at dinner. Grady or no Grady in her future, known evil or not, Ryder wasn't the one for her. When did she turn into such a fraidy cat?

Okay. That's enough. Her stomach was growling anyway, having hardly touched her dinner.

Claire slipped out of bed and tiptoed to the door. A sharp hunk of icy metal jabbed into her foot. She grabbed her foot and hopped as she silenced her yelp. What the hell was that? Claire bent down and found Ryder's belt on the floor. As he never left stuff on the floor, she knew he was as messed up as she was right now.

Despite her limp, she made it out of the bedroom, unscathed through the final stretch, and closed the door behind her. Looking down, she realized she wore nothing but tiny shorts and a paper-thin, spaghetti strap camisole, her nipples standing at attention in the cool air.

Nope, that would be downright slutty. If Bill or Patricia came down for a midnight snack? She shivered at the thought.

She didn't dare risk waking Ryder, so she grabbed the chunky cardigan that she'd left on the arm of the couch and slipped it on. It covered enough so she would be safe if anyone walked in. Slutty, but waking Ryder was riskier.

The tile kitchen floor was freezing, and her toes immediately curled inward. Claire shuffled quickly toward the kitchen to grab her snack so she could escape back upstairs.

As she rounded the corner, she lurched, flooding with panic and lust and thrill and stupidity and... *Dammit.* Sexy-as-holy-fucking-hell. Like her waking dreams of him suddenly materialized in the kitchen, along details that she would never have had the creativity to conjure. Her jaw lost all strength and her eyes hazed with unbridled appreciation like when Captain Kirk laid eyes on a scantily dressed alien with big boobs.

Grady gulped from a crystal-clear glass of water, his Adam's apple bobbing with the guzzle. The angle of his arm was... superb. As if he were posing to give her the absolute best view of how his deltoid and bicep and tricep all came together like a Platonian model. Not to mention those abs—sans shirt. Washboard, she believed, was the term. And those carefree jeans slung low on his hips, top button undone. *Puh-hoo.*

Gasping as he downed the last of his drink, he turned to see her standing and gawking. The corner of his mouth quirked up, a satisfied grin like she was exactly what he had ordered. "Hi," he said.

Shivers ran straight up her spine. When did "*Hi*," become the single most seductive word in the English language? Why again, had she lost her nerve and not ended things with Ryder?

Player or not, she could at least have a quick rebound before going home...

"Hi," she answered, hoping she didn't look like the eager horn-dog she had become. "I, uh, couldn't sleep."

His grin widened. "You couldn't seem to stay awake at Ahab's. Sleep too much last night so you can't sleep tonight?"

"Thanks again for taking me home last night. Or, well..." She glanced at the time. "Two nights ago, I suppose. I know you probably wanted to stay and hang out with your friends more."

"I see them all the time. All good."

"I like them."

"They're the best." He put his glass in the dishwasher and rested his hands on his hips. Not helpful. The pose was downright... *damn,* that man was appealing. "Hungry? I think there's some leftover pizza."

"Patricia and Bill ordered pizza?"

He opened the refrigerator and pulled out a lidded Pyrex. "Oh no. But the chef makes exceptional pizza."

Claire unlocked her frozen toes and moved close enough to check out the cold pizza, but maintained a maximum amount of distance between them so she didn't inadvertently jump him. Whole wheat thin crust, a variety of cheeses, tomato, jalapeno, green chiles. "Looks amazing. Hot or cold?" She grinned, baiting him to give the right answer.

"Trust me?" he asked, raising a devious eyebrow.

"Maybe."

He grabbed a plate and loaded it up with a pair of slices and hit the thirty-second button on the microwave, turned the oven to broil, then transferred the nuked pizza to crispen.

"Fancy."

"Every experienced bachelor knows how to reheat pizza. Since flying this coop, I usually live alone. When I don't have friends thinking my spare bedroom is an invitation for a roommate."

And she was reminded of exactly why she hadn't broken things off with Ryder yet. An *experienced bachelor*, even by his own admission.

"Lucky. I've never lived alone."

"Really?"

"I could never afford my own place."

"And that's why you and Ryder moved in together so quickly."

"Precisely."

Grady skillfully slid the slices out of the oven, onto the plate, and set them up at the island.

Stomach rumbling at the savory scent, Claire hopped on the stool next to him and sank her teeth into the crispy-melty goodness. As she filled her hollow belly, her leg relaxed against Grady's. The heat was toastier than the fresh-broiled cheese, but she needed it. Craved the connection. Thrived on the geomagnetic activity stirring between them, resonating deep to the mitochondrial level.

*Dammit.* She stiffened and pulled her leg away. She was not about to be the player Ryder had accused Grady of being. Six-letter fancy term for slut. *W-A-N-T-O-N.*

As he swallowed another bite, Grady wiped the corner of his mouth on a napkin and asked, "You didn't do much better at the stupid *I Never* game than I did." They'd kept things pretty PG, but she suspected there was nothing PG about Grady's sex life.

"I suppose I'm not very adventurous."

"I know that's not true."

"Really. I'm ridiculously ordinary. I don't break rules, I don't try dangerous things."

"You went ice skating alone, without ever having even seen ice, just for fun."

"That was different."

"Yeah? The next day, you rode trail into thick fog with a strange man that hasn't been subtle at the fact that he is attracted to you, even knowing that you're spoken for."

She pulled her lip into her teeth, not having a clue what to say. Wasn't he seeing someone? If not, would he think less of her if she sprinted up the stairs, woke up Ryder to dump him, then ran back downstairs and tore all her clothes off?

Appetite rapidly diminishing, she set down her pizza and adjusted her posture. "How was your dinner? Ryder said you've known Trace for a long time?"

His eyes brushed over her, his demeanor darkening, and he set down his pizza crust and slid the plate away. "For as long as I can remember."

"I'd love to meet her. Ryder thinks she's great." Dreading hearing him say more, Claire carried the plate to the sink, dumping their crusts into the trash. She rinsed and placed it in the dishwasher.

When she turned around, she reveled in his hungry ogle, wishing the forlorn weren't laced in there. Yeah, she probably should have worn more than the sweater. A few wrong angles, or right, depending on your perspective, and he'd get a hell of a show.

Knowing he was watching, that he had the player reputation, already confessing his attraction to her, while they were both seeing other people... well, she would hate herself for it later, but she needed to *know*, before saying *I do* or *I don't*. Or, *yes* or *no-thank-you*, as Ryder had yet to actually propose. She reached up into the cupboard, her sweater sliding up and flashing him a view of her tiny shorts, leaving no doubt that the lower curve of her butt was visible. Not looking back this time, needing that sliver of hope, she filled the glass and downed it, thirstier than ever.

Coming up for air, she glanced back at him, enjoying his jaw-dropped heated look.

"What?" he asked.

What had she asked him? Oh yeah. That. "How long have you been seeing Trace?"

"We're not seeing each other. We went out tonight, and I was hoping something would click, as I really don't enjoy lusting after my brother's fiancée, but Trace will always be my sister's friend." Blinking, he shook his head and took a deep breath, then stalked to the liquor cabinet. Even the man's walk was a nice sight. Hips steady, shoulders back, he maintained a casual elegance that was darkened by a tempered edge. "Whiskey?"

Unable to resist, Claire slid back onto the stool, her pulse pinging under her skin, wanting him to ask her again with that sultry tone. And again. And again. "Please."

Hands steady, he poured a double for each of them and slid her drink onto the granite, the glass gliding over thc stone, the amber liquid oscillating in rhythm.

She picked up her glass and asked, "To what are we toasting?"

Without shifting the stool further away, as he should, he sat next to her. His knee leaned against hers and swiftly jerked back. "Terrible relationships." He raised his glass in salute.

The phrase rattled through her skull. With a knowing nod, she clinked her glass against his and downed the whiskey in one long, burning gulp that seared her throat.

Eyes wide, he watched as she licked the final drip from her lower lip. Gaze not straying from her mouth, he downed his glass.

Breathless, she let the warm-and-fuzzy loosen her stiff shoulders. And her haywire brain. "If we I-Nevered bad luck at relationships, I would absolutely win."

"Not a chance. I am the reigning champ at that one."

The corners of her lips twitching as she turned the never into a dare, she nodded. "Prove it."

"Where do I start?" He rose from the island and grabbed the whiskey, then poured another shot for each of them.

"From the beginning."

"Jenny Mitchell. Kindergarten. I held my hand out to reassure her when the school nurse was delivering measles shots. She screamed. Not from the shot, but at the idea of holding hands with me."

"Ouch. That is terrible. Barry Minor. Eighth grade. Kissed me at the bus stop, then bragged to all his friends when we got to school that we'd had sex. I spent the next three and a half years trying to convince everyone that I was a virgin."

"Prick. I'm sorry. Three and a half years?" He didn't budge when she leaned into him. Instead, proving just how unlucky she was, he didn't move away and instead fused the connection.

"Backseat of Justin Malkovich's mother's sedan. It was as terrible and uncomfortable as it sounded. And he also bragged to the entire school. I gave up arguing. I made the unofficial school yearbook awards as *Most Promiscuous*. For one guy, once."

"Shit. How many guys have you been with?"

"Three. Come on, I'm winning here." She hiccupped the last word.

He nudged her. "You're drunk."

"I'm a lightweight." A giggle erupted from deep in her throat.

He bopped her nose delicately with the knuckle of his pointer finger. "I might be too."

"Come on, you're up. Terrible relationships."

"On my first trip home from law school, I, uh... I walked in on my girlfriend, with, um..."

"Who?"

"Doesn't matter. She seemed set on proving her point. And it worked."

"Didn't want to wait for you, huh?"

"Nope. Fast-forward a few more terrible relationships, and I met Sophie."

"Sophie from Ahab's?"

"The very one. Anyway, Lincoln had totally talked her up, saying she was the one for me. Pippa was even worse. And we did hit it off right away. I wouldn't say sparks, but a light simmer. Then... she met Asher, and I found out she wasn't interested in me after all when I walked in right after they'd enjoyed a little dressing room action. I hadn't even realized they were into each other."

"Ouch."

His body tensed, firm and blazing against her skin. He leaned forward and gripped his hand in his hair. "Worst one yet. I met this incredible woman. She's got a laugh that makes everything more colorful. Is charming as hell, but she doesn't seem to realize it. Brilliant. Her brain is always ticking with weird facts and has this quirky sense of humor that she rarely shares, and I wish she'd say it out loud."

This punchline wouldn't be what she was hoping for. Couldn't be. For either of them.

He continued, "Best date of my life, and I went to ask her out, only to find out she's taken. Worst of all, in this house that I hate, there she is, engaged to my brother, who absolutely doesn't deserve her."

His ocean blues locked onto hers, heavy and swimming, and she was drowning. Both glossy-eyed, from the liquor or the moment, she wasn't sure. Chest rising and falling with mountainous effort like she was wearing too many lead drapes to protect her from destructive x-ray radiation, Claire let her gaze lower to those irresistible lips.

Testing, hesitant, he leaned closer. Breath shared, soft, spiced, his lips were so close she could already feel the zap. She closed that last sliver of distance and broke that last line. *Just once.*

As she'd hypothesized, lightning struck.

Molten lava coursed through her veins. Her brain went all wonky as electrical connections busted and rebuilt again. Warm, pliant, he took it further, kissing, again.

Breathless, the world crumbling around them, she dug her fingers into his hair and wrapped around him. Deepening the kiss, he slid his tongue over hers, tasting, exploring, his hand cradling her jaw as he soared with her to a distant fairytale land.

A soft whimper passed her lips as the rest of her body pleaded to be included.

The south stairs creaked. A grumbling yawn preceded the intruder.

Claire leaped off the stool and booked it out of there.

Stealing one last glance, she found Grady sitting alone, rumpled and astonished.

# 10

## C-O-N-T-R-I-T-E

"**M**om, I messed up." Claire dropped into the blue suite sofa and buried her head in her hands, phone glued to her ear. Vibrant and cheerful, the sun was rising, but she felt the chill in the air through the triple-paned window anyway.

"Uh-oh. Tell me what happened."

"I... fuck. I don't know how to say it."

"Eek. I'd tell you to watch that language, but you must have a good reason for dropping that f-bomb," Val said sympathetically.

"I don't love Ryder."

"Oh, honey, I'm so sorry. The trip isn't going well?"

"I, uh... I'm such a bitch." She bit her tongue. "Sorry."

"You could never be a bitch." The b-word rolled off her mother's tongue awkwardly, but with a fierce determination that loosened the lump in Claire's throat.

"Have you ever had a crush on a guy that wasn't Dad?"

"Of course. It's natural to find other men attractive. As long as it's never more than an appreciation."

"I kissed his brother."

Long pause. "Oh my."

"Yup," she mumbled, popping the last letter with finality.

"Did you have a good reason?"

"There's never a good reason for kissing your fiancé's brother."

Gasp. "Engaged? Honey, you didn't tell me that."

"Well, we're not actually engaged. Long story. But a few days ago, it's what I thought I wanted."

"I can throw out a few reasons Ryder isn't the one for you. Should we start there, or do you want to focus on the brother?"

"That is part of the issue. I can't get my mind off his brother."

"Did you tell Ryder what happened?"

"No. I plan to break up with him first."

"Good plan." Long pause. Heavy sigh. Maternal supportive judgment. Claire wished she had gone for a video call so she could add the puppy dog eyes.

Claire blurted out, "Ryder says Grady is a player. But I'm not sure I believe that."

"He did kiss his brother's fiancée."

"Thanks, Mom. So helpful."

"Well he did. That alone doesn't exactly reflect well on him."

"What about me? I'm the one in a serious relationship."

"Not to worry, you're not off the hook. Who instigated the kiss?" Val's voice was stern but loving. But what Claire really needed was a hug. Or wine on the front porch while the hot afternoon sun settled into night, like they'd do when Claire's grad school classes would end early.

"Me. Maybe it was him. I'm not sure who started it, but we are both very guilty. And there was definitely whiskey involved."

"Well, there's your first mistake. Not that it's an excuse, but don't drink while alone with a man you have feelings for."

"No shit. Lesson learned." She snorted, and neglected to add, *in the middle of the night while both parties are grossly underdressed.* "When you met Dad, I know you guys hit it off right away. But... was there that electricity, like they talk about in sappy romances?"

"I know that's not an easy thing to find, but... yes. I knew." Her smile blossomed through the airwaves; Claire didn't need to see her mother's face to know she was blushing. "There was that instant lust, then that foolish feeling that he was my soulmate, then that level-headed, oh-crap, he's too stubborn and enjoys action figures more than a grown man should, and... I dumped him three weeks in."

"What? You never told me that."

"It's a scary thing, finding someone that upends your world."

"This may sound shallow. But, what if I leave Ryder, who I really do care for, even though he drives me crazy sometimes, and hang my hat on the possibility with Grady, and then three weeks in, discover that he's not what I thought?"

"Love is always a risk. Listen to your head and your heart. And if they are telling you gibberish, then wing it."

"Wing it. Okay. I can wing it."

"No offense Claire, but I've never seen you 'wing it.'"

"Not my thing, but I'll figure it out."

"Let me know how it goes. Call tomorrow?"

"You bet."

Angry at himself for his typical indecision and gut-lessness, Grady paced outside. He stalked out to his car, opened the door, then slammed it shut again. Why did he have to kiss her? Better yet, why had he poured them so damn much whiskey? Isn't that how Zane got himself hitched?

Answered his own question there. Yeah, he'd worked up the nerve to let her know how he felt... if thrusting his tongue down her throat counted as expressing his feelings.

This morning, he'd eaten the world's slowest breakfast. Which, yeah, he did every Monday morning, stalling as long as possible before dragging his ass in to work. Lincoln was going to dock him for tardiness pretty soon. As salaried partners, not likely. But as a friend, he would be fully justified to call him on shaving off the start and end of the workday as often as possible.

He'd left Trace with a friendly peck on the cheek. Nothing. Not a zap.

Not trusting himself to decide anything with regard to his pathetic love life, he picked up the phone instead and called a friend.

"Hey," Asher answered.

"Hey, man. I, uh... Fuck." Grady ran a hand through his hair, having no idea why he'd even called.

Asher laughed, teasing him already. "You're having a rough time there. What's going on?"

"I'm trying to figure out how to say this without sounding like a... I don't know. I... How quickly did you know Sophie was the one?" *Real manly there, Grady.* Totally normal conversation.

"Uh-oh, who is she?"

Grady had no idea how to dodge that little truth. Might as well be honest. "Ryder's fiancée."

"Figures. You two looked pretty cozy at Ahab's. I'd say I didn't think you were that stupid, but, well. You are you."

"Yeah." Non-phone hand in his pocket, he paced around the side of the house. Kicking a rock, he tried to land it in the pond. The rock flew wide, missing the target and sputtered to a pathetic stop in the shrubs. Why hadn't his mother enrolled him in soccer like Ryder?

Thankfully, Asher didn't sound condescending or judg-mental. More sympathetic than anything. "I'm sorry, man. One look, and I knew."

The next rock hit the decorative rockery around the pond and ricocheted back at him. He hopped on one foot to get out of the way and narrowly dodged a self-inflicted injury. "That's what I was afraid you were going to say. What would you have done if she were already with me?"

"Tough call. I can't say for sure. You know me, I wouldn't have waited in the wings. Besides, Sophie would have wanted to make an informed decision, on her own, without pressure. So, don't be an ass about it, but give Claire the choice. Think she's into you?"

"Um..."

"That's a heavy '*um*.'"

"It is that."

"And?"

"I kissed her." Grady grimaced, waiting for the reprimand he deserved.

"Good for you."

"No, not good for me. Did you miss the point about her being engaged to my brother?"

"Did she slap you and call you a jerk, or did she kiss you back?"

"She kissed me back. And it... it was incredible. But then Bill interrupted, and she took off. I haven't seen her since."

"So what are you going to do about it?"

"Hide. I'm going to work. Then to Black Op. Then I'm crashing at your place until she leaves."

"Real brave."

"Fuck off."

"Hey, I'm going to the damn gala for *you*. I can't believe you threw me under the bus like that. Your mother hates me."

Grady laughed out loud, grateful for the distraction. "And that's part of why I keep you around, takes some of the pressure off me. Besides, now you know why I look so good in a tux. Years of experience. Your turn to suffer with me."

"Tell you what. I'll go to the dreaded gala, if you go back home tonight. Talk to her. And if it's a no-go, you can hide at my place until they leave and whenever they're in town."

"Deal."

"Now promise me there will be beer at this affair. Not just champagne and those fancy cocktails Patricia hasn't noticed that no one enjoys but her."

"Black Op will provide beer for the event. She may think it beneath me, but she recognizes it's a high-end product."

Miraculously, he was smiling when they disconnected. Until he looked up and saw his brother kissing Claire in the library window. Hands cradling her face tenderly, he looked into her eyes before releasing her. She smiled back, just as lovingly.

Cringing, Grady clenched his fists at his sides. What did he expect? She was engaged to his successful brother for a reason. He wasn't exactly a prize by comparison. Ryder's depressed lawyer brother that lived with his parents at age thirty... Not looking good for Grady.

As home now sounded worse than work, Grady climbed into the car and took off.

Lincoln was already on the phone with a client when Grady wandered in. He offered a quick wave, then poured a massive cup of coffee and dropped into his desk chair. He booted up the slick PC and opened his schedule.

Thank fuck. No clients in person today. If Lincoln didn't kick his ass for his paltry schedule soon, Grady was going to do it himself. He crossed his feet in front of him and rolled up his sleeves.

Within the hour, his day got remarkably... worse.

"I need to speak with him now." A thunderous voice boomed over the assistant's desk, the fire behind it threatening the foundation of the building.

The assistant's voice crackled. "I'll take your information and Mr. Mallory will get back to you when he has time." Heavy footsteps rattled the ground as the intruder pushed past loyal Kent.

Grady rose to his feet, reaching the edge of the desk as his office door blew open. "Mr. Langford. Please direct any communications for your ex-wife to your own attorney, and he will pass along the message to me to deliver to Mrs. Langford."

"Fuck you."

Feet locked to the floor, Grady could have run. Could have swung. Could have done a lot of things.

But Mrs. Langford had been a cheating bitch. Mr. Langford was lucky to be rid of her. Another of Bill and Patricia's friends. And Grady had learned his lesson, having suffered this unbalanced couple for over a year, until last week when things were finalized. And Mrs. Langford had walked away with the house and most of their liquid assets.

When the block of a fist slammed into his cheek, Grady let his face ricochet back.

His jaw crunched as he tried to talk, his cheek throbbed with a contusion that ached deep to the bone.

Rubbing his hand over the injury, Grady checked that nothing was broken.

Fists up, Mr. Langford was ready to swing again.

"Mr. Langford. You had every opportunity to counter. Again, please raise your concerns with your own attorney."

"I know she was sleeping with you, too. Like everybody else."

As if. Mrs. Langford was a walking STD.

When the block of a fist aimed for Grady's other cheek, he ducked and cracked an uppercut into Mr. Langford's belly.

Doubled over from the force of the blow, Mr. Langford backed into the doorway and groaned.

"We can call it even, or I can call the police and let them handle it."

"Screw you." Mr. Langford grimaced, still holding his abdomen.

"I am truly sorry that your marriage ended on such unfriendly terms."

Scowl etched deeply between his eyebrows, Mr. Langford limped out of the office.

Behind him, Lincoln waited, waited, and finally let out a long sigh. "That was... tense."

"No shit." Grady flexed and relaxed his fist. "I'm done for the day."

He didn't look back to see Lincoln's reaction. Fury burning his gut, and his cheek, he floored it down Main and parked behind Black Op. Without pause, he unlocked the side door, locking it again behind him. He mustered a smile and waved to the crew already there, then dashed up the stairs.

Done with the monkey suit, he changed out of the lawyer uniform as quickly as possible and tugged on the jeans and Black Op tee he kept in his office. Kicking off his oxford's, he slid his feet into his brown leather Merrells and fired up the computer.

After completing the monthly budget, he pulled up his emails, then ensured their inventory was adequate to fulfill the orders from the local restaurants and grocers as well as anticipating growth. In three more months, if things continued at this trajectory, he would see about contracting with a distributor.

Zane popped his head in the door. "Hey, you're here early."

Grady clicked on his desk lamp, knowing the shiner was probably glowing purple by now.

"Shit. That's a good one. How's the other guy look?"

"Worse. Can't blame him; he got screwed in the divorce."

"You call the cops? Press charges?"

"Nope."

Zane bit his cheek and gave a subtle nod, but didn't push. Guy had a temper, but didn't let it show. Grady could use a dose of that subtlety.

Dropping into the chair across the desk, Zane leaned back and rested his hands over his abdomen. "Black Op is pulling in decent income. Why don't you cut back and just take cases you want?"

"I try to filter, but the ex-wife had seemed like a decent person. It wasn't until we got to the nitty gritty that I realized what a bitch she was."

"What does Lincoln think?"

"About what?"

"Did he witness... this?" Zane pointed to Grady's cheek that grew more swollen by the minute.

"Yes."

"And?"

"I didn't stop to commiserate. I came here."

Zane disappeared for a few minutes, then reappeared with an ice pack and tossed it onto Grady's desk, then parked in the opposite chair again. Settling in, they reported on the latest, and made plans for the next month.

# 11

## S-U-B-T-E-R-F-U-G-E

Watching her pacing across the room, Ryder clearly couldn't take it any longer. He never had cared for restless energy. Claire also knew he tended to be irritable when he hadn't slept, and she'd accidentally woken him when returning from her midnight make-out last night. He took her hand and pulled her over next to him behind the desk. Still, she couldn't stop fidgeting.

She glanced out the window, wishing she could ride out over the sparkly frost again. She couldn't keep up this fizzle, not when she had the chance to sizzle. Even if that melted to a drizzle. Claire bit her lip to hide her giggle, quickly remembering this was a somber occasion. "I know we agreed to wait on any big decisions until we got home, but I don't think this should wait any longer. I've been doing a lot of thinking. About us—"

As panicked as he must have been when Patricia pinned him down about their engagement, Ryder shook his head vigorously. "No, no, no. Not now. I know where this is going, and it's got to wait until we get back to Phoenix. I need you right now."

Of course. What was that saying about wanting to be needed versus needing to be wanted? He released her and stepped to the window that looked over the backside of the property, rubbing his hand over his jaw. Arms folded across her chest, she moved to stand next to him in front of the window.

Claire had never seen him so frazzled. "You've been thinking about it, too?"

"Yeah. Claire, we were stupid to move in together so quickly. I think we only lasted so long because we never see each other. You're an amazing person, and, I've got to say, you're the reason I've made it so far in my career. But we don't have a thing in common."

She hadn't realized he'd noticed. Maybe he wasn't as inattentive of a boyfriend as she thought. If he'd known this for long, he'd likely appreciated the status quo, like she had, so they could focus on work and school.

She powered on. "I've been thinking. I really like it here. I'll go rent a hotel room in town for the rest of the week and check out some of the vet clinics. Maybe drop off my resumé at a few places."

"Hold on, I hate to ask, but can we pretend we're engaged for a few more days? It'll make my parents happy, keep them from pestering me so I can get some work done, and... I just found out about a thing tonight, and I was hoping you'd come with me." His eyes pleaded, those obnoxious dimples flashing in an overly charming attempt to win her over.

Chest rising in a deep sigh, she wanted to jump up and down at the idea of seeing more of Grady. Even if it broke her heart. More than this tear-free breakup with Ryder, apparently. "That saves me the hotel expense. And it buys me some more time with... your family's horses. You owe me big time."

He scratched the top of his head and added, "Actually, I should have said something earlier, but I was selfish and was hoping you'd stick with me longer than the trip. A friend of mine's dad is a vet. I ran into him the other night at Ahab's and had considered introducing you, but you and Grady left before I had the chance. Dr. Parson takes care of the horses. Uh… he actually… might be looking for another full-time vet."

Typical. It wasn't convenient for him until now, so why would he have offered? She debated retracting her agreement to remain his pretend fiancée out of spite. Instead, she jabbed him in the sternum, covering her irritation with a genuinely appreciative smile. "Make the call. Today."

"Claire, you're a lifesaver. Really. You're too good for a selfish asshole like me."

"Damn right." She jabbed him again, more playfully this time.

Hands cradling her cheeks, he pulled her in for a friendly kiss. Well, a *we-used-to-be-intimate* friendly kiss. "Remember, we're engaged and are deeply in love at least until the gala."

"Sure." It wouldn't hurt if Grady knew. But how would she tell him? *So, now that I'm single, let's hook up.* That was going to sound classy. Regardless, thrill thundered in her chest as she pictured his response.

Ryder reached into his back pocket and pulled out a stack of cash. "About tonight. We'll be meeting at a swanky club in Seattle. If this goes well, I should nail that promotion. I saw there's still a boutique clothing store on Main, if you want to buy something to wear, and maybe pick up a black shirt for me? I can wear good jeans and the shoes I brought for the gala, but the shirt's too formal."

She snatched the cash and flashed him a wink. "I'll see what I can come up with. If you remind me how to get to town, I'll take the rental car once the stores open."

"I can't tell you how much I appreciate it. The head of marketing for the vodka campaign was supposed to meet us next month in Los Angeles, but he is in the area for a few days, and rumor has it, they're interviewing a few other consulting firms. Very last minute, and since I'm in the area, my boss put me on the wine-and-dine. We're to keep things social to avoid a high-pressure sales pitch, so I'm supposed to bring you."

"Get me that interview, and I will happily play the marketing consultant's date one last time. I'm psyched to get in touch with Dr. Parson. Mind looking at my resumé?"

She may as well take advantage of his expertise. He was good at his job. What would have taken her the rest of the day, he finished in minutes. While he touched up the aesthetics, she stared out the window, scheming about how to approach Grady.

"Alright, I'm going shopping. I, uh... I don't see a reason to keep any secrets from your brother."

"Sure."

"You guys are at each other enough. Some honesty might smooth things over." She hoped she didn't squeak with her pathetic attempt to... she chuckled under her breath, to *close the deal* with his brother as soon as possible. "Are you going to tell him?"

"About the breakup?"

"Yes. It's not healthy, being so distant with your brother."

"I guess so. Makes sense. Since Becca... yeah, I'll hash it out with him before we go."

At least he wasn't suspicious of her intentions. Case in point, however, as to why it was over. He really didn't notice her.

Claire slipped her arms into her denim jacket, her hallmark casual over the formal of the cocktail dress. She was glad this was her last social appearance for the sake of Ryder's career, but she had no idea when she'd be able to wear the cute outfits again. She'd tried on a dozen dresses, had even considered some leather pants that would look fantastic with her boots, but finally settled on a black cowl-neck. If it was on Ryder's buck, she might as well take full advantage. He didn't mind.

A knock at the door interrupted her musings. Turning, Claire saw Ryder opening the door. Grady leaned against the open door to the blue suite, looking downright edible. Still wet from a shower, his blond hair spiked in all different directions and his white t-shirt clung to his damp skin.

She tried not to stare, but she couldn't help but picture exactly what he'd just been up to in the shower. His eyes closed, letting the bubbly suds trail over those abs. Dramatically shaking the water out of his hair in slow motion like one of those shampoo commercials.

Ryder nodded to Grady's bruised cheek. "Who'd you piss off this time?"

"Fuck off," Grady muttered. "Claire?" he asked, his gaze softening and lips curling into a yummy smile as he caught sight of her.

"Yes, Grady?" Was that too hopeful? Too eager? Had Ryder talked to him yet?

"Do you have a minute?"

Ryder glared at his watch, shaking his head. "We need to get going."

Grady nodded and shifted his feet. "Freya and Sophie wanted to invite you over for breakfast before you go. Then, if you wanted to do something fun after, they're hoping to show you around Foothills."

"Oh, that's so sweet. I'd love to."

"I can, uh, I can give you a ride. If you want. Zane and I were going to meet up, too."

Ryder jabbed him in the ribs before pushing past him. "You hitting on my fiancée?"

Grady gritted his teeth. Claire worried for the integrity of his jaw, with that mastication muscle flexing so tightly. He shoved off the door frame and stalked down the hall.

After throwing his arms up in surrender, Ryder clicked the door shut and turned back to Claire. "I'm sorry about Grady. He's always had a short fuse, but he's particularly pissy this visit."

"You didn't talk to him yet?"

"I haven't had time. I'll go talk to him while you finish up. But we need to get going so we're not late."

And they were nearly an hour early. Her butt had gone numb from the wooden stool by the time their guests arrived at the club. Fortunately, this head of marketing for the vodka company was still jet-lagged and called it a night early. Ryder had floated the entire drive back, thrilled that he'd nailed the meeting. Despite the exceedingly long drive back to Foothills, he talked the entire way. Claire tuned him out before they even left the city limits. Maybe she didn't listen to him, either.

She was exhausted by the time they got home. At well past ten, her bedtime had passed hours ago. The adrenaline from the lights and sounds of the club was still raging though, so she left Ryder while he crashed on the makeshift bed on the floor.

Restless, she headed to the kitchen, but she wasn't hungry. Not for food, anyway. With the rest of the house asleep, she headed down to the entertainment room, considering trying her hand at billiards to take the edge off the edginess she always found after a long evening of entertaining strangers for the sake of Ryder's career.

Crashing through the cluster of balls and sinking into the corner pocket, Grady's cue ball was another nail in the coffin of a weird, fucked-up week. His cheek was throbbing, and that wasn't the half of it.

Watching Claire stroll out, arm-in-arm with Ryder, grinning and downright beaming, was more than he could take.

Then he'd about torn Ryder's head off. Not Ryder's fault that Grady couldn't stop thinking about Claire. But after Becca, he didn't give a shit about Ryder's dating habits. Sort of.

He shouldn't care about romancing Claire right out from under him. But, despite both Hattie and Asher telling him to fight, he wasn't that guy. If she loved Ryder, he wouldn't stand in the way.

Rolling his eyes, he recalled his latest awkward moment with his brother. Just as they were leaving for their hot date in Seattle, Ryder stopped in to have about their strangest chat yet. Dressed in a slick outfit with slim black jeans and coordinating shiny black tee, hair styled with flawless attention, Ryder looked the part of the successful marketing schmoozer. "Hey man. I'm sorry about what happened between us before."

"Okay..." he'd responded.

"She'd said it was already over before anything happened, I swear." Ryder's eyes had been wide with regret, and he'd nodded meaningfully.

"Good to know." Know what, exactly?

"Anyway. Claire said you and I should communicate more. She's... too good for me."

Grady stared at his brother blankly.

"We're done. Just wanted to, uh, you know, get back to the way we were. You know. Talk to each other more. Like brothers." Ryder had patted him firmly on the back and left Grady oddly confused in the green room, standing awkwardly as he watched his self-absorbed brother heading out with a woman that was *way* too good for him.

When they got back from the club, Grady hadn't been nearly prepared enough to handle Claire. Having learned from his mistake with the whiskey that had led to the kiss that had knocked the entire planet off its axis, he planned to keep a clear head until she left. But nothing was as intoxicating as Claire. In that outfit. With that lip parked between her teeth.

At the sound of footsteps that he shouldn't know as well as he did, that shouldn't set his pulse into critical rhythm, he turned and felt warmer and fuzzier than all the whiskey in the house could have induced. Claire sauntered into the room. A narrow window of skin was visible between the top of the tall boots and the bottom of the short dress. The drape of the dress revealed a hint of shadow between her breasts.

When his brain recovered enough to shift his gaze up to her face, well, at the sound of her clearing her throat anyway, he tried to hide his breathless ogle. She smiled back at him, her hazel eyes hooded with quiet confidence. Must have had a hell of a night.

Chiding himself and the whisper of hope he'd nearly succumb to, he lowered the cue stick.

"Want a partner?" she asked as she stepped close and slid the cue out of his hand, teasing her fingertips along the smooth shaft.

He tried to respond, but he couldn't manage to form a coherent thought. Not that it would have made a difference; his tongue was tied into so many knots a sailor wouldn't have been able to loosen it.

Claire reached into the pocket that he'd recklessly knocked the cue ball into. Without comment, she set it back on the table and took his next shot for him. Across the table, she leaned forward, giving him the closest look at heaven he'd ever seen. A hint of her strapless pink bra peaked out. Just a little more shifting, and those magnificent breasts would be free. With a crack, she nailed it and sank the ball he'd been going for earlier.

Clearing his throat, he found his voice. "Nice time at the club?"

A husky laugh escaped her lips. "I hate schmoozing. My clientele doesn't care what I look like, as long as I have a soothing voice and a gentle touch. Last time, thank goodness."

Grady got lost on "gentle touch," picturing those long fingers of hers gliding along his own shaft.

*Last time?*

"Grady, I've been wondering. Where did you come from? You're not anything like the rest of your family." She leaned against the side of the table and held out the cue for him.

He blinked his way back to the present and accepted the offered pool cue. "I appreciate the compliment. Apparently, I have a lot in common with my father."

"You do look a lot like your mother."

"Ouch."

"Seriously. It's not a bad thing. She's beautiful. You've got her eyes, almost, plus her height and fierce set to your jaw."

"I've got the same eyes as Ryder."

"No, yours are softer."

He raised a single eyebrow at her before lining up his shot. "Guys don't like hearing they look 'softer.'"

Again, that rich laugh vibrated deep into his bones. "As in, yours are meltier. His make a person feel judged. Yours are ocean deep and pull me in like the calm center of a storm."

*Uh-oh.* Completely missing the cue ball this time, he tried to close his gaping jaw. Perhaps the view down her top wasn't accidental.

She didn't seem drunk.

What happened to the goofy woman at the skating rink? Or the sweet woman grooming the horse? The prim and proper one at dinner? The shy one that kissed him?

This was the vixen of the mix... had to say, he couldn't come up with any objections to this version of her. Maybe he would tomorrow. But for the moment... maybe it was time to fight for her.

With a deep breath to calm the lurching stampede in his chest, he stepped back and took his next shot. Not as bad this time. "We're a little dysfunctional, that's for sure. What about your family?"

Leaned back against the table, she shrugged. "My family's pretty awesome. I have two younger brothers that are the best. My parents are supportive. They'll love Foothills."

"You seem to like Foothills pretty well. Ryder hates it. How is that going to work?"

"I'm staying."

Shit, if she and Ryder settled in Foothills, he'd be miserable every damn day, rather than being tortured only for their biennial visit. He'd have to emigrate.

He glanced over at her again, her eyes heated and lips looking particularly lush in a serious fuck-me expression as she stepped closer.

Yeah, she could be persuasive and would get what she wanted.

"Claire? I..."

"What is it?"

"Nothing." *Don't be a dumbass. Fight this time.* He hesitated, then held out the cue.

Claire moved to take her shot. Grady bit down on his tongue, struggling to shift his attention *anywhere else*. Her dress inched up as she bent forward, her posture enticing him to pay attention. He couldn't have looked away if his life depended on it. If she were his, he'd slide that dress up another few inches...

*Crack*. She nailed the next shot and stood up straight. View gone, he was able to tear his eyes away and shifted his body so she wouldn't see his physical reaction. He lined up his shot and focused on the game.

Leaned against the table next to him, she was waiting when he stood tall. Her eyes weren't releasing his. Her intentions were loud and clear. "I fell for you the moment you caught me on the ice. How you came to my rescue, and you laughed with me."

Later, he'd blame the concussion from the fight that morning. Or his determination to stand up and fight for the woman he wanted. In the morning, he'd have a serious talk with his brother. And apologize.

For now, he was foolishly caught up in the moment. That knowing that turned Asher into the sap he'd become, that left Zane foolishly watching his wife when he thought no one was looking.

He tossed the pool cue onto the table behind her and wrapped his arm around her, splaying his hand across the small of her back. Lost in those mysterious hazel eyes, he waited for her to object. To kick him in the nuts and tell him she was off limits.

"Don't marry my brother."

"We were never even engaged." She clutched his shirt in both hands and held him snug against her. Those lush lips were soft and pliant against his. Grazing his tongue along her plump lower lip, he teased her mouth to open for him.

Incredibly responsive, the velvet of her tongue rubbed along his, meeting him stroke for stroke. Her hands shifted and clutched at his waist. He pulled her closer, so her breasts were pressed tight against him as he devoured her.

Shifting, he tasted his way down her jawline, nipped her earlobe, nibbled the side of her neck and shoulder.

Hands busy, she tugged at his shirt and teased her fingertips under the cotton, caressing the bare skin of his abdomen, gripping his waist.

Breathless, she murmured, "Please tell me I'm making the right choice. I want you."

"I want you so bad," he groaned. Hungry, desperate, his hands moved lower and pulled her dress up to her waist and clutched her spectacular ass.

She hooked her curious fingers into the waistband of his jeans, grazing along his skin in sensual torture, driving him out of his mind as she hinted at more, his cock twitching as her fingers teased inches away.

Driven by her response, he slid his hand along her thigh and down the front of her panties. A rich sigh escaped her lips, and she pressed against his hand, urging him on. Quickly, he found her sensitive core and rubbed and caressed until her breaths came faster and higher and she came against his hand with a honeyed moan.

*Dammit*, as the orgasm rocked through her, he remembered exactly who she was. Who he was. What they were to each other.

He pressed his forehead against hers. "Claire, I'm so sorry. I shouldn't have done that. I'm not, we can't—"

Furious with himself for behaving like his asshole of a brother, he stormed out of the room without a backward glance.

# 12

## P-E-N-A-L-T-Y-B-O-X

Claire awoke to the bright, perky sunshine infiltrating her bedroom. She rolled to her side and yanked the pillow over her head.

Grady was a decent guy and must have been horrified. Walking in with that marketing-schmoozer outfit, taunting him like that. If only she'd indulged in those drinks that the vodka guy had offered, then she'd have an excuse for being so forward. Instead, she couldn't blame anything but lust. He'd been so disgusted, he'd left her standing there, completely aroused and then totally cold and alone.

Perhaps moving to Foothills wasn't such a good idea. There were plenty of small towns like this. Probably. It would be hard enough seeing Grady over the next few days. Maybe she could avoid him at least until the gala, if she played her cards right.

There was that stupid ache in her chest again. She wasn't foolish enough to ignore it, but what the hell? It had been only a few days since she'd first laid eyes on Grady. Things didn't move this quickly. Emotions shouldn't build this easily.

That afternoon skating had been the best date she'd ever been on. She'd never laughed so hard, nor had anyone laugh so hard with her. Ryder would have thought she was nuts, sitting on the ice and not feeling at all embarrassed by her own ineptitude.

And she'd completely blown it. Over the past few years, she'd worked so hard in school that her social life was nil. No friends to speak of. Ryder was the closest thing she had to a confidante; an embarrassing statement as to her current situation. She wanted to call her parents or her brothers more than anything, but she really didn't want to tell any of them how she'd acted like such a slut and driven away Grady.

A knock at the door interrupted her pity party. Ryder poked his head in. "Babe, your interview is in two hours. I wrote down the address so you can take the rental and, if you want to explore town after, go for it. Your resumé is on the table out here."

Couldn't he call her by her actual name? She was a grown woman. Albeit a stupid, slutty one, apparently.

He looked down at her sprawled across the bed, only her head poking out from under the covers at the side of the bed. "You ok?"

"I'm fine." She wiped away the stupid tear that threatened to fall from her brine-blurred eyes.

He lowered to the edge of the bed and patted her foot through the blankets. "Okay. If don't you want to talk about it, I get it. But I'd like to stay friends." He paused, then tried again. "Did something happen last night? You were in a great mood when I went to bed."

Her chest rose and fell as she took in a deep breath. "Really, it's nothing. I'm just overwhelmed with everything going on."

"Ok. Hattie left you breakfast in the fridge. Although, it's almost lunch now. Good luck today." He gave her ankle one last pat and left her to her thoughts. Her cruel, self-berating thoughts.

Once she heard the door close, she tossed off the covers, but remembered she was still wearing only the panties she'd worn last night. Foolishly allowing herself to get lost in memories from last night, she remembered Grady's capable hands on her body, driving her straight to a rip-roaring climax... in a matter of seconds.

Dammit, when she wanted something, she went for it. She didn't beat around the bush and bat her eyebrows until someone else made a move. If that didn't work for him, then he wasn't right for her. She was not about to feel foolish for being herself. And enjoying it.

With a bolstering nod, she dragged herself out of bed and got ready for her interview. She'd get that job, move to this adorable town, and figure the rest out along the way.

Unfocused in front of the glaringly bright computer screen, Grady struggled to complete the document he'd spent all afternoon working on. The words swam around the page, becoming more elusive the more he tried to finish the damn job. After ditching early to go to Black Op so much lately, Grady had a lot of catching up to do. But it wasn't happening.

Lincoln hollered from across the hall, "I can hear your brain from here. Stop thinking so loud. It's deafening."

Kent had already gone home for the afternoon, leaving the office painfully quiet. Lincoln had been pushing him to spill on why he was in such a lousy mood. He was always cranky at work, but even Lincoln noticed how much worse it was today. Finally, when Grady was too far gone to respond with his pathetic groans anymore, having deteriorated to whimpers, Lincoln crossed the hall and dropped into the leather chair across Grady's desk.

"You look like hell. What gives?" Friends in law school, although a year apart in school, he'd set up shop as soon as he graduated a year and a half ago, and Lincoln had joined him last summer. His partner still seemed to find the job interesting and worthwhile. Grady couldn't let him down, especially so early in their partnership.

Shit. He should at least talk to someone about his more acutely pressing predicament. Other than Hattie. She was too supportive. And Asher would either pat him on the back or call him a fucking moron. Lincoln would be less biased.

Hopefully. Or hopefully not. It could go either way. Frankly, there was no outcome of this current mess that would be palatable.

Not bothering to hide the sleepless rasp in his voice, he went for it. "I fell in love with Claire and then fucked it up." He dropped his head in his hands and pulled at his hair.

Silence.

Leaned back, he waited for Lincoln's response. Long pause. Lincoln shifted his posture. "I'm sorry. I'm not sure I heard you correctly. Didn't she just get into town a few days ago? With your brother?"

Weakly, Grady looked up at his friend and nodded.

"How the hell could you, A) Fall in love so quickly, B) Put yourself in a position to fall for your brother's fiancée, and C) Are you stupid?" This is why Lincoln still enjoyed what he did. He was going to lawyer the shit out of this.

"A) It happened in a matter of seconds. She arrived at the skating rink a few minutes after Sophie and Freya left last Friday. I didn't know who she was. She's absolutely gorgeous with this chocolaty brown hair and eyes that seem to change color depending on her mood. She didn't flat-out say that she was engaged, and she was there alone. So, naturally, I hit on her, and we joked around and I've never laughed so hard in my life. B) It wasn't on purpose. I tried not to, but every time I turn around, she's right there being so gorgeous and sweet and funny. C) I am a complete idiot. I was irritable last night and threw myself a pity party, and, uh, I made out with her. She looked so hot in this sexy little black dress, so damn appealing and... determined."

Lincoln leaned back in his chair and considered, his fingertips tapping against each other. "Define 'made out.'"

Exasperated, Grady pushed his chair back from the desk and stood to pace the room. "The act of rubbing one's tongue against another's."

"Mutual?"

"What? Of course. I'm an idiot but not a creep. Her tongue was just as far down my throat as mine was down hers."

"Was she drunk?" Lincoln's eyebrow raised up like it was under the control of a damn fishhook.

"No, we were both sober and consenting."

"Was that all that happened?" Damn lawyers.

"And... I sort of... skipped past second and stole third base. And she was giving me the best damn glimpse at her version of second. Or third. Fuck, I don't know which. I mean, there's no established system for delineating the base system, but please don't make me go into detail. However you want to classify things, it was consensual and... incredible. And then in my usual graceless stupidity, I made it worse and walked away."

Scowling, Lincoln shook his head in sad judgment. "Mr. Mallory, you definitely crossed the line, but so did she. What are you going to do about it?"

He walked to the window and looked over the alley behind the office. "Last night, I'd decided to fight for her, like Hattie and Asher had insisted. I meant to tell her how I feel. To give her the choice. But things quickly got out of hand. It was just going to be one more kiss to let her know how I feel about her. So, new plan. I'm going to hide."

"One more?"

"Always on the details, aren't you?"

Lincoln stood from his chair and nodded grimly. "You may need to do more than hide. Either a plea bargain or run like hell. Are you going to say anything to Ryder?"

Grady shook his head madly. "Hell no. Serves him right after Becca. He deserves to be cheated on."

He hated even thinking that of Claire. Maybe he didn't know her as well as he thought, to consider she would be so forward with someone when she was with someone else?

But, fuck, he was a little fuzzy on the details. He'd replayed their pathetic excuse for a conversation over and over last night, trying to make sense of things, and he could swear she said they were never even engaged. But when he'd left for work this morning, Patricia had been on the phone with wedding venues.

C laire was floating on her way back from the interview. The temperature had dropped to well below freezing, but the skies remained clear. Too bad; she really wanted to see snow. Then she might be able to call the trip a win. If she could stay in town, doing exactly what she wanted, she might be able to convince Grady that she wasn't a slut that bounced from one brother to another. If she could first convince herself.

They had offered her the job before the interview was even over, pending reference checks and successful completion of her boards, of course. And she already liked her new boss. Parsons let her shadow him for most of the morning and even let her jump in on a few procedures. It was clear he wanted to see her in action as much as she wanted to get a feel for his style before she signed the dotted line. The clinic was exactly what she was hoping for. She would get to spend half the time in the clinic, and the other half going out to tend to the larger animals. With three other vets in the clinic, she would have tons of support while she got her boots wet.

The sun was getting low in the sky, so she stopped off to eat a late lunch at the local diner. Alone. And, more to the point, she wasn't ready to face Grady. She shot a quick text to Ryder that she'd be back late.

Inside Larissa's Diner, an adorable place with décor a few decades out of date, the scent of fresh-baked pie and cozy atmosphere warmed her more than the radiant heat. A bubbly server met her at the door and guided her to an empty booth. The place was hopping; must be good food to be so popular, with all the other options she'd seen on the main drive through town.

"Can I get you anything to drink?" A woman with a thick southern accent inquired as she approached the table with a menu.

"I'd love a cup of tea. Whatever you have that's hot and decaf." Her toes were still numb from the few steps in from the car. It would take time to acclimate from Phoenix. And thicker wool socks.

"Coming right up. If you're hungry, the lasagna will warm you straight down to your bones." The woman winked at her. Larissa herself, according to the nametag.

"That sounds perfect. Thanks."

"You're not from around here, are you?"

Claire suspected her violent shivering gave her away. "I'm from Phoenix."

Larissa threw her head back in joyous laughter and slapped her thigh in delight. "That would explain why you look like a popsicle. It took me a decade to get used to Washington weather. This is about as chilly as it gets, but not unusual for January at this elevation."

"A decade, huh? That's not reassuring," Claire joked. Mostly. She may as well invest in fleece-lined pants for the winter days she'd be spending in barns and pastures.

"What brings you to Foothills?" Rather friendly, the woman may as well have a seat in the bench opposite.

"I actually just interviewed with Parson Veterinary Hospital. I'll be starting in a few weeks." She already liked saying it.

Her parents would freak, but they were ready to get out of the heat and would happily follow. The real challenge would be in convincing her brothers to move, as Cole had only recently moved home.

"Doc Parsons was in here this morning telling me all about the new grad he was interviewing today. I'm glad to hear it's you." Larissa disappeared and returned a few minutes later with her tea. And a spare mug.

Larissa poured a cup for them both and sat across the booth. Big change from Phoenix. Apparently small towns were as friendly and casual as many a TV show had implied. "Claire, right?"

She nodded.

"I can't believe Ryder agreed to move back to town. Every so often, we raise a few hot shots that are too big for our little town." Larissa bobbed the chamomile tea bag in the steaming mug.

This woman seemed a little too intuitive and would see right through Claire. "He, uh... it's complicated."

She grinned knowingly. "Honey, it always is. I left Alabama, many years ago, to come to Foothills with an ex-boyfriend. He that hated it here and didn't stay long. I fell in love with this town, and a local man, and have spent the last few decades happily married in the most beautiful place in the world."

Claire tested the hot tea, blowing the steam across her mug. It was risky, but she sipped safely and without a tongue burn. "Was that your daughter that seated me?"

Larissa nodded. "That's her. Good kid." Funny, she looked to be the same age as Claire. At thirty, Claire no longer considered herself a kid.

"Grady was in for lunch earlier, sporting a heck of a shiner, but he didn't say anything about Ryder and your visit. You see much of him over there at the Mallory place?"

Claire gulped a sip of tea too quickly at the mention of Grady and burned the back of her throat. "A bit," she coughed.

Larissa smiled knowingly. "That Grady is too good for his own good, if you know what I mean. Raised in a pretty rigid household, he struggles between doing the right thing and doing what he needs to for himself. Needs a little TLC, that boy." She subtly nodded at Claire as she stood. "That lasagna should be out in a minute."

Maybe he wasn't the player Ryder had insisted. He'd been teased about his innocence at that stupid party game, and this diner owner—who seemed to know everything about everyone—thought well of him. Clearly, the slutty billiard game had not been her best approach.

Tonight, she'd hash things out with him.

After wolfing down the lasagna, the heavy meal doing the job so she could feel her toes again, she paid her tab and slipped outside. She scanned up and down the street, realizing she had no idea where his law office was. Quickly googling it, she followed the path laid out, getting a few crazy looks as she rechecked the map and turned herself around a few times, then finally caught sight of the inconspicuous converted house not far off Main.

Shoulders back, hair probably frizzy from the wind, Claire swallowed the shiver in her throat and pushed open the door. The front was dim, the receptionist desk empty, as if they'd already closed up for the day. A voice from the back hollered, "Hang on."

From the sole glowing room in the office, Lincoln popped out, immediately smiling when he saw her. "Hey, Claire. I wasn't expecting you to drop in, and I suspect Grady wasn't either. He left a bit ago."

"Oh." She glanced around, wondering how rude it would be to turn tail. The office was nice. Soothing mountain pictures, natural wood and metal furniture, and walls of books. But it lacked the energetic, positive vibe of Black Op. "I'll catch him later."

"Claire?"

"Yeah?" Shit. Did Grady tell him anything? Judging by the concerned, curious, amused smile and elevated eyebrows, he knew everything. Her cheeks flamed red.

"I know I should stay out of it, but Grady's had a hell of a time of it lately. Are you planning to string him along, or do you have feelings for him?"

Lungs heavy, as if filled with fluid, Claire worked her lip between her teeth as she decided how to respond. "What did he tell you?"

Lincoln lowered to sit on the corner of the receptionist's desk, folding his arms over his chest. Earnest, he settled his gaze on her. "That he feels awful about what happened, and that he knows he crossed some lines he shouldn't have."

"That's utter bullshit," she huffed. "I'm the one that crossed the line. Do you know where he is? I need to talk to him."

"Probably still over at Black Op."

Claire backed up and murmured, "Thanks."

"Claire?"

"Yeah?"

"Go easy on him."

She offered a weak smile and returned to the chill evening air. The wind had grown stronger the few minutes that she was inside, and she pushed against it to make her way into Black Op. As busy as it had been the other night, she waved to the greeter and snuck up the stairs.

The far office was glowing, a shadow pacing in the soft light. Claire inched past Grady and Zane's darkened offices and found Freya painting madly in what was clearly her studio, a large space with tall windows and dozens of blank and completed canvasses. Freya silenced the music and smiled knowingly. "Hey, Claire."

"Hi, Freya. I'm sorry to interrupt."

"No worries. I should have stopped an hour ago, but sometimes I get sucked in."

"Did you paint the one in Grady's office?"

"Since when were you in Grady's office?" Eyebrow halfway to the ceiling, Freya grinned. "Never mind. Yes, that was me. He needed the breath of fresh air."

Why did everyone seem to think Grady was helpless? Sure, he'd said himself he was struggling, but it was as if all his friends encased him in heart-protective bubble wrap. "I really need to talk to him. Lincoln said he might be here?"

"You just missed him."

"Okay. I'll catch him at home, then." If she could avoid Patricia and Ryder. That house seriously had ears.

"Actually, he's crashing at Asher and Sophie's tonight. The guys have some... things they need to take care of."

"Oh. Okay. I'll call him."

"Claire? I mean this in a good way, give him a few days to collect his thoughts." Freya rinsed her brush in the jar of water and pulled her apron over her head. "It's all about timing."

"Timing." Claire mulled on that one for a moment. "Did he tell you what happened?"

"He didn't have to. He looks as miserable as you do."

Cringing, Claire rubbed her eyes and stepped back. "I messed up."

"Funny, that's what he was muttering to Zane while I was pretending that I wasn't listening." She chuckled and flicked off her studio light before joining Claire. They stood and looked into Grady's office, her expression brightening as her gaze landed on the painting of the wind curling over the mountain peaks that hung behind his desk. "It's going to work out. But sometimes you need to let him stew."

"I prefer to be up front about things," Claire began.

"As do I. But Grady doesn't. You two struck like two meteors that were on separate trajectories. It will take some adjusting."

Claire's vision fuzzed over as she tried to understand Freya. The woman was a mystery.

"I'm sure you noticed Grady has a hell of a temper, and is a lost soul. I love him to bits, but he needs to wallow at the bottom right now, or he'll never figure it out."

# 13

## F-L-O-U-N-D-E-R

Grady had resolved to stay with Asher and Sophie until Claire and Ryder cleared out. Maybe he could play sick and skip the gala too. Proving to be the best friends a guy could have, Zane didn't say a word when he dragged him out of Black Op, and Asher and Sophie ensured he had a bed to sleep in, no questions asked about how things had gone with Claire.

Until Thursday morning. Pippa stopped by the office before heading off to school. She'd twisted his ear like the naughty schoolboy he was the moment he entered. Not that she ever grabbed her students by the ear. She was too gentle of a person, but Grady had deserved it.

"You're a complete cad," she admonished. He heard Lincoln chuckling from his office.

"I know. Trust me, there's nothing you can say that will make me feel worse." On seeing her punishment wasn't nearly as agonizing as what he was already going through, she released him from her iron grip.

Obediently, he followed her into the kitchenette where she poured him a cup of coffee and gave him a look that would have any troublemaking kid confessing his every misstep. He should have paid Lincoln a retainer to secure his silence. Otherwise, the trouble with telling your married friend a secret, is that he didn't keep secrets from his wife, and while the others seemed to appreciate Grady was wallowing in his own misery, Pippa was too meddlesome. She already took it upon herself to help Lincoln's bachelor friends, since they didn't have women of their own to keep them in line. He tried telling her it was sexist, but she didn't seem to care.

In full lecture mode, Pippa's hands rested on her hips while Grady crashed into his office chair like a dejected student. "The sparks were obvious the other night at Ahab's, but come on, when she's still engaged? It was going to happen, but you have to wait for the breakup to finalize so she's not put in an awkward position. I can't believe you'd take advantage of her like that."

"Hey, she took more advantage of me than I did her. She was... she was... hot." That was not his best defense.

"Sure. Just keep telling yourself that. You can hide, but you're going to have to face her, eventually. What's your plan?"

"I don't have a plan."

"Exactly the problem. You need a plan. And that starts with apologizing."

"I will again."

"Again? When did you apologize?"

Shit. His hand had still been down her panties when he apologized. She'd still been leaning on him and in the haze of orgasm when he'd run away. Green guilt washed over his face like a seasick sailor in the middle of a typhoon. *Fuck Grady, way to make her feel worse.*

Seeming to read his mind, Pippa gasped, staring at him in horror with her hand over her mouth. "You didn't—"

He nodded, biting his lip very much like Claire might.

"Grady Mallory. You really blew it this time. You're on your own with this one."

With no hope of rescue, Pippa ditched him, too. Lincoln left him alone for the day, not commenting when Grady left for Black Op at lunchtime. Even Zane and Freya avoided him for the rest of the day. By evening, Grady was convinced that he'd done irreparable damage.

"I think you should go with the truth." Asher's eyes were locked on the TV as his Xbox quarterback threw a twenty-yard pass for a first down.

Lincoln took a swig of his beer and nodded. "The truth shall set you free." Lincoln was running a terrible defense, having chosen players based on his fantasy football league alone. It hadn't worked out well for him all season.

In no mood to play, Grady had the feet raised on the leather recliner like an invalid. He rubbed his eyes and pretended he wasn't in the pickle he currently found himself in. "Not sure the truth is going to make anything better. How about this: *Ryder, I'm in love with your fiancée and made it to third base with her Monday night? By the way, she might have fidelity issues. Although you two deserve each other, I still want her for myself, because I'm that pathetic.* Think that will go over well?"

Rolling his eyes, Asher managed a successful running play while mocking Grady at the same time. "I meant, talk to Claire first. You said yourself, she doesn't seem the type to fool around when she's in a committed relationship. Trust me, the Claire we met at Ahab's was not a cheater. Maybe there's more to the story."

Grady's brain sloshed inside his skull. He felt like sandbags coated his entire body, pinning him to the chair. He hadn't slept much since Claire had walked into his life. Shit, he didn't even know her last name. Yeah, he was seriously fucked up. "Why do you have to be so logical?"

"Aren't you a lawyer?"

"Supposedly."

After scoring the extra point, Asher set down the controller while Lincoln reconsidered his strategy. "Remember when you made Sophie feel like shit for making out with me in the dressing room before Lincoln and Pippa's wedding?"

"Don't remind me." Pressure was building behind his eyes. Not another damn tension headache.

"As soon as you got your head out of your ass, you came over and apologized. Now, Sophie's one of your best friends."

Zane strolled in the front door and didn't hesitate to add to Grady's misery. "Is his head still in his ass?" He grabbed a beer from the fridge, popped open the bottle with his titanium wedding band, and plopped on the couch next to Asher.

"Asher, did you call everyone over to make me feel worse?" Grady groaned as he realized he was in the middle of an intervention.

With a deep belly laugh that had been scarce six months ago, Zane whacked Grady on his foot. "What are friends for?" He took a massive swig of beer. That man didn't do anything small. "From what I hear, you fooled around with your brother's fiancée, then checked out as soon as you'd gotten your play."

Sitting the recliner up rapidly, its electronic gears complaining from the swift movement, Grady glared at Zane. "That's not—" Grady cringed, realizing that was exactly what had happened.

"Look, do you want her or don't you?" Zane's expression grew serious, without a hint of amusement.

"More than anything."

"Then get off your self-pitying ass and go talk to her."

Catching his breath through his heavy chest, Grady braced his hands on the arm of the chair to stand.

Zane laughed and shoved him back down with barely a tap. "Not now, you lovesick puppy. It's late, wait until tomorrow. No offense, but she'd have to be out of her mind to consider necking with you right now. You look like shit."

Eyes glued to the game, Asher added, "She's having breakfast with Freya and Sophie day after tomorrow. They'll feel her out. Maybe put in a few good words for you, after they make sure she's not a faithless bitch."

His phone buzzed in his pocket; ripping it out, he juggled to catch the damn thing, pathetically hoping it was Claire. Not that Claire had his number, but Ryder did, even if he never called.

Nope.

"Haley?" he answered. She hadn't called him in months.

"Hi Grady," she said with a waver in her voice.

Sitting up, he walked into the kitchen. "Everything okay?"

She sniffled, but cleared her throat and powered on, tripping over her words. "I'm leaving Nate. I walked in on him with my friend Mariella in our bedroom, and, and, I don't think it's the first time. I feel like such a fool."

"I'll be on the next flight out."

"No, don't come. I'll figure it out. I just needed to say it out loud."

"Seriously, I can be there tomorrow. Do you have friends you could stay with in the meantime?"

"I don't trust any of them right now."

He gripped the phone tighter and wanted to chuck it at Nate's pretty face. "That piece of shit. Tell me what you need."

"I just needed to talk to someone *normal*. That isn't a creep."

Grady snorted under his breath, wishing to hell that was him. "Is he moving out?"

"Yeah. He's in a hotel for now, then he's looking for his own place. But I hate this house. I can't stay."

"Come home. I'm looking for a new place anyway and can get something with a spare bedroom so you can crash with me until you know what you want."

The sniffling calmed, but there was still a fire to her tone. "I will come home." She seemed to smile, her voice lightening. "I'll fix up my house."

"I thought you sold that after your dad passed."

"No... Honestly? I hadn't even considered it until just now. Nate didn't think it was worth anything, so I continued on with the rental management company Dad had used, and I get an update every year or so. It's been vacant for a few years because it needs updates. I'm going to fix it up and *you* can stay with *me*."

"That would be awesome, but that's a long way off, I can't stand another day under Patricia's roof. Especially while Ryder's there with his fiancée."

"Ryder's engaged?"

"You didn't know?"

"I've been avoiding Patricia. I don't want to tell her."

"For all her faults, she'll take your side. When she found out my dad was cheating on her? She threw him to the street and didn't even take us to his funeral." Grady rubbed a hand over his jaw and dropped to the kitchen barstool. He knew his dad hadn't been a decent guy, cheating on Patricia and then wrapping his car around a tree while drunk driving a year after she'd left him. But he'd still been his father, and Grady knew next to nothing about him. Except as Patricia's excuse for where Grady's temper came from. Or any of his inadequacies.

"Ugh. Maybe I'll call her."

"Better yet, get away for a few days and come rescue me from the gala."

"Shit. I was using Nate's annual holiday party for work as my excuse to avoid coming."

"I'll cover for you if you don't want to come."

Haley paused, and he heard a heavy exhale as she considered.

"Hey, Haley?" Grady said as he glanced out the window, but as full dark had set in, all he could see was his own reflection, the shiner from the shitty case he'd taken glowing bright as the moon, his hair frazzled like a madman, and his jaw clenched so tight he might break a tooth.

"What's up?" she asked, her tone sympathetic before she even knew he needed it. As if her problems disappeared as she worried after her big brother. Luckily, she'd had a decent dad to take after, unlike Grady, who was stuck between two terrible choices of parents.

He released the breath he'd been holding in, suddenly glad his sister had called. "I'm the same sort of jerk. I fell for Ryder's fiancée."

"Uh-oh."

"And I made a move, then ditched her before we could hash it out."

"You are a jerk." The words were harsh, but she held the sympathetic tone. "Does she feel the same?"

"I think so."

"Did you tell her how you feel?"

"Sort of." Closing his eyes, he shook his head. "I will."

"How does Ryder feel about it?"

Shit, he hadn't even thought about Ryder's feelings. He really was an ass. "I don't think he knows."

"Okay, Grady? As your baby sister, a pissed-off, cheated-on woman, and a human being, I'm going to be bossy here. Ready?"

Chuckling mirthlessly under his breath, he agreed. "Shoot."

"Where are you now?"

"At Asher's."

"Okay. Tonight, you're going to plan your case. You're a natural orator and will come up with something great. In the morning, hit the gym or something to burn off that temper, or you'll blow it. Then, you're going to talk to Ryder and see how he feels. Finally, you're going to talk it out with her. Tell her how you feel and, if she's the right one for you, she'll be thrilled you did and you can sweep her off her feet."

"You make it sound so easy."

"Trust me, as a woman that is finally free of the jerk of a man that she's been saddled with for the last ten years, I'm realizing the importance of honesty and fighting for what you want. And you, Grady, you never fight for what *you* want. You swallow your pride and accept what others want for you, and then you take it out on the ice or the field or wherever you can throw that negative energy."

Needing a long draw of oxygen, Grady nodded. "Got it."

"Just don't get hurt."

"Sure," he said, glaring one last time at the distorted reflection of his shiner before turning away.

"And I'm coming to the gala."

"I was kidding. Don't do that to yourself."

Her voice vibrated with snarky enthusiasm. "It will be perfect. I have a plan."

Avoiding Ryder hadn't been difficult. In yet another meeting, he was already in the office before she got out of bed. Now that he had no reason to set aside time for her, he wasn't even pretending to be on vacation.

Claire hid in the stables and visited the horses until the stablemaster arrived, then snuck back into the house. Hattie hung around longer than necessary to make sure Claire ate something. While she didn't pry, she unsubtly regaled Claire with stories of Grady's heroics and adorable antics. The puppy he'd rescued from the side of the road as a kid. The bully he'd knocked flat that had pushed Haley into the mud.

When Patricia and Bill returned from a charity brunch, Claire was suddenly finding Mallory Mansion too small for comfort. Hattie tipped her off about a nice hiking trail and packed her a snack, ensuring she had a warm hat and gloves.

The Riverside Trail was as gorgeous as she'd hoped. After following the thundering river for a mile, she hooked to the upper loop, too fired up to notice the temperature was dropping.

Her phone buzzed in her pocket. Ripping off her gloves, she dug into her pocket and bumbled the phone, only half disappointed when she realized it wasn't Grady. And then remembered he didn't even have her phone number.

"Hi, Mom," she answered.

"Uh oh. I called to see how you were. You don't sound good." At the sound of her mother's voice, her eyes welled with that damn pressure behind them, and her vocal cords rattled.

"I made it worse."

"Oh. Honey. What happened?"

"I don't even know where I went wrong. I broke things off with Ryder." She tugged her lip into her mouth, squeezing until it hurt. "That went okay, better than I thought. But... I tried to tell Grady how I felt."

And her maternal patient pause. "He didn't feel the same way?"

"I thought he did. We... I kissed him again, and it was amazing. Fireworks and lightning and all that good stuff. But he left. Apologized and stormed out."

"What? Why would he apologize after a fireworks kiss?" Val's voice was fiery on her behalf.

"I was trying to wing it, and you know I'm not good at that. I had gone out with Ryder for one last schmoozing dinner. Anyway, I wore this really cute, but maybe too come-hither dress for Grady's taste? I don't know. I may have been a little too direct, hoping a big gesture would show him how I felt. But, I got carried away and threw myself at him."

"Your grandmother would have something to say about you being too forward, that men want to be the aggressor. But that's a bunch of baloney. If he doesn't appreciate your moves, then he doesn't deserve you."

"In that moment, it was so perfect. Honestly, we seemed to connect." She spared her mother the details, but hadn't been able to spare herself as she remembered too well the sensation of him seeming to sense exactly what she needed. "But then I... I don't know. I think I got too carried away."

"Not possible. Have you talked to him?"

"No. I plan to hide from him for the rest of the trip."

"Honey, I'm going to be stern. I'll be waiting at the airport when you get home, and if you haven't straightened things out with Grady, one way or another, then I'm turning you right back around to catch the next flight back."

"So he can reject me again?"

"So you can *know*, that the man that upended your world in a matter of hours truly isn't the one. A lifetime of regret? I don't think you want that. If I had stayed broken up with your father, imagine where I would be? You were right to break things off with Ryder. He wasn't the one for you, and I'm glad you figured it out on your own. But don't leave things unsettled with the other one."

"Okay." She nodded weakly. Her teeth were chattering, her hand numb as she grasped the phone.

"How'd the job interview go?"

A few flakes fluttered around her like butterflies, and a miraculous giddiness bubbled in her tummy. "I got the job."

"I'm so proud of you. You must be thrilled."

"I am. You need to come see this place. Dad will have the house on the market before you can say yes."

"Until he hears I'll take advantage and cut back on my hours. Although, if you move up there, you'll be seeing more of Grady, anyway."

"Spoilsport."

"Talk to the man."

"I will."

"Before you leave."

"I will. I'm going to have breakfast with some of his friends tomorrow, and I'll pick their brains."

She shoved her phone in her pocket, slipped on her gloves, and started the hike back. As the flakes began to stick to the trail, she did a victory dance. As more and more flakes accumulated, she picked up the pace.

# 14

## W-H-I-T-E-K-N-I-G-H-T

For the first time in his career, Grady was grateful to spend the day in court. Admittedly, he was stalling. Hattie had called him a few hours ago and said that if he didn't come home and talk to Claire, she was officially disowning him.

Part of him was desperate to get back to Claire and talk it through. Most of him was terrified of getting slapped in the face and being called out as the biggest jerk she'd ever laid eyes on.

He pictured Dr. Strange holding up a single finger. One chance to get it right. There was no snapping his fingers out of this one.

"You make it sound so easy. Pippa was your high school sweetheart." He loosened his tie and crashed into his office chair.

Lincoln dropped into the seat opposite. "Not that she made it easy. She insisted we needed to focus on our careers and spread our wings to be certain we were right for each other. Officially broken up through college, we dated other people. It was awful, knowing the love of my life was out there, but she wouldn't have me." Lincoln's day had been much more sedate, and he'd skipped the suit and tie today.

"How do I even open the conversation? *Claire, I know it's only been a few days, but I'm desperately in love with you, even though you're a cheating whore.*" That sounded even worse out loud than it had in his head.

"Let's not go with 'cheating whore.' How about you start with, '*Hello,*' and possibly add, '*How are you?*'" Lincoln looked him up and down, lingering on the yellow shiner that was enhanced by the dark circles under his eyes. "You know, I think you should go exactly as you are right now. Don't change a thing. Go get her."

Grady rose from the chair and looked down at himself. He re-tucked his shirt, straightened his pant legs, and smoothed his hair.

Lincoln pushed Grady out the door, knowing he'd hover and fret for hours without a good shove. "Don't overthink it. You're a good lawyer, so pretend you're in court and she's an unsympathetic judge. Work out your opening statement on the drive over. You've come up with utter brilliance in less time."

Grumbling, Grady headed out the door in front of Lincoln. He hopped in his Forerunner and fired up the engine. Not even the windshield wipers could keep up with the increasing torrent of snow, but he managed to clear the layer of snow that had accumulated in the few minutes since he'd returned from the courthouse.

Lincoln hovered outside the passenger door. Grady opened the window and inwardly rolled his eyes. Not one more *helpful tip*, as his entire, happily relationshipped group of friends had decided he was too dense to figure this out on his own and had flooded him with advice all day. They weren't wrong. "What?"

Lincoln leaned in the open window, a gust of snowflakes whirling into the car around him. "Let her know how you feel, then give her time to think it over. And hear her out. If her defense is shoddy, she's probably worth forgetting anyway."

Grady rolled his eyes at yet another helpful suggestion. "Got it. Thanks."

Traffic was sparse in the freezing evening. Grady forced air into his lungs, leaving the windows down, counting on the wintery chill to revive him. Stronger by the minute, the oversized snowflakes melted on the leather interior. Maybe this was a bad idea.

Thick clouds darkened the sky, casting one massive, eerie gloom over the region. Folks were turning in for the night, yet it was only four in the afternoon. The forecast had been updated in the last hour, calling for the snow to pick up overnight, but it looked more like a dumping was on the way.

The flakes coated the county road on the way to his parents' house. No, these were fluffy golf balls plummeting from the sky... flake was way too tame of a word for these monsters.

He clutched the steering wheel as the tires raged against the thickening snow and tried not to focus on what a shit-show his life had become lately. No home. Balancing two jobs, the career he'd invested his entire education on, and the business he actually liked, but didn't have time for. And his love life was about as precarious as it could get.

He didn't bother parking around back, as his mother preferred. He probably wouldn't be staying long anyway. If this didn't go well, he might have to skip town entirely.

At this point, he didn't give a shit how much of a disappointment Patricia found him to be. Come the gala, she had Ryder to present, with his gorgeous fiancée and his successful career. No one would notice if Grady wasn't there.

He took a bolstering breath and stepped out. Movement from the barn in the distance caught his attention. Of course, Claire would be out with the horses rather than spending the afternoon under his mother's scrutiny. Although she was a good sport, Patricia was an overbearing force of un-nature and would probably push wedding plans on her.

His toes were freezing in the leather oxfords, and the cuffs of his pants likely irreparably water damaged from the rapidly accumulating snow, but he didn't care.

As he got closer, he heard breathy moans and high-pitched squeaks. Damn, apparently she and Ryder were doing ok after all. He backed away slowly before anyone saw him.

*Wait... that's not Claire.* Wow, he really shouldn't know the sound of his brother's fiancée in the grips of... yeah.

Quietly, he crept closer to be sure, following the indiscrete sounds. Cozy in the stable office, Sasha, their stablemaster, was wrapped around Ryder, and the pair was making out like a couple of eager teenagers.

Recoiling, Grady backed away. What the hell? Should he tell Claire what he'd seen? Did they have an open relationship, hence the coming on to him?

Not worth deciding today. Run and hide was a much more enticing option considering recent events. He stalked toward his SUV, his pulse firing faster than Sasha's squeaks.

His tracks from the walk over were already filled in, the snow halfway up his shins already. He'd better move fast to get to Asher's before the roads were impassable. Nearly back to his car, he had his hand on the door before Ryder came running out of the stable. At first, he hadn't even seen him through the dense snowfall.

"Dude. I'm sorry you saw that. About Sasha..." Ryder at least had the gall to look guilty. For once, his perfect brother looked disheveled. Of course, that was probably more from the frantic make-out rather than guilt.

"No. That's just messed up. What about Claire?" Despite what had happened between them, he wasn't going to say anything to throw her under the bus until he talked to her.

Ryder's face contorted incredulously. What did he have to be mad about? He was the one caught cheating with the stablemaster. "What about Claire?" he fired back.

Jaws and fists clenching, images of the last time they'd fought over a woman came crashing back. Black eyes, swollen cheeks, his hand fracture that still nagged at him now and again.

"Where is she?"

"Hell if I know," Ryder said.

The disinterested shrug was more than Grady could handle.

"You're necking with a family employee while your fiancée is inside, enduring Patricia's wedding plans for her?"

"Whoa, what? No. First, Sasha is a grown woman, and what happened in the barn is between us. Second, Claire's not here—"

Grady's heart plummeted. "Where is she?"

Frozen, Ryder's skin paled. "Hiking."

"You let your fiancée go out in the middle of a blizzard?" Fuck it. Grady's fist flew.

Smashing into his brother's jaw, the force rattling them both. Unsatisfied, he swung with the left.

Ryder let the first one land, but he dodged back before Grady nailed him with the second.

"I had no idea it was coming down so hard—"

"Because you were too busy nailing someone else—"

"Whoa. I wasn't *nailing* her, nor was I planning on it, not yet anyway. And why are you so messed up about *my* sex life?"

"Why? What? You're missing the point. Again. If you'd stop and think before screwing around—" Grady shook off the rage and backed toward his car, blowing right over Ryder's response. "Where is she? I'm going after her."

Ryder's phone rang.

Grady looked around. The snow was coming down so hard now he couldn't see the barn anymore. Sasha came running up behind Ryder. Her face was scrunched up in remorse, but her flushed cheeks told a different story.

Ryder looked worried. "Claire? Where are you? It's really coming down out there."

He could barely hear her on the other side of the call. Stepping closer to his brother than he liked, he could hear her shaky voice. "I was out hiking, and there were a few flakes, but now... I can't see anything. This stupid car is so utterly stupid I can't get enough traction to get up this stupid hill."

"Where are you right now?" Ryder interrupted.

"I was hiking at the Riverside Trail and I started back when the snow hit. I turned onto the main road a few minutes ago. The last landmark I saw clearly was the bridge and I think I passed the sign for the park, but now all I can make out is the edge of the road, but it's becoming less visible by the minute."

Without thinking, Grady ripped the phone out of Ryder's hands. "Claire, how far back is the bridge?"

She started at the sound of his voice, but didn't hesitate. "I'd say I'm about a hundred yards past it."

Ryder took off into the house at full speed.

"You're only two miles from Asher and Sophie's place. They're at the top of the hill. Think you can make it that far?"

He heard the overpowered engine whining. "I can't get this stupid car up the hill. I can walk it."

Grady dove into his SUV and started the engine, shoving into gear without pausing to consider. "I want you to roll back down the hill and park next to the trailhead sign before the bridge. There's a wide gravel turnoff right at the sign."

"I can do that."

Ryder appeared and swung open the passenger door before Grady could take off. He tossed in a stack of white and cream-colored blankets he must have grabbed from the parlor. Ryder's expression drawn tight, he said, "Go get her."

He didn't wait for the door to close all the way before he took off down the driveway, letting the force of his acceleration slam it shut. "Talk to me, Claire. Are you at the sign yet?"

"I, I'm not sure. Yes. Yes, I can see it. I'm pulling off the road."

"Keep your headlights on bright and turn your flashers on until I get to you. I'll be there as soon as I can."

"Ok." She sounded scared. Dammit, he'd better make it.

Like driving blindfolded, the whiteout was near complete. He couldn't see shit, but he couldn't leave Claire out there, alone in the storm. "Stay with me, Claire, I'm not leaving you."

How could such a gorgeous whiteout make everything so blindingly dark? Her heart was beating so hard it filled her entire ribcage, threatening to burst out of her chest. And her hands were vibrating like that little toy she'd kept in the bedside drawer that was probably covered in dust and nonfunctional by now. These were nothing like the pretty little stars that fell from the sky in the movies. These were Godzilla loogies.

Grady's voice kept her in the present. "I'll be there soon. It's going to be ok." He sounded absurdly confident in an uncertain situation.

"Are you crazy? I can't see two feet in front of me."

She flipped on her high beams, her emergency flashers, and hoped she kept the ridiculously red car as close to the road as possible so he could see her, but not so close someone else would run into her. Blinded by the whiteout, she squinted so she could just make out the trees that lined the road.

"Keep your heat on and sit tight. I'm on my way."

"You'll get lost trying to find me. Go back home. I'll walk up the hill and find your friends' house."

"Have you always been this stubborn?"

"Me? You're the crazy one driving through a blizzard so we can freeze to death together. How can you even tell where you're going?"

"I grew up here. I could make this drive with my eyes closed." It didn't make any sense, but she believed him. Needed to, she supposed. He sounded so sure. He'd better be right.

She watched the minutes drag by. Where was he? It had taken her twenty minutes to reach the trailhead from downtown, and that was in clear weather. It could take him hours in this mess.

"Tell me about your hike today. Was it the Riverside Trail?" He chatted, for him or for her, she wasn't sure.

"Yes. It was so pretty. I looped up to the Sundown Trail for a bit. When the snow began to fall, I started back. By the time I reached the car, I was turning into a Claire-cicle. I didn't know snow could be this intense."

"I'm not sure I've ever seen it dump like this. Typical, Claire, your first snow is a goddamn blizzard. Do you do anything halfway?" His voice had a desperate edge.

"Apparently not."

Silence for a moment. She could practically hear him white knuckled on the invisible road, trying to not get stuck in a ditch or wrap around a telephone pole.

"Claire, what's your last name?"

How did he not know? Thoughts of him filled her every waking—and sleeping—moment, and he didn't even know her last name. She laughed with relief. "Dabney."

"What's your middle name?"

"Carmichael. It was my mother's maiden name."

He chuckled. "Claire Carmichael Dabney. I like it."

"What's your middle name?" Although she appreciated the distraction they both needed, she wanted to scream and beg him to hurry out of the storm. She was safe enough for now, but knew he'd rush to get to her if she sounded scared or unsafe. He was already risking life and limb for her. The least she could do was keep *him* safe by staying calm.

"August. After my father."

"Ryder doesn't say much about him." *Sure. Safe subject. Way to go, Claire.*

"He died shortly after I was born. Drunk driver. Patricia had already divorced him and forbidden him from seeing us."

"That's terrible. Did they arrest the driver?"

"No, *he* was the drunk driver. Fortunately, he didn't take anyone else out with him."

"Grady, I'm so sorry."

"It's okay. Patricia married Haley's dad shortly after and Haley came a few months later." He cussed under his breath, but quickly started talking again, as if nothing was wrong. "Apparently, I can thank him for my attitude." A loud crack shattered the air, and Grady cussed as a thunderous boom resonated through the call.

"Are you okay? What was that?"

"I'm good. Just a tree in the road."

"Falling? Grady?"

"Yeah?"

"Please don't get killed because of me."

Long pause. *Way to go, Claire.* She couldn't help the thrill that prickled over her, the hope that he was coming to the rescue because he loved her. But she knew he would do the same for any troubled creature. "Come on, it's a nice day for a drive."

"I like your attitude. You're not a pushover."

He snorted in a derisive laugh. "Nor are you." After a long pause, his voice lightened, shifting back to safer territory. "What's your favorite food?" He was too adorable for his own good.

"Anything with green chiles. Can you tell where you are?"

"Shit, shit... Yeah, found the bridge." His voice strained, he cracked a laugh of relief, reassuring her. "I'm turning around now. Almost there."

Claire exhaled a sigh of relief. Not only that he was close, but that he hadn't found the bridge by flying over the side. She quickly flashed her high beams to show him the way. Diffused headlights appeared right in front of her, and he turned his SUV around so he faced the road, barely visible, although he was only a few feet away.

Grady was at her window moments later and eased the passenger door open, scraping through the mass of snow. Heart pounding in her chest, her eyes welled at the sight of him. His cheeks were pulled tight with stress, but he masked it with a devilish grin.

A lightness washed over her face as she released a hitched exhale. "You made it."

"Barely. I think we're stuck here for the night." He glanced back to where the road should be. "Power's out anyway. We'll wait until the snow slows down so I can at least see where I'm going."

She nodded weakly and grabbed her half-consumed water bottle and her winter coat. "Okay."

He took her coat, and she crawled over the center console to meet him. Knee-deep in the snow, she rose to stand. Thanks to the glow from the car lights, she could make out Grady, but nothing else in the darkness of the night.

Legs teetering as she steadied herself, he wrapped his arm around her and held her tight against him, her worry melting despite the chill. "You okay?" he murmured.

An emotional outburst festered under the surface. She forced it down and nodded. "Thanks for coming for me."

His eyes were as glassy as hers were. Probably from the cold. He nodded, then stepped back. Close behind, she waded through the foot and a half of snow that had accumulated in the last hour. Maybe it was two feet. Whatever it was, it was past the wheel wells of the stupid sports car Ryder had splurged on. Death trap is what it was.

She gripped Grady's hand for the lifeline that it was. She couldn't even see the ends of his car. He held open what she realized was the back passenger door.

As soon as she was inside, he murmured, "Hang on."

Where could he be going? She couldn't see two feet in front of her face, and he disappeared completely. While she waited, she noted the stack of blankets. Good thinking. Patricia would be pissed.

Back a few minutes later, he reappeared, looking like Frosty. She pulled him in onto the leather seats next to her and uselessly brushed the mountain of snow him off. Out in freezing weather in nothing but his work clothes, his suit jacket was damaged beyond repair as snow melted into the fabric. He was frozen solid, his cheeks blazing red. And that shiner was glowing in contrast. She traced the edge of the healing bruise with her fingertips.

He stilled her hand and gritted his jaw tight. "I dug out as much snow as I could around the exhaust pipe. We'll need to check it whenever we turn the engine on in case the snow covers it."

Grady was soaked to the skin—sopping, she amended—as the massive snowflakes melted in his wild blond hair. Ryder had been on the phone with her and was about to talk through directions. Not Grady. He'd taken the phone and gotten to her in recklessly fast time.

Shit, tears were full streaming now. She hadn't admitted even to herself how scared she'd been.

Those ocean blues softened, and he wiped away the tears that poured down her cheeks. She didn't sob, managing to hold back the snot-storm, but she felt like a leaky faucet.

As he held her tight against him, he murmured, "It's ok."

Desperately, she wanted to ask him why. Why would he risk his own life for the slut that had thrown herself at him a few days ago?

"Let's figure out the next few hours." Mind-reader. "Hop in back."

Not easily in her snow-encrusted clothes, she climbed in the back of the SUV. He joined her a moment later and flipped down the seats. From under the back compartment, he pulled out what looked to be an emergency kit.

He set up a flashlight and turned off the dome light, then sat back on his heels and glared at their surroundings. Each on opposite sides of the car, they laid out the blankets into a makeshift bed. He gathered up water bottles and a handful of protein bars. He even had a reflective blanket to lie over them from his emergency kit. She chuckled as the remaining chunks of snow from their clothes had melted and they looked like bedraggled cats that had been dunked in the bathtub.

Without a word, Grady kicked off his leather shoes that were irreparably damaged by the snow, and he leaned against the side of the car. The flashlight cast deep shadows, accenting his fatigue.

Claire peeled off her soaked sweater. "I'd never seen snow before today." She smiled with the goofiest smile she could muster.

As hoped, he grinned at her humor and let out a quiet laugh. "Well, you're making up for it now. I don't think I've ever seen a storm hit quite like this."

"I checked the weather before I left this morning. It was supposed to be an inch or two. I thought that would be pretty."

"*That* would have been pretty. I'd say we're over two feet by now. If this keeps up, I'm not sure we'll be able to get out in the morning."

His phone buzzed, and Hattie's name popped up on the screen. "Hey," he answered.

Ryder's voice came through in a near panic. "Did you get to her? Are you guys ok?" Claire glanced at the front and saw Ryder's phone propped up from where Grady had talked to her the whole way over.

Grady rubbed a hand over his face and leaned against the side of the car. The dark circles under his eyes told of more than just today was bothering him. Good. At least it hadn't just been her, selfish as she knew that must sound, but his pain was oddly reassuring, that maybe he felt something for her.

"Got her. We're safe. Roads are getting worse by the second, visibility limited to about twelve inches, so we're set up here for the night."

"Ok. Check back in the morning so we know you made it through the night. Sooner if you need anything, not that we'll be able to get to you. Patricia's already been trying to bribe the road crews. They've had lots of calls from people worse-off than you, so you're stuck for the night at least."

"We'll be fine. Don't let her do anything rash. 'Night." Grady clicked off the call and tossed the phone to the driver's seat.

He leaned forward and turned off the engine. At her worried look, he said, "We'll turn it back on throughout the night whenever we get cold. I don't want to run out of gas."

She nodded and kicked off her shoes, then scooched her sopping pants over her butt and peeled them off, too.

When she looked over at Grady, he was looking everywhere other than her. At least she'd worn fairly modest underwear today for the hike. Expression drawn tight as he avoided looking at her, he flipped off the flashlight and the car was suddenly pitch black. It was too early for sleep, but she supposed they'd need the supplies if they were stuck here more than just tonight.

Cozy under the blankets, she rolled her big winter coat inside out to make a large pillow for them both. She felt Grady slip off his wet clothes before following her under the blankets. Side by side in the dark, each tucked as far against the side as humanly possible, Claire breathed a long sigh. Her visions of snuggling to stay warm were rapidly fading. If they didn't talk this out, it was going to be a long, long night.

Brain a complete and utter blank, she strained to find something to say. In the distance, although not nearly distant enough, she could hear the cracking and occasional thunderous boom as a tree or large branch broke under the weight of the snow.

She hadn't moved, or didn't think so, and hadn't noticed Grady move, but with each passing minute, he felt closer, like a magnet was pulling them together. Eventually, his arm was against hers, sending heat rushing over her.

"I'm sorry about the other night." She blurted out. There. Conversation initiated.

Gravel coated his voice, his words cautious, his tone flat, sapped from fatigue. "No, I'm sorry. I shouldn't have taken advantage."

Had he been berating himself when she was the instigator? "I was a perfectly willing and eager participant."

"Fair enough, but I shouldn't have taken it so far."

She snorted, "And I probably shouldn't have flashed you."

Still lying flat on his back, he chuckled under his breath. "So, that *was* on purpose?"

An indelicate cackle escaped from deep in her gut. "Of course. What kind of person doesn't notice their tits and ass are hanging out of her dress?"

Grady's rumbling laugh shook the entire car. Delighted at hearing him happy, she lost herself in laughter alongside him. After several minutes, the laughter faded. She wiped the tears from her eyes and coughed as she caught her breath. When had she ever laughed with anyone quite like she did with Grady?

After a moment of the quiet, well, aside from the world collapsing around them, he said, "I appreciated the view."

She smiled and shook her head. "Well, I rarely share that view. So, I'm glad you enjoyed the show. I'm not usually so forward."

The pause that followed was palpable. There was something bothering him, but would he say it?

He curtly responded, "Goodnight, Claire."

"Goodnight, Grady," she whispered, completely, utterly, naively, and foolishly confused.

# 15

## T-E-M-P-E-S-T

C laire awoke a few hours later, convulsing with cold in the freezing car. It was still pitch black out. She had no idea what time it was, if the world still stood, nor if the snow was still coming down.

Her teeth chattered so loud, she woke Grady without even trying. Grumbling, he turned on the flashlight and sat up. Claire shielded her eyes from the invasive light and grimaced, but quickly adapted as she realized Grady was stripped to the skin, aside from his boxer briefs. He clicked open the rear door and hung out the back to check the tailpipe, scooping away the few inches of snow that had accumulated around the exhaust. Once he had ensured it was clear of snow, he quickly clicked the door closed again.

Breath whooshing from her lungs, she bit her lip and pulled the blanket up to her chin. That view was going to reign in her imagination for... the rest of eternity. Damn, she'd enjoyed nice views in the past, but that was one fine ass. And back. And legs. And... did he have to look so good? Sleepy and grouchy, but so damn hot.

As the rear door clicked closed, Grady's eyes were at half-mast from sleepiness, his face scrunched tight to block the shocking brightness of the dome light. His five o'clock shadow was already darkening his jaw. Worse than usual, his hair was tousled every which way. He was ridiculously sexy, so disheveled and groggy.

Grady crawled forward and leaned over the driver's seat to start the car again. Cold air blasted from the vents, and she huddled tighter in the blankets while waiting for the car to heat.

Still without saying a word, he sat atop the makeshift bed with his arms draped over his knees and turned to face her. Were her lips as blue as his were? He looked far wearier than even the cold or late night could have done to him. Was it wrong that she hoped to hell he was as miserable as she was?

Wary as a skittish horse, but he wouldn't let it show. She sat up and cradled her ice cube hands around his jaw and pressed her freezing lips to his shiner, then rested her cheek against his. He didn't resist. They sat and breathed together for a moment, savoring the scrap of warmth each could provide for the other.

And he didn't run away. Mouth over his, moving with him, the heat raised a degree. His freezing hand reached around and gripped her waist. His icy touch radiated heat across her skin as she reacted to his touch.

As quickly as it had come on, the dome light shut off again. At the interruption, he pulled back again hastily. "I can't do this again. I'm not *that* guy."

"Grady, I don't think I've ever wanted *any* guy as much as I want you. I guess I can't read you at all. I... Okay, I know I'm in no position to be pursuing you, but, I thought... I don't know." Her confidence waned, totally uncertain about his feelings for her.

"I don't cheat, and I'm not sure I'm comfortable that you're ok with cheating, no matter what my asshole brother is up to. And if you tell me you have an open relationship, I am absolutely not comfortable with that either. Sorry, but I don't share well."

The pit that had been hanging out in her gut the last few days melted away in an instant. An ironic chuckle escaped her lips. "I think I like you even more now. Grady, I'm not cheating." She knew he couldn't see her in the darkness, but she tried to look him in the eye, so he knew she was dead serious. "Cheaters have their own special level of hell, and open relationships are disgusting. Why do you think I pulled away every time things got close?" Her teeth vibrated so loudly she could hardly get her sentence out.

She could feel his confusion. And his shiver.

"Wait, I'm not following. At what point do you consider it cheating versus not? Do you wait until you've said your I do's, or is it once the ring is on your finger? I note the cheap bastard didn't even buy you a ring."

Tone clipped, shoulders tight, he was clearly slipping into that temper. Very understandable. Dense, irritating man. With his odd relationship with his family, she had little doubt he had self-confidence issues. "No. No. Grady. First, we were *never* engaged. Second, and most importantly, Ryder and I broke up. It had been coming on for a while. Since before I met you. That's why I said it was complicated when I saw you at the skating rink, and I've pretty much been working on ending it since. This trip was supposed to save our relationship, but I was already realizing it wasn't salvageable. Ryder said he'd told you."

Her palm rested on his chest, and she could feel his heart accelerating under her fingers.

"What? When?" She couldn't miss the exasperation, the hopeful confusion in his voice.

Taking pity on him, she wanted to get it through his thick skull that he wasn't a cheat or a fling. "Okay, I admit I kissed you before we officially broke up. Wait, I'm backing up a minute. I had planned to end things the night after we rode together, but you know how hard it is to pin down Ryder to sit still and pay attention. Then I meant to end it the night he took me out to dinner, but he told me you were on a date and I got jealous and sad and lost the nerve. Anyway, after we kissed, I knew I couldn't go another day with things the way they were, so I ended it the next morning. I couldn't... it was physically painful to pull myself away from you. Hell, at the skating rink, I watched you getting into your car and I started to go after you, but by the time I worked up the courage... you were gone."

Long pause. Hopefully she hadn't bungled it too terribly. Finally, he asked, "So, you're not engaged to my brother?"

"No."

"Wait. He told me something about 'we're done.' Wow, that was about Ryder-level of communication. That night when I... at the billiard table, you said you were never engaged, and the more I thought about it, I convinced myself I'd heard wrong. Then when he was making out with the stablemaster, I assumed you had some open relationship or something."

"He was what? That slimy bastard. Although, I'm hoping to be doing a lot more than making out with his brother in the next few minutes. What I'm trying to tell you is he and I were over before we said the words. Honestly, we were barely more than roommates. I never loved your brother, and I'm pretty sure he's figured that out about me, too. We were convenient. And then... getting to know you, feeling this breath-stopping, gut-wrenching fluttering in my chest and total loss of thermoregulation whenever I'm around you—"

His hand that had stilled at her side, squeezed gently in sweet contact, his thumb brushing along her skin. "Then you... You're not..."

She could feel the moment it really sunk in. Poor guy. "I want you. Only you." She pressed her defrosting lips against his before he could doubt again. Although, the car was finally warming up, surrounding them both with a penetrating warmth that tingled deep into her skin.

Slow and steady, he kissed her with a testing curiosity. His fingertips trailed along her jaw.

"Say it again," he said, smiling against her lips.

"I want you," she murmured.

"So if I hadn't left the skating rink in such a hurry, you would have come after me?"

"My hand was on the door." She nipped at his lip. "And if you hadn't invited us out with your friends that night, or gone out on that date the next night... really, it's your fault it took me so long."

Hand on her back, he whispered, "I've never been so miserable as I have been since meeting you."

Impatience taking over, she wiggled out of the blankets and wrapped her legs around him. "Is it bad that I'm pleased about that?"

He tugged her up against him and grinned. "As you chose wisely in the end, I'll let it slide. This time."

Building, urgency mounting, he kissed her back with a pent-up hunger, quenching the thirst she'd been struggling with for days. Tilting her head back, he deepened the kiss and poured everything into it that he'd been holding back before.

Breathless, she demanded one more answer. "Were you going to tell me how you felt, or just sit back and let me marry your brother while he's nailing the stablemaster behind my back?"

He chuckled against her mouth. "That night at the billiard table, I had meant to talk it out with you, but, well, I was distracted. You looked amazing in that dress, by the way. Anyway, then I felt like an ass for taking it so far and tried to give you space. And then tonight, I came home to hash it out with you. My plan was to convince you to dump his sorry ass and give me a chance. Plus a fair amount of groveling for leaving you like I did. That's when I heard Sasha and him making out in her office."

"Heard?" She teased, expecting him to correct his statement, that he saw the pair. "How did you know it wasn't me?"

He moved downward, his icy cold hand sliding her top up. Shifting lower, his breath hot against her cold skin, his mouth opened over her breast and took the tight bud in his teeth, then sucked her hard until she let out a gasp. She felt his grin pressed against her breast. "That's how."

For a moment, she considered smacking him, until he pulled her top the rest of the way over her head and continued right where he'd left off. His breath against her, he circled the tight nub and took her breast into his mouth, pulling, and again, she moaned as he sucked and tantalized.

No longer cold, from the heater or his touch, Claire couldn't stand the remaining clothes that separated them. Grady released her long enough to peel off his briefs.

"Damn this darkness. I can't even find you." His deep laugh vibrated through her. "There," he said as he found her and nipped the side of her breast.

His hand shifted down, uninhibited this time, and massaged her wet center until she cried out, begging for release that was moments away. Her back arched as he drove her to the edge.

"Grady, please," she gasped.

Mounting pressure inside her boiled over as he brought her higher and higher. Teetering on the cusp of something earth-shattering, she pleaded again.

"Please, what?" he teased, driving her on until she couldn't speak at all, and cried out in blissful release as she came in his hand.

As her breathing calmed, he kissed her until her brain melted. "Please, what?" he asked again against her lips.

"Make love with me," she whispered.

With a cruel, tempting laugh, he refused. "I'm not letting you off that easy. Not that I can see anything." Shifting down, he trailed his lips down her abdomen, lighting a fire as he went, kissing each square inch of skin along the way.

Beyond ready for him, she opened for him as he settled between her legs. Pressing the exquisite velvet of his tongue against her core, he applied just enough pressure to elicit that moan again. Crying out at the intensity of the already building orgasm, she urged him on.

Lightly tasting, tickling her swollen clit, he drove her wild with anticipation. Circling, he methodically increased his pace with her gasps. Licking, vibrating, he laved. Her voice echoed through the snowy car as he drove her beyond the edge of reason.

As she crested again and again, he mercifully pulled away and moved up her body. Both overcome with desperation, needing more, he nuzzled against her neck, hard against her as he was clearly struggling to keep his lust in check.

"Now, Grady," she whispered against his ear.

"Are you sure?" he asked, the hope in his crackling voice unmistakable.

She gripped his hips and moved under him. "Yes. I want you. Now."

Without further argument, but maybe with a hint of a chuckle and the feel of a grin against her neck, he thrust into her deeply and completely, before she could finish her thought. Stars flashed before her eyes at the rush of ecstasy. His hips pumped with hers in harmony against the destruction of the night. A resonant groan escaped his lips as she tightened around him. The only two people in the world of confusion and darkness, she was absolutely, one hundred percent certain, he was hers.

G rady awoke shuddering as daylight glowed through the snow-encrusted windows of the Forerunner. Well, the rapid clicking sound of Claire's teeth chattering woke him. Carefully, to avoid waking her, he pulled his arm out from under her to check the tailpipe. She didn't even stir when the dome light came on.

With a silent expletive in response to the mound of snow that had covered the exhaust pipe, he used the ice scraper to dig around it so he could start the engine to warm up again. Thank goodness no one was around to see his naked torso hanging out of the back of his SUV, shoveling snow like a polar-bear club lunatic. Hands now totally numb, aside from the intermittent burning stab of cold, he shut the back door and moved up to turn the engine on again.

Claire stirred at his side, groaned and wrapped around his bare waist while he sat next to her, but she drifted right back to sleep. Just after six in the morning and a message from Hattie buzzed.

*It's Ryder. You alive?*

Fingers finally defrosting as hot air settled over their makeshift bed, he texted back, *Doing fine. Any word on the snowplows?*

*Slow going, but you're on their list. A lot of people in similar situations and trees blocking critical roads, so it might be awhile. Patricia's been after them all morning.*

His stomach grumbled a noisy complaint. In his rush to get to Claire, he hadn't eaten dinner last night. The midnight protein bars hadn't done much.

*Don't worry about it. Think we can get up the hill to Asher's and will crash there for now.* And hide there as long as possible. He had no idea how he was going to explain the switch-a-roo to his mother.

*K. Haley's flight landed in the nick of time so she's at a hotel next to the airport. I'll borrow Bill's truck to run get her as soon as the roads are clear enough.*

Grady breathed a sigh of relief. The gala sounded like such a nightmare, but maybe, just maybe, having his brother and sister there to have his back would make it okay. If Ryder understood... which, after the stable incident, Grady suspected Claire was right, she and Ryder had been over long before the official breakup.

It looked to be at least three feet of snow out there, but he had decent ground clearance and four-wheel drive, so they might be able to push through. Hopefully. Worst case, they could wrap up in blankets and it would be a gorgeous morning hike up the hill.

Still sopping wet, his pants were hardly a degree above freezing. He felt Claire moving at his side, waking fully this time in the cozy cab, her lips no longer as blue as they'd been a few moments ago. Her eyes fluttered open. Confused at first, she scowled and looked at the snow-covered windows. Then the giggles started as she assessed the situation. And kept going and going.

"Good morning," he said, chuckling with her. Yes, she was totally nuts.

She sat up in the makeshift bed and the blankets fell to her waist as she tried to contain her giggle fit. A total cad, he thought about making conversation, maybe even eye contact, but his eyes locked onto those spectacularly rounded breasts.

Rather than complain about his lack of manners, she calmed her laughter, but her grin didn't relent, and she pulled his hand to her and pressed her breast into his palm, a delicious grin on her face. Fascinated, he inspected each, weighing and pressing his thumbs over the pert pink nipples. "Battery be damned, we should have risked it so I could see this sooner."

His empty stomach took the hint and shut up as he appreciated the moment. He ran his tongue across the tops of her breasts, and her back arched in response. Circling around each tight bud, he took each in his mouth and sucked and tormented until she cried out in that husky moan that was uniquely hers.

In the light of day, she was just as insatiable. Reaching his hand between them, he slid his fingers along her slick folds. Caressing her, bringing her to orgasm within seconds, he'd quickly discovered exactly how to drive her wild with just his touch.

As she crested, he was so hard and ready, he slid into her. Squeezing around him, she climaxed higher and rolled her hips with his. Each time they joined, it was a little more intense, more satisfying, more... everything.

She came again and again, massaging his thick cock until his vision was clouded and they released with electrifying finality together.

Collapsing atop her, he groaned with exhaustion. Breath gradually calming, she stroked her hand through his hair in a lazy motion.

Stunned, he realized how foolishly impulsive they'd been. He groaned and said, "We, uh... we probably should have had the condom conversation about twelve hours ago."

Her cozy chuckle soothed him more than anything she could have said. "Excellent point. I'm blaming the hypothermia. If it helps, I have an IUD and haven't had sex in months."

Pausing, he calculated, struggling to figure out how that had happened. "Didn't you and Ryder just break up a few days ago?"

"Yeah. As previously stated, it had been coming on for a while."

He sat up and smiled devilishly at her. "Well, you won't hear any complaints from me on that end of things. Now, let's never mention it again." Reaching across the blankets, he found his pants again. "I just had my annual physical. Clean bill of health, STD screening included." He flashed her a grin and winced as he pulled his damp clothes back on.

She found her jeans, saturated and a few degrees above freezing, and whimpered as she pulled them over her hips. She glared at her wet socks.

# 16

## F-A-M-I-S-H-E-D

Covered in snow and chilled to the bone, they hopped back in the car after manually digging out a path to gain traction before trudging through the wall of snow. Dark circles shadowed under his eyes, and she knew he hadn't slept more than ten-minute intervals. Every time she'd started shivering, he'd started the engine again.

Claire peered over Grady's shoulder as he checked his incoming text from Ryder via Hattie's phone. Grady tossed the phone down and fired up the engine. "Now that she knows we're alive, Patricia has requested to redirect the plows so her party can go on as scheduled. I suspect the road crews are laughing their asses off at her request. They might have other priorities, like the hospital and the power company."

"At least she prioritized your life."

He chuckled under his breath. "That is a plus." Gaining traction, the SUV puffed up the hill, every few wheel turns skidding despite four-wheel drive and hefty tires. "I don't want to go to that damn gala."

"Me neither." Claire couldn't suppress a whimper. "I'm so hungry."

"What, half of a protein bar for breakfast wasn't enough for you?"

"Puh-hoo. I have a caffeine headache. And I'm cold." She rotated her side of the air vents toward her and shifted the driver's side vents toward him.

"Me too. No sleep, no food, no caffeine." He warmed her blue fingertips in his slightly warmer yellow ones. "On the bright side, we found creative ways to stay warm."

Smile at half its normal strength, he showed the fatigue he tried to hide with humor. Claire still couldn't believe he'd risked life and limb to come for her. Not that she couldn't have survived on her own without some basic safety tips, theoretically, but she was so grateful she hadn't had to go through it alone.

"I'm thinking we should sleep for the next eighteen hours."

The incline sharply climbed, and the SUV whined at the extra effort. Grady pulled his hand away to shift gears. With a tight grimace, he held his breath. "Hold on to your butts," he murmured through gritted teeth as he fluttered his foot on the gas pedal.

She snorted. "What?"

"Are you kidding?" He smiled tightly, as if his grip on the wheel would help overcome the mound of snow thickening as they pushed against it. "How about 'must go faster?'"

"Nope. Nothing."

"Jurassic Park? What kind of veterinarian are you?" He hissed as they halted, then shifted to reverse, rocking the car backward, then forward again while attempting to angle around the snow pack that had accumulated in front of them.

"You're such a nerd. I'm the kind of vet that treats living creatures, not the extinct variety." She felt her feet pushing against the floorboards, as if she could somehow help.

The engine hummed, swelling to a roar as they powered forward and seemed to gain traction. Steady on the gas, he built up enough momentum to keep them moving. Hands gripped tight on the wheel, he turned widely and eventually straightened out. Regardless, they were moving, the snow had stopped falling from the sky, and the air was clear.

Claire marveled at the winter wonderland around them. Fuck that, winter wonderland was a gentle term. This was a snowy fortress leading them to the evil ice witch, not the kind snow fairy. Thick branches, bowing under the weight of caked-on snow, hovered just above the road. Cracking branches added to the ominous ambience as they traversed the spooky forest.

Knuckles now white from the ridiculous drive rather than the cold, Grady kept a steady pace up the slope, occasionally having to veer to the side to unload the snowpack that accumulated on the grill. Snow crunched and groaned as it compressed under the wheels, the underbelly of the SUV scratching the top layer of snow as it attempted the labor that belonged to snowplows.

"What are we going to do when we can't hide anymore?" He sighed and shook his head, his voice lost, eyes locked on the road.

Her mouth quirked up in question.

"As in, about us?"

"Oh. Yeah. A small complication I should have mentioned sooner. I sort of promised Ryder I'd continue the engagement ruse until after the gala."

Grady laughed mirthlessly. "He is such a suck-up."

With an overdramatic eye-roll, Claire shook her head. "I think he's more about looking good than aiming to please. Patricia has extended some invitations to a few Seattle-based CEOs that may be looking to up their marketing game. Regardless, he got me the job at Parson's, so I agreed."

He glanced away from the road just long enough to shoot her a massively sweet grin. "You're staying?"

Biting her lip, this time in utter delight, she grinned so wide her cheeks hurt. "I am."

"Then I will be patient for another few days." His grin was as eager as hers. "But he and I are swapping bedrooms. He can stay in the nauseating green room."

As they reached the top of the hill, a thick trunk blocked most of the road. Grady eased around the tip of it and turned into what was probably, hopefully, a driveway. The engine whined at the turn, but powered on. After a sketchy drive in which they lurched over several branches, the driveway opened, and she saw a cozy blue craftsman-style home settled in front of a broad field that overlooked the snowy valley beyond.

Smoke puffed out of the brick chimney and the windows were glowing like a cozy homing beacon. To the left, Zane carted a backpack down the steps of an over-the-garage apartment. From the front porch of the house, Freya held her arms around her middle, until she caught sight of them approaching and waved madly.

Grady parked in front and pushed his door open.

From the foot of the steps, Zane nodded. "Rough night?"

Claire trudged through the snow, aimed for the house and warmth and coffee. Grady grinned like a smitten fool and said, "I've had worse."

She smiled back at him, a blush flaming her cheeks that were already pink from the crisp air. Grady's grin was irrepressible, and Zane nudged him on the shoulder, teasing as he looked him up and down. "You look ridiculous."

His sleeves were pushed up, his dress pants soaked to the thighs, and his leather shoes were irreversibly damaged. Claire laughed and dashed up the front porch to wait with Freya. Claire found herself enveloped in Freya's snug embrace as Freya laughed. "I can't believe that just happened. Zane was determined to attempt the storm to go rescue you guys, but I wouldn't let him. Well, I would have if things were getting dicey, but Grady's got survival skills."

Claire looked back to see Grady grinning wide and pushing back at Zane. After Grady stomped his snow-caked shoes on the porch, Freya jumped and hugged him. "My hero."

Zane snorted, arms open as if waiting for his own hug. "Hey, I didn't have to trudge through all that snow to bring your sketchbook *and* your fuzzy socks. What about me?" Grinning, Freya looped her arms around him and nuzzled close. "You already know how I feel about you." Freya turned to Claire. "Tell me the harrowing tale of how Grady drove through hell to rescue you."

Asher was waiting, leaned against the doorframe, and waved them in. He knocked Grady on the arm as they passed into the house. "And how you warded off hypothermia all night, all alone, just the two of you."

The house felt like a welcome sauna after last night. Claire kicked off her snowy boots and set them in the boot tray, while Grady and Zane did the same. Grady slipped his hand into hers, the easy affection sending her pulse aflutter.

From the kitchen, Sophie smiled and flashed her a wink. "You guys must be starving."

Stomach rumbling on cue, Claire nodded. "We missed dinner."

"Coffee?"

Sleepy grin widening, Claire whimpered, "Yes please."

Sophie poured a pair of steaming mugs in the homey kitchen. The lights over the island were on, and a lamp in the attached living room, a fire blazing in the hearth, but otherwise the house was dark.

Asher caught her perusal. "Power's out all over town. Probably the state. We have a generator."

As Zane returned from the back of the house where he'd dropped the bags he'd carted in, he tossed Freya a bundle of pink fuzzy socks. "For which we are grateful." He looked to Claire. "Freya and I live in the apartment over the garage. As we are saving up for a house, we hadn't even thought about investing in a generator. And there's no fireplace in the apartment."

Asher shrugged. "Can't say I thought about it either, but my dad owns the hardware store in town and ensured we had this thing properly installed before winter hit."

"Oh, I've been wanting to go in there but haven't had an excuse to. I was hoping it was locally owned." Claire gratefully accepted the coffee from Sophie and leaned back into Grady, the zing fluttering through her as he wrapped his arms around her before accepting his own coffee.

"Unless you're gainfully employed, don't risk it. He's hiring."

Grady stood behind her and laced his arm around her waist, and she melted into him. Voice light, he said, "Not to worry, you are looking at the newest veterinarian at Parson's."

Cozy in her socks, Freya curled up on the couch and whooped, "You're staying in town?"

Grady nuzzled close, his smile palpable as he held her close.

"Damn right," Claire beamed.

Leaned against the kitchen island, Sophie asked, "How do the roads look?"

Grady's voice rumbled against her. "Awful. Mind if we crash here for now?"

"You'd better," Sophie answered. "Freya and Zane already claimed Freya's old bedroom. You guys can have the other one. We already tossed some sheets on the bed when we heard you were coming. I'll grab some dry clothes for you, and there should be plenty of hot water for showers, but I'm fixing breakfast so don't take too long."

Zane rolled up his sleeves and headed into the kitchen. "I'll give you a hand."

R elief was a paltry understatement to describe how Grady felt on getting Claire to safety. That treacherous drive to reach her last night had been the stuff of nightmares. No visibility, creaking and snapping branches all around, utter darkness. All amplifying the fear of finally finding the love of his life, only to lose her before he even had a chance to tell her.

Like they'd been made for each other, each piece fitting together like an intricate puzzle, last night was extraordinary. The fact that she hadn't been a cheating bitch certainly hadn't hurt.

Grady tugged Claire against him and whispered in her ear, "Let's go warm up."

Biting her lower lip, she grinned and leaned into him. "Quickly. I'm starving."

Before his friends could drill him any further, he dragged her into the back bathroom. Stealing her coffee, he set their mugs on the counter and peeled her top off. Lips warm and pliant against his, fluidly joining without hesitation, he was lost in her.

They must have disconnected long enough to remove the rest of their snow-encrusted clothes. Must have turned on the shower and stepped inside. But Grady noticed nothing but her in his delirium. Her lips trailing along his shoulder. Her clever fingers teasing along his hard shaft and gripping him tight.

Sensation returning, her skin pinked and pressed against his, he lifted and braced her against the shower wall. As the steaming flow rushed over them, he thrust into her. Gasping on impact, she moaned as he moved inside her.

A thousand words, infinite hope threatened to cross his lips as he made love with her again. Biting his tongue, he restrained himself from confessing his love to her in the midst of a shower quickie. Really romantic. His timing was already nightmarish, his words continually inadequate around her, he didn't dare risk it.

But fuck, he was in so deep.

On a moan, as she ascended into her climax, she whispered in his ear, "Come with me, Grady."

Hazel eyes thick with emotion, she held him in her trance, moving with him, pulling him over the edge until he was well and truly and eternally hers.

They managed to pull away, but he craved the sensation of her skin against his as the water flowed over their joined bodies. He poured shampoo into his palm and massaged into her hair, but she giggled and said, "We need to get a move on, or your friends won't let us stay."

"I'm fast." When he didn't scrub fast enough, she snagged the shampoo and turned his hair into a mohawk, laughing out loud at how ridiculous he looked.

At the impatient knock at the door, Grady winced. Asher growled, "Get your asses moving, or I'm not saving any bacon."

"One sec," Grady yelled back.

"Clothes on the bed," Asher said before leaving them alone again.

Claire rinsed out the last of her conditioner and shut off the faucet, suppressing a giggle at their delirious foolery. They toweled off and dashed into the bedroom. Cozy joggers and a top of Sophie's waited in a neat stack for Claire, and Asher had loaned him a pair of jeans and a sweatshirt. Grady tugged on the jeans and dropped to the bed, taking a gulp of the freshly refilled coffee that was waiting on the bedside table.

He heard Sophie's bellow across the cavernous great room, her voice bouncing off the refinished hardwood floors. "Asher, get your ass off the couch and come help me in the kitchen. I like your bacon better than mine."

Asher answered in a goofy tone, "Sorry, sorry. On my way."

They had at least another ten minutes, maybe more with how charred Asher made bacon. Outside the bedroom window, the forest was coated in a thick blanket of white. Undisturbed, as if the entire world stood still.

Claire lowered next to him on the bed and leaned into his side, slipping his fingers into hers. "I love the snow."

He kissed the back of her hand, then reached the table to hand her coffee over. "When we were kids, Ryder, Haley, and I used to have these snowball fights that would last for hours. Patricia would usually go to the hospital ahead of the weather, thanks to the urgent calls from the hospital requiring staff to make plans to get to work no matter what. Haley's dad was often away on business anyway, so we three would let loose. Hattie would have hot chocolate waiting, and we'd warm up in front of the fire."

"It was lucky you three had each other."

"Yeah. I miss that."

"Know what? I'll bet they miss it, too. Ryder's got a lot of colleagues, but aside from me, he has no real friends."

"We used to be close." Grady caught the scent of cheesy, eggy, savory goodness emanating from the oven. His stomach rumbled and reminded him how long it had been since he'd eaten anything. "Let's eat," he said. As they walked into the kitchen, he saw Zane pulling pie pans from the oven. "Zane, please tell me that's the quiche you were thinking of adding to the lunch menu."

"It's your lucky day." He set down the oven mitts and started to slice into an avocado. "Sophie added jalapenos and green chiles."

Claire leaned into Grady and wrapped her arms around his middle, her tummy rumbling so loud the entire room heard it. "I might pass out from happy hunger."

Asher flipped hunks of well-cooked bacon in the cast iron pan with a series of sizzles and pops. He laughed out loud, shaking his head as he said, "You and me both. We were up hours ago and had to skip our morning run, but Sophie insisted on holding breakfast until you guys got here."

Freya skated across the hardwood toward them in her pink fluffy socks, coming to a halt alongside Claire. "Thin walls. Trust me, he was well entertained while waiting for you."

Jumping back to avoid a bacon grease splatter, Asher laughed and said, "Don't steal my martyr moment."

Grady slipped out of Claire's arms to refill their coffees. Within minutes, they were all seated around the table, cozy in the dim kitchen that was brightening as the cloud-diffused sun reflected off the snow.

Like a starving horde, they dove into the meal. Claire laughed at his side.

"What?" Grady nudged her and grinned through his over-stuffed bite of quiche.

"My brothers would feel quite at home here."

"I avoid appropriate, dull conversation and impeccably mannered dinners with my parents as often as possible," Grady groaned.

Out of the corner of his eye, he saw Claire eyeing the last piece of bacon. And she wasn't the only one. After a fair enough pause, she swiftly snatched the precious morsel. But Sophie was there just as fast and grabbed the other half.

"You've got some incredible reflexes. Like a freaking gecko," Claire teased her new friend.

With a mischievous grin, Sophie broke it in half to share. "And you're a bacon fiend."

While Claire munched the last of the bacon, Freya watched as Claire leaned into Grady and he wrapped his arm around her, leaning in and taking a long breath as he snuggled closer. "What did it take," Freya asked, "For you two to figure it out? Last we saw, Grady was a miserable lump."

Claire grinned. "I'd been working on it since the moment we met. But apparently it took being locked up in the middle of a blizzard to get him to listen long enough to hear that he's all I want."

Grady grabbed the pot from the kitchen and returned to pour a round for the table. "I tried to warn you, I'm terrible at relationships."

"He's not wrong. Poor guy's had his heart broken more than his fair share," Freya said.

Leaned back in his chair, Grady held his stomach and groaned. "Thanks for letting us crash here. Even if we could make it all the way to the house, I don't think I could handle it right now."

"I promised Ryder I would pretend we were still engaged until after the gala. In return, he helped me to get the job at Parson's."

Asher glanced at Sophie, his eyebrows raising a question in a secret lover's code. Smiling sympathetically, she nodded, and Asher said, "You're both welcome to stay here as long as you need. We can pretend the roads are impassable for at least another few days and skip the damn gala if you want."

Sophie jabbed her finger into his ribs. "You just want to skip the gala. I want to see you in a tux again."

He grimaced. "I would kill to skip Patricia's party to celebrate herself. But if Grady wants us there, I will go."

"Seriously, I know you wanted to give us space, but please, both of you, do you want to move in here for a month or two while you find a place? Or two places, whatever you decide, but at least to get *both* of you out of Mallory Manor?" Sophie dropped her eyebrows and smiled.

Claire threw her head back in laughter, slapping her knee in enjoyment. "I call it Mallory Mansion."

With a shrug, Grady nodded. "I call it Patricia's Vanity." He looked to Claire, and her eyebrows raised. The corner of his mouth turned up in question, like the exchange Asher and Sophie had shared. The simple, familiar gesture stirred a tendril of heat that ran through his veins like a shot of smooth tequila.

Still holding his gaze, Claire grinned. "Yes, please. If you're sure you don't mind. I have to go back to Phoenix to pack, and then I start work in six weeks."

Suddenly shy, Grady felt a bubble of anxiety in his gut. "Want some company? If you have much stuff, we could drive it up. Make a vacation out of it."

"I'd like that."

A frown lowering his brow, Asher looked out at the snow-covered front yard. "Grady, while you're on such a roll, proving to be a normal, decent human being, and therefore not what your mother had hoped for you, while stealing your brother's fiancée, pretty much fucking up your parent's gala anyway, are you going to quit your job?"

"What? No. I can't—"

"You can't keep doing what you're doing. It's sucking the life out of you."

"Lincoln—" Grady tried to reference his business partner.

Sophie interjected, "Lincoln loves his job. He's resilient and clever. He'll be fine without you. No offense."

"Do you know how much my parents invested in my law degree? How much blood, sweat, tears, and time *I* invested?" Grady leaned back in his chair and ran a hand through his damp hair.

Zane shrugged, rising from his chair. "Did I mention my architecture degree? Twelve years in the Navy? And now I brew beer. Things change." He poured a warmup and leaned against the kitchen counter, sipping the boiling hot liquid with a satisfied grimace.

Freya hopped to her feet and nodded to Claire. "Come on, let's raid Sophie's closet."

Brow scrunched, Claire sported a puzzled grin. "Um, okay."

Sophie shrugged as she said, "It's a thing."

Asher stacked the licked-clean plates from the table and set them in the sink. Turning on the faucet, he methodically hand washed the dishes. A month after Asher had returned from the

Navy, he'd hardly been able to make much more than toast, having lived in a tiny apartment and eating takeout or galley food. Now, he was cooking breakfast—albeit bacon so crispy it melted in your mouth—and doing dishes. Grady took a lot of credit for that from their time as roommates.

Grady rose from his chair but was dizzy all of a sudden and gripped the kitchen counter to steady himself. "Intervention?"

With a careless shrug that Grady knew was anything but, Zane said, "A tardy one."

Asher's mouth turned downward in concern. "It's scary, fighting for what you want. But maybe it's time."

Nodding, Zane moved closer and patted him on the shoulder. "Your family will come around. Or, if they don't, on the plus side, Patricia may stop talking to you."

Grady stood upright and pushed down the anxiety, washing it away with a heavy inhale. "That would be amazing. Imagine not having to deal with my mother anymore... Who am I kidding? I'm not that lucky." Continuing to steady himself with regular influxes of oxygen into his lungs, he paced the kitchen.

Asher plucked the towel from the hook and wiped his hands dry before leaning against the counter across from Zane, the pair of Navy SEALs flanking him like they were going in for the kill. "You can't keep doing this to yourself."

Zane shrugged. "It's not like you're drowning in student loans like I was, and you're not going to be waiting in the unemployment lines. Black Op is young, but you know our financials. It'll be tight for the next few months, but we can afford for you to take a regular income."

"I'm not worried about the money." He shook his head, digging his hands in his hair. "I mean, I have a decent savings account, but I don't want to dip into that. The security blanket of my steady paycheck has been my excuse. But you're not wrong. I'm so burned out."

"See? You know it's time. Your cheek is still purple from one of many assholes you've pissed off," Asher said.

Zane winked and said, "I don't know, I think Grady will find a way to get coldcocked all on his own."

Mug raising to toast after topping off Grady's coffee, Asher said, "Stop worrying and rip off the Band-Aid. Take a few weeks to just exist, without thinking about it. Give that overactive brain of yours a break."

Zane nodded. "Take that vacation. Just leave me some notes on what all I need to do while you're out."

"I fucking hate being a lawyer." Nodding, Grady's eyes wandered the ceiling, considering what it might be like to actually relax. He hadn't taken time for himself in... ever? "Okay. But—"

Zane whacked him on the arm. "Stop butting."

Grady nodded, nauseous as he thought about it. What idiot wound up with two of his best friends counting on him as business partners? Didn't matter what he did, he was going to let one of them down.

Zane winked. "If it helps, you have to survive your mother's party first."

"Fuck. Let's hope the roads will still be impassable. Cross your fingers it snows again."

"If all hell breaks loose and Patricia condemns you in front of her peers, or if she's completely humiliated by your antics... Well, let's just say Zane and I know how to raise hell."

Chuckling, he flexed his crossed arms and grinned mischievously. "Hell, yeah. Like that party in Syria that we weren't supposed to infiltrate."

Asher winked. "Exactly. Those greedy assholes didn't know what hit them."

Hysterics shuddering through his broad shoulders, tears flooding from his eyes, Zane said, "Or what they were smelling."

Grady couldn't help but laugh, rolling his eyes at his friends. Although he'd love to see the look on Patricia's face if her party were to turn disastrous, he'd rather lie low and suffer a quiet night.

# 17

## G-R-E-A-T-E-X-P-E-C-T-A-T-I-O-N-S

While the guys seemed to be having some sort of intervention, Claire followed Sophie and Freya into the main bedroom. Humming as she carried the lantern into Sophie's closet, Freya asked, "Claire? Do you have what you need for the gala?"

"Um. Yes."

Sophie laughed, winking at Claire. "She's a terrible closet thief. If you have anything you don't want stolen, lock it up."

"I heard that. I always return them, plus some," Freya hollered from across the house.

"Correction, she returns them. And she usually adds a fun sketch as payment."

Claire stood back and laughed, enjoying the distraction, and knowing Grady would appreciate a smaller audience for his intervention. "I saw the charcoals in the bathroom. My favorite was the cedar branch, but the one with the jagged mountain peaks was gorgeous too. It sounds absolutely worth it."

The main bedroom was as airy as the rest of the house, even in the gray morning. Freya popped out of the walk-in closet a moment later. "I'm going to have to go for the green one this time."

Fingernails in her mouth, Sophie winced. "I have a small addiction. It's Freya's fault. I had a few cute dresses that I never wore until she made me start wearing them. Turns out, I like them, so I keep adding to my stock."

Raising her eyebrows, Freya pulled a slinky, pink silk dress from its hanger. "Asher appreciates them as well." Turning to Claire, she handed her the dress and winked. "Grady's fond of silk."

She didn't want to think of how Freya knew he liked silk. He'd mentioned he had a thing for Sophie when they'd first met, but otherwise she was unaware of Grady having any romantic involvement with his friends. Not that she was the jealous sort, but it helped to know this sort of thing. "Actually, I'm set on that end. The dress I brought is silk."

Sophie added, "By the way, Freya just knows things. Not to worry, neither of us has any personal experience involving Grady and silk."

"I wasn't worried. I'm really not a jealous girlfriend. But I am possessive."

Freya tugged off her cozy power-outage yoga pants and sweatshirt in a blink, leaving nothing more than a miniscule pair of lace panties. Blushing, Claire looked away. Sophie laughed. "You'll get used to Freya."

Nodding, Claire didn't argue. "I'd love to be that comfortable with my body."

Freya slipped a green velvet number over her head. "Claire, you have an amazing body. If you're not comfortable with it, I'm going to kick your ass."

"I appreciate your violent response. It's taken me a while to get here, but I like me. Although that doesn't mean I'm comfortable enough to undress in front of you guys."

Sophie nodded, sorting through the pile. "Me neither, so we're good." She fussed with the choices, sighed, chewed on her nails a bit more, then put her hands on her hips. "I can't decide what to wear."

Claire wandered into the closet. "You do have cute stuff. What about the pink one?"

"I love that one." Sophie said as she came up behind her and ran her fingertips over the smooth fabric.

Freya groaned, "Sadly, we don't share a shoe size. Claire? Please say you're an eight and a half?"

"Nope, sorry."

Sophie grabbed a pair of suede heeled booties and rose to her feet. "Claire, I have to admit, I was worried when Grady decided to move in with his parents when the house burned down. We tried to get him to stay with us, but he insisted Asher and I needed the privacy." Sophie sighed before continuing, pacing and looking out the window. "Don't break his heart. He's good at everything. Really, it's ridiculous. Except for relationships."

Walking closer to Sophie, she stood at her side, the snow twinkling as the sun peeked out from the clouds. "I've gathered he doesn't have a great track record. You're getting at more than that, aren't you?"

Freya nodded. "He's had his heart broken more than his share, and I think it's taken a toll. Catching Ryder with his girlfriend in law school was probably the worst of it, as they'd been close until then. Then it really didn't help when he showed interest in Sophie.

Sophie groaned, her lip turned out in a guilty pout. "I'd actually wanted things to work out between Grady and me, so initially I didn't exactly act not-interested, but I fell for Asher so quickly... Actually, Grady found out about us when he overheard, a, uh, a rather intimate moment in a dressing room." Sophie blushed.

"Really?" Claire raised her eyebrows, intrigued.

In glorious green velvet, Freya joined them at the window. "Between the two of us, maybe we can get out of her the many interesting places they've impulsively done it."

Full blush, Sophie had those nails in her mouth again. "Hey. You're one to talk. Laundry room?" She pulled her nails out, clearly a habit she was fighting tooth and nail.

Ha, *tooth and nail*. Claire swallowed the bad joke, not quite ready to reveal the full Claire-quirkiness just yet.

"Anyway, back to Grady." Sophie grinned. "It's been, what, not even twenty-four hours, and you've already done it in the car and the shower? I'm impressed."

Claire blushed and shook her head. "I guess I can't remember the last time I've had girlfriends."

Veering from the impulsive sex-capades topic, Sophie said, "Aside from relationships, Grady is good at everything, because he won't allow himself to fail. As he was always under so much parental pressure to excel, he holds himself to inhumanly high standards."

Freya nodded vigorously. "Enviably well rounded, yet he's so afraid of failure, he's... fragile."

Blood rushing turbulently through her veins, Claire fisted her hands at her sides, feeling impotent in her ability to make Grady see how genuine and normal he was. That he didn't have to try so hard. "I know we're still so new, but trust me, there is nothing I want more than for Grady to be happy."

Claire found herself enveloped in Freya and Sophie's octopus arms. Lip quivering, Claire bit down, nearly drawing blood as she struggled to stop the tears that threatened. Lack of sleep and adrenaline and... dang emotions. The last week had been one of the best, but, well, also one of the worst.

Her new friends were as teary as she was. Freya looked deeply into her, the corners of her mouth turned up in a subtle smile. "I expect to pick out my own bridesmaid dress."

Grady's eyes fluttered open to find Claire draped over him, waking from the best dream only to find he had landed in a better one. As he stirred, she shifted her hair out of her face to reveal a sleepy smile. He slid a stubborn lock of hair off her forehead.

Fully awake in a heartbeat, Claire rose to her elbows and pinned him in her hold, so he could see nothing but her. Grady leaned up and indulged in a lingering kiss before rolling her under him to draw out the kiss. Her fingers teasing in his hair, Grady slipped deeper into the fantasy.

Until his phone buzzed. And buzzed again. And buzzed again.

"You should answer that," she whispered against his mouth.

"They can wait," he said.

And again.

"Fuck." He reached over and checked his phone.

"What is it?"

"Patricia." Sitting up, he tugged the blanket over his lap and glared out the window at the sparkly blanket of snow.

Claire wrapped her legs around him, encircling him from behind, trailing kisses along his shoulder. "Just get it over with. In a few days, we'll be on our way to Phoenix and vacation. You can meet my family and they will adore you."

Hand over hers, he relaxed into her. "If they're anything like you, I think we'll get along brilliantly."

Clicking send, he held the phone to his ear. Claire nuzzled against him.

Patricia's grating voice clanged against his eardrum. "Grady. I can't tell you how relieved I am that you're okay. And Claire. She's okay?"

"Yeah. We're both fine."

"Wonderful. Bill had a friend plow our driveway so the guests can get in, and Ryder's off to the airport to pick up Haley. Did you know she was coming?" Patricia fired away with rapid speed. "I can't believe she's coming. Apparently, Nate couldn't make this trip but she says she's got great news to share."

Grady cringed, trying to figure out exactly what Haley's plan was. As far as he could tell, it was a disaster waiting to happen. Or, fuck, what if she was pregnant? Shitty timing.

Patricia powered on so he couldn't get a word in anyway. "Won't this be incredible? Ryder engaged to an intelligent woman, Haley and her surprise, and I'm sure you'll figure out some way to shine."

His eyes rolled back in his head and he leaned into Claire. Nope. This was going to go exactly how he'd feared.

"Please say your friends aren't afraid of a little snow and will make it?"

"They're planning on it. Are you sure you don't want to put it off, with the power still out? I'm sure most of the out-of-town folks won't be able to make it."

He could picture her huffing and stiffening. "We have already heard several regrets passed along, but many are still looking forward to coming. It may not be as grand as usual, but I think it will be even more magical with an intimate group and low lighting. And most importantly, all three of my children together. I can't remember the last time you've all been in the same place at the same time. I hope the photographer can make it. But the champagne truck turned over on the highway."

"What? I hope the driver's okay."

"I'm sure he's fine. But, well, we're making adjustments. Do you have any extra stock? Of that beer that won the award? I mean, we always share a toast to the year ahead. And wouldn't that be a great way to celebrate your new business endeavor, with toasting your award-winning brew instead?"

Grady tensed. Her angle was clear, but unexpected. If he had no fiancée and no other accolades, perhaps his "little hobby" would make an acceptable brag after all.

Claire traced her fingertips along the curve of his arms. He clutched his free hand over hers and finally responded. "Zane just left to check on things, and I was going to head up in a few. I'm sure we can make it work."

"Wonderful. That's great."

Grady held the phone from his ear and groaned. He finally answered, "Of course."

Clicking off, he tossed the phone across the bed and turned to haul Claire onto his lap. "Let's book an early flight and get the hell out of here first thing tomorrow morning."

"It's a date." She grinned and tugged him back to bed.

After a brief delay, they were dressed in borrowed clothes and at the door. Chuckling, Grady pulled Asher's sweatshirt over his head before slipping his feet into borrowed boots. Boldly imprinted across the shirt, the word *SEAL* commanded attention. He shook his head at Asher.

Snuggled up with Sophie in front of the fire, Asher grinned. "I'm sure Patricia's patriotic, or thinks she might be. But I know how she feels about me. Just wanted to rub it in."

"Can't say I object."

Grady and Claire trudged through the knee-deep snow to the car. Stopping in front, Claire grabbed Grady by the arm and pulled him back. "Wait."

"What is it?" he asked, his brow dropping low with worry.

She pulled out her phone. "Just..." She dragged him against her and said, "Bear with me. Smile." She snapped the image and winked. "Okay, let's go."

Astonished by her sudden photo op, he grinned and hopped into the SUV. After letting the windshield defrost, they were on the road within minutes, the snow scraping along the bottom of the car, despite trying to make use of their old tracks and Zane's. He cringed, picturing the damage to the chassis.

As they reached the end of the driveway, Claire's phone chirped with an incoming text. She grinned and handed the phone over. A stream of teary, happy, hearty, smiley emojis took up the first line. *You both look so happy. When can we meet him?!?!?!*

A lightness washing over him, Grady handed her the phone back. "Let's definitely book that early flight out. I like your mother already."

The drive into town was a fucking mess. Zane had the generators already running at Black Op, tossing out the few things that couldn't be salvaged. Not wasting time, Grady rolled his sleeves up and joined him. He fired off a text to the crew that they were closing down, at least through the rest of the day and tonight, and would touch base again in the morning.

When he came up for air, he searched for Claire. Bundled to the teeth, snow past her knees, she was out on the front patio, clearing snow from the sidewalk while Zane was on a ladder checking the integrity of the patio roof.

"Hey." She grinned and leaned on her shovel as he came outside. "All set?"

"Yeah. Too short of notice to move over anymore kegs than the ones we already brought last week. We've got plenty of bottles for that toast."

Zane climbed down the ladder and tilted his head to the side like a confused puppy. "She's still having the party?"

"Gala. And yes, nothing would stop Patricia from flaunting her own successes. Not even a natural disaster."

They loaded up the SUV, securing the boxes in the back. While Zane hopped in his truck to go back home, Grady waved and climbed into the SUV. Reaching over the center console, Grady brushed a light kiss over Claire's cheek, but couldn't seem to move away, cradling his hand around her jaw. "You are incredible," he whispered.

"Well thank you," she said with a playful grin. "What for?"

"This has been a... let's go with an *altering* week for me. And I haven't gone through even half of what you have. How are you so calm? You roll your sleeves up and dive in."

"I'm not known for spontaneity. I rather bumble things when I don't have a plan and end up saying stupid things and feeling awkward. So, when in doubt, I duck my head and work."

"Do you feel awkward now?" He pulled away and studied her expression.

"Not at all, actually."

He shifted into gear and kept his eyes on the road, mostly. He couldn't help but keep checking back, watching her expression light up at the blanket of snow that illuminated the scenery. With a shake of his head, he realized his cheeks had been pulled into a dopey grin. Best damn week of his life.

When they finally pulled up to the house, Hattie came flying out and threw her arms around Grady. Satisfied he was alive and well, she didn't release him, but grabbed blindly until she found Claire and pulled her in for a cozy group hug.

Haley stood behind, her wavy hair well past her shoulders, and, as usual, she was dressed utterly flawlessly in a funnel-neck sweater, skinny jeans, and wool socks pulled up past her ankles. A quiet held behind her smile, she waited until Hattie released him, then took her turn and said softly, "You look happy."

Before releasing her, he whispered, "And you look... ready for a break."

She gave him a brave smile as she pulled back. The weary look faded as she looked to Claire and smiled in earnest. "You must be Claire. I'm so glad to finally meet you."

Claire sighed and nodded. "Likewise. Your flight was okay?"

"Interesting, anyway. I think I was the last flight in before they canceled the rest for the night."

Ryder stood back and watched. Grady looked over at him and tried to read his expression. Raising an eyebrow, he silently asked what he was thinking. With a mysterious smile, he shook his head and mouthed, *Later*.

Cheeks flushed with a brilliant gleam, Hattie seemed completely content as she said, "Come on in. Claire, Grady, you two go upstairs and freshen up. I'll bring up some coffee. It's nearly ten, have you eaten?"

"Not yet."

"Well. I'll bring something to your rooms...?" She grinned expectantly.

"To the blue room," he answered.

Beaming, she disappeared inside. Haley followed behind, flashing him one final look. "I expect a full report."

He winked. "Ditto."

In the foyer, Claire paused next to Ryder. She opened her mouth to speak, then shook her head again, finally saying, "Let's chat later."

He nodded, looked back and forth between Grady and Claire, and turned to follow Hattie into the kitchen.

Grady paused at the green room door, and Claire continued toward the blue room. She turned and smiled softly. "Meet you in a few?"

"As you wish," he whispered.

She chuckled softly, resting her hand on the doorjamb as if she needed to steady herself. "That one I know."

In the heart of his bedroom, he turned and shook his head at the lack of his stuff in here. What little could be salvaged from the fire was in storage. Packing his gear took a grand total of eight minutes. And that was because he stopped to brush his teeth.

He heard the shower running when he got into the blue room. Hands on his hips, he looked around the suite in disgust. Despite Ryder's tidy habits, he was everywhere in here. Grady picked up the odds-and-ends that marked his brother's territory, grabbed the suits and other fancy-pants non-sense from the closet, plus the garment bag and overpriced backpack, and dragged all evidence of Ryder's presence to the green room.

Within a few minutes, he had their stuff completely swapped. He'd always liked the blue room better anyway.

Shit. A simple swap, no big deal.

Sure.

Huge deal. He didn't take relationships lightly. Which, in part, might be why he was always too late in snatching up the good ones.

This time... this time, the best of the best chose him. Deep in every aching muscle in his body, warmth and relief soothed away tension and fear, knowing that she'd fallen as hard and fast as he had. Not that she'd said it, but he knew. As they say, when you know, you know.

By the time he finished, he heard Claire shutting off the shower. Moments later, she came out fresh as a wildflower on a spring afternoon, sleek brown hair dripping wet and brushed neatly down her back. Not a trace of makeup, she looked like a forest nymph that had miraculously chosen him, a mere mortal, as her lover.

She looked at him with a question in her eye at his breathless look. "Nothing," he muttered on a small exhale. If she knew half of the corny shit floating around in his brain, she'd... no, she would think it was sweet.

Claire sunk into the leather chair across from him and nearly cried when she saw the huge cup of coffee and mountain of food from Hattie on the tree stump table between them. That moan of pleasure passed her lips when she took the first bite of grilled cheese. Still wiped out from the snowstorm, he devoured his sandwich in four bites.

As soon as she'd finished eating, Claire leaned back in the chair and closed her eyes. Within seconds, she was sound asleep. Not exactly drooling, but... no, she was definitely drooling. Mouth gaping open.

He scooped her up and laid her in the bed, sliding off the bathrobe that she'd tossed on for their late breakfast. Before crawling in next to her, he stripped off his clean clothes and eased into the bed. The gala wasn't for another few hours, and he was toast. The hypothermia hadn't helped, nor the last two nights caught up in Claire, but he hadn't slept a wink since that first day on the ice.

It was just past three when the creak of the bedroom door opening woke him. Groaning, he sat up enough to see who had dared interrupt the most satisfying nap he'd ever taken. Vision blurred, he rubbed away the thick haze of sleep.

# 18

## S-W-I-T-C-H-A-R-O-O

Ryder stood in the door, mouth drawn in full *what the hell*, with the puzzled eyebrows to match. In case Grady had missed the meaning of the look, Ryder mouthed, *What the hell?*

His poor brother probably didn't have a clue what was going on. Why would he? He couldn't imagine when Claire would have told him. Although, his frantic exit in the middle of a storm to rescue Claire was a pretty damn good clue. But he'd already figured out that Ryder didn't understand Claire.

He slid out from Claire's arm and stood from the bed.

Ryder groaned in horror at the show. "Come on, man," he whispered, arm shielding his eyes from the view of Grady, buck-ass-nude.

Grady hid his grin as he slid his jeans on and grabbed his shirt from the floor. "Hey, you could have looked away," he whispered back.

"I wasn't exactly expecting... that." Ryder gestured to his sparsely dressed brother as Grady buttoned his jeans, and motioned to Claire, sound asleep on her stomach, the blankets not covering much.

Grady pushed past his brother and moved the conversation into the sitting room. "Yeah, about that—"

Ryder dropped into one of the sitting room chairs and poured a cup of coffee from the fresh, insulated carafe Hattie had clearly brought up when she took the dishes down. "Yeah, about that?"

Grady pulled his shirt over his head, poured himself a cup, then dropped into the other chair. He bit his cheek, having no idea where to start.

"Ok, let's start with an easy one. Where's my stuff?" Ryder's body language was calm as he leaned back in the chair and slowly sipped his coffee, eyes watching his brother closely over the rim of the mug.

Posture mirroring his brother's, his long legs spread out from the small leather club chair, Grady took a long drag of his coffee and shrugged. "In the green room."

"Okay. I guess I should be glad I won't be sleeping on the floor again. How about this one... you stole my fiancée?"

Grady's feet shifted on the plush blue rug. An impish grin tugged at the side of his mouth. "I'm not sure that was a question."

Eyes set fiercely in a threatening squint, Ryder growled under his breath, but he lacked the fire he usually harbored beneath that glare.

"First, I know the fiancée business was a sham to earn some brownie points with Patricia. Second, you and Claire broke up."

"What, you waited all of forty-eight hours to fuck my ex-girlfriend?"

"Ouch, that sounds so crass." Grady cringed when he remembered his own similarly vulgar words to Asher last summer. "You're not exactly one to talk."

Ryder shifted awkwardly in his chair. "That's different—"

"Is it?"

Ryder shrugged innocently. "You and Becca had broken up *weeks* prior."

*What?* "Uh, no. We hadn't."

"Wait. She said... That... Fuck." Shaking his head, Ryder grimaced. "I should have figured. We both should have figured. What were you doing with a manipulative bitch like that anyway? For the record, she told me you dumped her when you left for law school."

He considered for a moment. "Yeah, I guess I should realized. She'd been convinced the long-distance thing would lead to me cheating on her. Wow. Yeah. My first trip home, and she found her revenge. I'm sorry she used you to get back at me. More, I'm sorry I was pissed at you all these years because of a lying bitch."

Chuckling mirthlessly, Ryder kicked him gently with his foot. "I guess we're both a couple of jerks." Sullen, both sipped their coffee in unison. "With Sasha, that was... I don't know, we got to talking, and she's just out of a relationship and, well, next thing I knew we were consoling each other. Whatever you think of me, I wouldn't take advantage, nor was I planning on taking it further."

"If you really like her, ask her out. She seems pretty decent."

"Nah. It was nice to remember that I'm still human, but, fuck, I don't have time for—"

"Anything?" Grady laughed under his breath. "When was the last time we sat and... coexisted without firing insults at each other?"

"Not since you broke your hand on my face." The corner of Ryder's lips turned up, a lightness seeming to melt over him. "Haley, too. I can't even remember the last time she or I called each other. And we talked the whole drive home this morning. I'm glad she's going to move home."

"When we were kids, we got each other through. Fresh start from here on out."

"I'm on board with that. Maybe even try to see each other now and again. Somewhere far from Patricia's beady eyes." Ryder laughed, sprawling his legs as he sank further into the chair.

"We'd have to be sneaky."

"I think you've got the sneaky thing down pat. Seriously. You and Claire, without me noticing? When and how and…?"

The corner of Grady's mouth quirked up as he imagined all the whens and hows. If he'd known she was single that night at the billiard table, hiked up that dress a little further… maybe he could have taken her from behind like he'd imagined, and she would have made that breathy moan—

Ryder scowled and kicked him a little harder, pulling him out of his daydream. "I am a little weirded out, but I should have seen it coming. She'd never even met you before dinner the other night, and she watched you all night, blushing and gnawing on that lip like it was going out of style. I'd figured she was weirded out by how much we look alike."

"I'm surprised you noticed." He grinned and leaned back further into the chair. "We'd met that afternoon on the ice. You must have been working?"

"Fuck. Yeah. Guess this is a pretty obvious wake-up call that I work too damn much. My pansy-ass brother steals my fiancée out from under me, in broad daylight."

Raising an eyebrow at his brother, Grady downed the last of his coffee.

Ryder grinned smugly at his sneaky jab. "We'd been over for months, but, hell, we hadn't spent enough time together to notice we weren't where we assumed we'd be by now."

"I thought I'd died and gone to heaven when she stepped out onto the ice. Imagine my surprise, when I came downstairs for dinner and discovered that you were the 'complication' she mentioned when I tried to ask her out at the rink. Your loss, my gain. Then, you were too busy to go horseback riding with her. See a pattern?"

Ryder ran a hand through his hair and mussed the meticulous style. Grady couldn't help but enjoy seeing him having a very human moment, feeling the full extent of his self-absorption. "I really am an asshole. I've been ignoring her for months. Hell, we were both too busy for each other. Kept saying we'd make time for each other once she graduated from vet school and I had a handle on my career. Shit, why didn't we dump any whiskey in this coffee? I can't handle this gala."

Cloudy vision and an even hazier brain enveloped Claire as she struggled to wake from the thick nap. The sun was just beginning its descent on the jagged, tree-filled horizon. Things sure had a way of abruptly shifting gears around here. Blizzard conditions yesterday and bright blue skies today. The combination would be gorgeous for the gala, moonlight twinkling over the untouched blanket of snow.

She grumbled as she dragged her lead-laden limbs from the bed, pulling on cozy jeans and a cotton sweater. Feet padding over the dense carpet, she made her way to the sitting room, where she found Ryder responding to emails on his phone. At her entrance, his eyebrow raised in question. "Feeling better?"

The last remnants of fog faded as she blinked away the nap. She took advantage of the steaming carafe of fresh coffee and poured herself a cup before dropping into the chair opposite.

Ryder's expression wasn't helpful. Those damn dimples were deep in his cheeks, and his eyes gleamed with amusement.

"Yeah. What's going on with you?"

Leaned forward in the chair, he rested his elbows on his knees and stared at his fingernails. "It appears I have been moved to the green room."

Unsure how to proceed, she didn't try to stop gnawing on her lower lip. She took a soothing sip of the liquid fortification and nodded. "You ok with that?"

Eyebrow raised again, he shook his head. "Guess I'll have to be. I am a little weirded out though. I... there's no good way to ask. He and I look a hell of a lot alike. Ignore the hair color and dimples, and we could be twins. We sound the same, similar mannerisms. Obviously, we have different interests and goals. But, what is it that drew you to him so quickly that wasn't working with me?"

She started to respond, but he clearly wasn't finished yet.

"You know what, don't answer that. I... I know I've been a workaholic—"

"We both were."

"But you had good reason, and an end goal that was clearly defined. I should have been there for you this week."

Her cheeks slackened with a twinge of regret that comes with a breakup. Even a necessary one. "Yeah, you should have. All for the best though."

His smile reached his eyes this time. "You seem really happy."

"I am. You and I will always be good friends. Grady is... Grady. He's got this honest, thoughtful, passionate way about him."

"Which is exactly why Patricia doesn't understand him."

"True. Mostly, I feel comfortable being my odd, quirky self around him."

"You're not odd."

"Do you know how much effort it takes to not mention weird things at social functions? Remember the time I told one of your clients that there really is more than one way to skin a cat?"

He chuckled. "You do occasionally say some gross things."

Snorting, Claire covered a hand over her mouth and nodded. "Sorry about that. I promise to behave myself tonight."

"I can't ask you to be my fiancée now. This would take the awkward in this stark mansion to new heights."

"I got the Parson's job. Grady already knows I promised you this first. If all those bigwigs that Patricia groomed and enticed to hear you out are traversing these roads to meet you, I'll be your cheerleader."

"I know you never wore a pleated skirt and did cartwheels across the football field."

"Hell no. And I know you were the slick, rocker-wannabe Ryder back in those days. Football gear or no, I think you were as quirky as me. Just less nerdy."

"Yeah, you may be right." He nudged her foot and smiled softly. "Thanks, Claire. I wouldn't have survived the last two years without you."

"Damn right. But, ditto. Now, if we can all survive tonight..."

Breathing slowly in and out, counting rhythmically so he wouldn't hyperventilate and pass out, Grady inched down the hall. It was stupid. Days. Just days. He shouldn't be doing anything so foolish. What if she said no?

Cool and heavy in his pocket, the metal band circled a thousand doubts in his mind. Not of Claire, but... The timing was epically awful. Hardly more than a week. He couldn't know already. But he did. Did she?

Maybe this was why he got dumped so much? Too chicken-shit to make a big move. Or, leaping ten steps ahead of where he should be.

A few nights back, he'd heard Patricia telling Ryder she was glad he hadn't bought a ring yet, as she'd been saving her grandmother's ring for him. Far too embarrassing to be engaged to a Mallory without a dazzling diamond on her finger. Patricia had sent Ryder to fetch it from the box of heirlooms she had set aside for him. So, Grady raided his own box of heirlooms and found their great-grandmother's ring that he had inherited. The band was simpler, but lovely, and much more Claire.

Grady paused outside of the blue suite, bracing his knees tight before he passed out from a full-on panic attack, equally terrified of Claire being present or absent. One final muster of his courage, prepared for rejection, or the dreaded *I'll think about it*, he opened the door.

Her legs were draped over the arm of the leather club chair, her head leaned back over the opposite arm. Hazel eyes twinkling when she saw him, she grinned and bit her lip.

Phone to her ear, she was deep in conversation with someone. "There's snow. Tons of it. I almost died in it." Chuckling, Claire paused and listened to the other end of her call. "Ok, kidding. I wouldn't have died. Probably. Maybe I would have. Regardless, I survived... It was a freak storm... Mom, stop, don't let it scare you from Foothills... Grady drove through hell to rescue me... Yes, he kept me warm all night." Filled with another bout of laughter, she wiped a tear from the corner of her eye, the laughter on the other end as bright as hers. "I miss you, Mom... I'm not kidding. Put the house on the market. Dad can work anywhere, and you've been looking for an excuse to slow down anyway. You've both been wanting out of Phoenix for a while now."

Grady's breath hitched. He was in so deep. What was he thinking? Way too soon.

After placing a silent upside-down kiss on her lips, he dropped into the other chair and rested his elbows on his knees, too restless to settle. She chatted with her mom a moment longer, then promised to email their flight information before hanging up. No wonder she was so comfortable in her own skin. Her parents sounded incredibly supportive.

She spun around in the chair to mirror his position and faced him, their knees inches apart. Her knees jiggled in excitement. "I've almost convinced my parents to move up here. My brothers will take more convincing. Dad's already packing his bags. He's always hated the desert."

"I am genuinely looking forward to meeting them. I talked Ryder into giving me his return ticket, and he's going to head straight to his next meeting in Portland. Honestly, I don't think it's out of kindness, I think he's avoiding the breakup packing."

"You might be right. He doesn't do emotion. What if I were to cry? He'd be so uncomfortable."

Grady paused, not quite sure how to ask. Knowing he'd screw it up, he dove right in. "So, Patricia is planning to have you wear our grandmother's rather ostentatious engagement ring for the party tonight. I... I hated my grandmother to be honest. She was less warm and fuzzy than Patricia."

Claire's grin morphed into a grimace. "Let's hope it doesn't fit."

Catching his breath, his ribs tight against his hyper-inflated lungs, he continued, "My great-grandmother, on the other hand, was rumored to have been a decent person. A hard worker and a feminist. So, I have a better idea. Well, I hope you think so. If tonight is going to be an engagement party, even if not for me... shit, I'm terrible at this."

Raising an eyebrow, Claire put her hands around his and stayed quiet, letting him sort out his thoughts.

"It's too soon, but I'm sick of taking the safe route, of protecting myself from inevitable rejection. Will you marry me? It can be as long of an engagement as you need, or you don't even have to say yes, just please don't wear someone else's ring tonight. Wear mine, at least for the night." He pulled the simple band from his pocket and held it in his palm.

Mercifully, she didn't say no right away. Eyes wide and glassy, she bit her lip and stared at the ring. Instead of the large diamond that would get caught on everything or not fit in her gloves, this ring was a thin gold band of fine woven leaves and a pink gem he didn't know the name of, set into the pattern like a blossom. He hoped she appreciated the simplicity of it, like he did.

Claire slid the ring onto her finger. Hand held high, she spun the ring in the rays of sun. With a soft smile, she finally answered. "It's perfect." She climbed onto his lap and brushed her lips against his. "Some might say it's too soon, but if you and I think the time is right, then it's right. We'll worry about the details later."

With a grin so wide his cheeks hurt, the heaviness in his chest dissipated, morphing into tendrils of heat spreading throughout his body. "So that's a yes?"

"Yes. And I'm not giving the ring back after the gala. It's mine now. As you are."

"It's just a zipper. I don't understand how this particularly delicate piece of hardware can be so mechanically inferior to ordinary zippers. I had no difficult with the one on my pants." Grady's hands gripped either side of the zipper of her dress, barely able to even grasp the tiny pull.

Claire laughed, and he hoped to hell she was admiring how adorable he was, rather than his struggles at getting the damn zipper to cooperate. Her voice danced with glee as she said, "The fabric was expensive, so I guess they had to save money on the zipper." Turning in his arms, she grazed her hands down his bare abdomen, then tucked her hands in his waistband to demonstrate. "Your pants have a rather persistent escape artist behind the zipper and needed the durability."

He dropped his hands to his sides and hissed, backing out of her reach. "Hey, trying to help here. We're expected downstairs in six minutes."

Laughing out loud, she raised her eyebrows, as if hinting at the many things they could accomplish in six minutes.

"No." He shook his head and laughed out loud. "You are insatiable."

Calming her laugh, on the verge of an unshakable giggle fit, she moved her hair off her back and turned away again. "One more try. If you fail, you're going to fetch Haley, so I don't have to wander the house like this."

He growled and traced his fingertips along the edges of the zipper, sneaking in a final feel of her soft skin before having to keep his distance for the next few hours.

"Hello? Claire, are you ready? I thought I heard you from down the hall." Patricia's shrilly cheerful voice shattered... everything. "I was hoping we could chat before the guests arrive." The door to the suite was closed, but that had never stopped his thoughtless mother before. How did she know Ryder and Claire weren't having a moment in here?

"Shit," Grady muttered, gripping the pull and tugging it up as quickly as possible, then remembered he didn't even have a shirt on yet.

"Claire? I have a gift for you and Ryder downstairs for the party. He's waiting for you in the parlor." *Oh yeah*.

Patricia stormed right in like the intruder she was, assuming the open bedroom door meant nothing personal was going on in here. Eyes wide as an owl's, as piercing as an eagle's, and as stupid as a chicken's, she looked from Grady to Claire in puzzled horror.

Grady stood tall at Claire's side, hands out in a futile attempt to calm a frightened bull. "I can explain."

Dim in the evening clouds, the last rays of sun filtered in through the window, casting a gray light that brought out the furrow between Patricia's eyebrows. Seething, foaming at the mouth, she was rendered silent for the first time in history.

Finally, after hemming and hawing until he thought steam might actually puff out of her ears, she spewed out, "Explain?

No, there is no explanation that will suffice. I'm downstairs, setting up what will be the gala of the century—in celebration of your brother's engagement—and you're fooling around with his fiancée?"

Biting his tongue, Grady struggled to not throw back every angsty, bitter sting he could.

Instead, Claire cleared her throat. "Patricia, I understand why you are upset. If you'll give us a few moments, I'd like to talk this over in a civilized manner. With you and Ryder and Grady."

Patricia couldn't say no to manners, despite her fury. Her eyes raked across the unmade bed. "Unfortunately, we don't have time for civilized. Our guests will begin arriving any moment. I suppose for tonight, we shall say nothing of... of *this*... and address the issue tomorrow."

When the metallic taste of blood trickled into Grady's mouth, he released his raw cheek from his clenched teeth, but tightened right back on, knowing he'd blow up if he opened his mouth. This was a shitty situation for her to walk in on, but maybe, for once in her life, she could try to hear him out.

Nostrils flaring, she turned on her heel and stalked out of the room.

Grady clicked the door closed behind her. Turning to Claire, he shook his head and apologized. "I'm so sorry."

Gliding toward him in ice blue silk, Claire wrapped her arms around him. "One more night under this roof." With velvety hazel eyes, she looked up at him and rose to her toes. She brushed her lips against his, soothing away the hurt.

"You're amazing. Thank you."

"Nothing is going to make what we have anything less than miraculous." She ran her fingers along his jaw. He managed a nod, still dizzy from the jolting transition between enjoying a light moment with his fiancée, to being on the direct receiving end of the angriest he'd ever seen Patricia.

# 19

## H-A-N-D-I-N-T-H-E-C-O-O-K-
## I-E-J-A-R

Claire wished she could storm downstairs in jeans and manure-encrusted boots and stomp and yell. Yeah, she could understand his mother's bewilderment, finding the wrong son half-dressed with her future daughter-in-law. She could see how it would be distressing without knowing the details.

But, come on, what sort of future mother-in-law didn't knock before barging in? The woman needed some serious lessons in manners. But, she supposed Patricia had led a charmed life, brilliant and beautiful and having never been told *no*, even as a child, from what Ryder had told her.

Grady came out of the bathroom, his expression drawn. He'd smoothed his hair, so it was neatly styled. Claire hadn't realized it was possible to tame that marvelously unruly surfer hair. She hated that he was so often coerced into changing himself to make others happy.

Stepping into her towering heels, she fastened the buckle before stepping up to Grady. Up on her heels, she stole a soft kiss. "I'm thinking, we give it an hour, then sneak back up here."

"Brilliant." He sighed against her mouth, his voice thick with a painful blend of affection and melancholy.

Sliding her hand into his, she let him set the pace. She nudged him as they neared the bottom of the stairs, needing to see him crack a smile before braving his impending scolding and said, "Bet we can mess with her, keep her guessing about which brother I'm with."

His laugh was raw, but at least he was laughing. "I'm game."

When they reached the foyer, Patricia was nowhere in sight. As the sun set outside, the generator-run lights glowed, illuminating a path past the parlor and down the corridor, opening to what she expected was normally a bright, decked-out ballroom. Old-style lanterns and candles lit up the center of each table instead of the flower arrangements she'd known had been planned. Above the wide-open middle of the room, a dance floor, Claire supposed, the chandelier was dimmed, and its crystals reflected the candles like stars overhead. Through the oversized windows and glass doors, the snow sparkled in a puffy blanket as far as the eye could see, the clear evening sky reflecting off each frozen flake. The music was a simple quartet of strings, the musicians beginning their song as voices from behind hinted at the arrival of the night's first guests. A roaring fire filled the medieval fireplace across the way, keeping the cavernous room warm in temperature and ambience.

Drink in hand, Haley came gliding over in mile high heels and let out a heavy exhale, clutching her frothy IPA with a twitching gleam in her blue eyes that perfectly matched her brothers'—down to the stressed-out wildness and all. To any that didn't know them, Patricia's three offspring would seem as arrogant and elegant as their mother. Yet Haley's opening line completely betrayed the flawlessly styled half updo and black velvet gown. "Fuck."

Grady chuckled and mirrored his sister's rabbit-in-head-lights look. "Yeah," he agreed with a slow nod. "You holding up okay?"

She nodded and handed him her beer. Grady took a long pull and handed it back. Haley smiled softly at Claire. "You?"

"Um," Claire said dryly. "How many minutes until we can bail, do you think?"

Ryder dashed up from behind them and halted next to Claire. "I don't know what you guys did to Patricia, but I've never seen her so pissed. I think there's a hair out of place, but I didn't dare point it out."

Grady looked to Haley and asked, "Did you give her your news?"

She shook her head and held her shoulders back. "I have a plan."

Ryder raised an eyebrow and snagged his sister's beer, taking a gulp before handing the drink back. "Why does that frighten me so much?"

"Everything is lovely. Thanks so much for inviting us." Freya's voice resonated down the hall. Zane and Asher playfully jabbed at each other, the sounds of their laughter bolstering Claire with a glimmer of hope that Grady wouldn't be miserable through the entire night, particularly his guest list already outnumbering Patricia's.

Claire whispered, "You have good friends."

"I've never been so relieved to hear those two messing with each other."

They appeared a moment later. Grady flashed them a desperate grin and took a deep inhale.

Arm linked with Asher as they caught up, Sophie nodded and cringed. "She was the ultimate, polite hostess on greeting us, but I think she's brewing an aneurism."

Ryder chuckled under his breath and muttered, "Maybe she'll try to operate on that herself. I'm not sure she'd trust anyone else to do it."

Asher asked, "Going well, huh?"

"Just get me through the night." Grady cringed.

Haley laughed under her breath. "I'm on it."

An amused gleam flashed in Asher's whiskey eyes. "The notorious Haley is back with a vengeance."

Freya laughed out loud and said, "Holy crap. Haley, I hardly recognized you." Without a hint of hesitance, Freya crossed the circle they'd formed and wrapped Haley up in an emphatic hug. She delivered a few quick introductions, then turned and said again to Haley, "I think you were, what, thirteen the last time I saw you?"

"Yes. But I'm moving home as soon as I get a few things wrapped up in San Francisco." Apparently at ease on the outside, Haley downed the last of the drink and said to her brothers, "I've been hiding in the kitchen. What did you do to Mother? Did she find out already?"

Another cluster of guests filtered in, and Ryder headed to the corner, the others following so they could chat on the other side of the quartet. Claire chewed her lip and closed her eyes. "She walked in on us. I mean, we weren't doing anything, but Grady didn't have a shirt on and was trying to fix my zipper."

"Fuck." Ryder laughed under his breath, his smile widening. "Well. That's one way to break the news to her. I wondered why she gave me about the darkest death glare I've ever been at the receiving end of. She stomped her foot, and I could swear she growled."

A giggle bubbled up in her throat, and Claire snorted a laugh. She covered her mouth, but the giggle fit wouldn't be contained. Chest convulsing, eyes watering, she shook her head and said, "You should have seen her face."

Haley giggled and watched her mother across the room. "I'm so glad I came home after all."

Claire turned to see Grady watching his friends, siblings, and fiancée laughing like a bunch of idiots. Raising an eyebrow, he said, "In a decade, I might enjoy looking back on this. But why is this so funny?"

Ryder knocked him on the shoulder. "The power's out and half the guest list isn't going to show. Instead of her engaged son bringing his fiancée, she's now stuck with a potentially awkward love triangle—not to worry, the third corner is actually happy for you—thus she has no idea how to introduce Claire. Haley's here without Nate, a first, and I know Patricia suspects something... and she's going to lose all three of her kids if she doesn't get her shit together."

Studying that was slowly filtering in, Zane asked, "Was she *always* this...?"

Grady nodded. "For the most part. I mean, it's gotten tragically worse the last few years. It was more of an overexcited cheerleading perfectionist when we were kids, whereas now it's..."

"Patricia's empire of success?" Asher finished for him. "Grady? Come on, I'll buy you a drink."

He followed, muttering, "It's an open bar, and it's my beer anyway."

Hand extended to Claire, Ryder gestured to the center of the dance floor. "Shall we show them how it's done, and royally confuse Patricia as to which brother you're with?"

"You read my mind," she said, letting the absurdity of the evening roll off her like a bad eighties movie. Draping her arms over his shoulders, swaying on the dance floor as they had at so many of his work functions in the past, the familiarity was appreciated, but it felt so much more natural without the romantic pressure. "Still trying to win a few contracts thanks to Patricia's impressive guest list?"

"Always. But the ones I actually wanted to connect with aren't going to make it. Two decided they didn't want to brave the snow, and the third planned to come anyway, but he called an hour ago because the road's blocked and he can't get here."

"Wow. What does it feel like?"

"What?" His brow drew together in question, but his smile was pure amusement.

"You have an entire evening to yourself. No work, no fiancée to keep happy, and a mother expecting nothing respectable out of you."

"Feels pretty damn good, actually."

"Are you really going to keep this up? Working through your vacations, through weekend dinners, never taking a minute for yourself?"

"I take time for myself."

"When? At the gym on your way to work? Staying up late reading when you can't sleep? And even then, I suspect you're working in your head."

He shrugged, and his baby blues almost looked tired. "Once I get that promotion, I'll be able to set my own schedule. Cushy corner office, take only the contracts I want, delegate the little things, hit the slopes every weekend."

"Sounds tempting."

"I'm sorry I invested more into my job than you."

"You're doing what's right for you. And now I'm doing what's right for me."

"I'm going to miss you, Claire."

"Ditto." The song drew to a close, and Grady was waiting on the sidelines, patient and almost looking relaxed. Did any of the Mallorys know how? Ryder released her and disappeared as she connected with Grady, melting into his arms on contact, unsure if she could truly snuggle, or what would make the night easier on him. For all her teasing, she didn't want to make the evening any more awkward.

As the guests settled in for, all marveling at the fairytale field as if this were an ice castle, she caught sight of Patricia smiling and laughing with friends, her uneasy gaze wandering in Claire's direction. Claire teased her fingers on the back of Grady's neck and asked, "How on Earth did you survive growing up in this house?"

Grady rolled his heavy eyes. "Not sure I did."

"I don't get it. I mean, not all parents understand their offspring. You're a mother's dream come true. Capable, kind, generous, brave." She ached to lean in and rest her cheek against his, but she kept her distance. "And incredibly attractive."

He laughed out loud and shook his head.

"How do they not see all these wonderful things about you?"

"Likely my fault, almost as much as theirs," he answered flatly.

"How so?"

"I practiced the French that my preschool academy immersed us in, but at recess, I'd stomp in the puddles while hollering the words to *Frère Jacques* at the top of my lungs. She'd insist I play Mozart for the piano recital, but I'd play U2." He paused, reflecting. "I'd get booted from the hockey game when she was trying to teach me temperance." His hand splayed across her back, blazing through the thin fabric, and held her as close as the situation allowed. "I couldn't tell you if it was intentional or not, but I always seemed to do my best to subtly defy her."

"Always doing what you're told, but never quite the way she intended, huh?"

"Exactly. Hell of a way to live. And it is precisely how I ended up wasting so damn much time in law school and burning myself out in less than two years in practice."

"I know you have the obligation to Lincoln, and to your clients, but they'll get over it. You need to take care of *you* first."

"Asher and Zane think I should quit. I love it at Black Op. It's tempting, but... I don't know. It's complicated."

"When I was a kid, we counted every dollar. We never lacked for anything important, but we were careful. Living simply is scary, but doable."

"You make me feel spoiled and whiny."

"You are spoiled. And practical. If it helps, you're engaged to a veterinarian."

He pulled her closer, undoubtedly drawing curious looks from around the room. "I'm really not worried about the money. It's more fear of losing the security that comes with knowing my job's never going anywhere. Of staying the course I set for myself years ago. But... fuck, just thinking about getting a place with you, getting to focus my energy at Black Op, coming home without feeling like I've been run over by a truck? Sounds too good to be true."

# 20

## M-O-M-E-N-T-O-F-T-R-U-T-H

The music was light and soothing in the candlelit ballroom, and Grady had to admit, his mother did know
how to throw a party. Gala. Whatever she wanted to call it,
the setting was brilliant.

Lincoln and Pippa strolled into the ballroom, with Patricia
escorting them. Her hand was gripped tight over Lincoln's
wrist, seemingly clinging onto a source of stability, despite her
attempts to mask it with a contented smile. Lincoln caught
Grady's eye and raised an eyebrow like the question mark he'd
fired across many a lecture hall in law school, but, in classic
Lincoln style, he played it calm and soothed Patricia with a
confident nod and a smile.

Claire followed his gaze. "What are you thinking?"

His lips turned up in a hesitant smile. "I have an idea. Trust
me?"

"Maybe." She winked, moving with him to the music, close
enough that the silk of her dress brushed against his pants, but
she felt a mile away with all the air between them.

He grazed his fingertips along her back and along the edge
of the silk. "I can't figure you out. Jeans with thick wool socks
when you're tending to the horses, that sexy dress that night

we..." He cleared his throat, remembering the moment too vividly. "... At the billiard table, the sweet skirt and sweater at dinner that first night, and now you're a vision in an elegant silk gown. I don't think I could begin to guess what you'll be wearing tomorrow."

"Snow pants."

"See what I mean?"

She giggled and spun in his arms. "I've never built a snow-man. Or made snow angels."

"What time does our flight leave?"

"Five in the evening."

"Plenty of time."

Lincoln slipped from Patricia's grasp and joined Asher and Zane by the window overlooking the gleaming white blanket that coated the hillside, the mountains glowing in the moon-light. Freya had dragged Ryder to the dance floor and joined them at the end of the song, arriving as Grady and Claire did. Freya was laughing, amused as she always seemed to be, and said, "You'll regret that invitation soon. I have always wanted to paint the desert, and I may settle in for weeks until I capture all the colors of the Arizona sunset."

Ryder seemed more relaxed than Grady had seen in years, smiling and accepting a beer from Zane. Asher still hadn't dropped the glare, but the others seemed to realize Ryder wasn't the creep Grady had believed him to be all these years. Because of one misunderstanding. "Absolutely, anytime. It's not like anyone ever uses the spare bedroom."

Grady motioned to Lincoln and asked, "Have a minute?"

Lincoln nodded to the empty corner next to the bar. As soon as they were out of hearing distance, Lincoln said, "It appears you finally apologized to Claire. Looking awfully cozy with your brother's fiancée."

Lips pulled tight in a grimace, Grady sighed. "She's... so much cooler than I'd thought."

"So, not a cheating whore?"

Grimace morphing into a full-on mirthless laugh, Grady accepted a beer from the bartender and chugged it down by half as they wandered toward the fireplace. His thumb traced over the foamy drip on the smooth glass. "No. Not even close."

Gaze steady, Lincoln watched the bustling party and said over his glass. "That's not what you wanted to talk about though, is it?"

Grady shook his head and stared into the amber brew in his hands. "I'm not... I hate being a lawyer."

"I wondered." Lincoln sighed and stuffed his free hand into his jacket pocket. Not looking anywhere in particular, he said, "I kept figuring that you'd settle. After Sophie, and then the chaos of starting Black Op, then the fire, getting stuck here, and Claire... I assumed you were just burned out."

"I was. I am. But it's more than that. Every day I have to go to court, I stare in the mirror in the morning and tell myself it's not that bad, that I'm good at it, that it'll get easier."

"But it isn't."

"No. It's getting worse. I can't do this anymore."

"Why didn't you say anything? If you want to cut back on your hours, anything, I'm there for you."

"I think..." Grady took a heavy breath and pushed his shoulders back. "I'll stick around until you find a new partner, but I'm done."

Lincoln took a slow sip of his beer, a suspicious twinkle in his eye. "Rumor has it, you're going with Claire down to Phoenix tomorrow, then taking your time moving her up here?"

"I, uh, was getting to that."

"No worries. How about you go on vacation, and when you get back, help me catch things up? I don't mind taking over your cases, but I'll need a hand until I find a new partner."

"Sounds great." He exhaled a long breath, the weight already starting to lift from his shoulders. "I'm so sorry."

"Don't." Lincoln shook his head, calm when he should be pissed. Then again, Lincoln always looked calm. Born to be a lawyer, he didn't rile easily. Unlike Grady. "Not going to say I'm not disappointed. I love working with you." He smiled and took a long pull on his beer. "I mean, how am I going to find another partner that isn't afraid to take a punch or two?"

"One punch. I won't put up with a second." He smiled back, the crunch in his jaw reminding him that even the first was a bad idea.

"March thirtieth."

"What?"

"That's your last day. It'll give me plenty of time to start recruiting, or at least thin out the workload, while you transition to Black Op full time."

"Thanks. I wasn't sure how to even begin to tell you."

"Any idea how you're going to tell Patricia about Claire?"

Grady groaned and drained the last of his beer, setting the empty glass on the catering tray that brushed past them. "She already knows."

"That would explain the vague comments about how wonderful it is to have honest people like me at the gala."

"Ouch."

"And that she's hoping Pippa and I will help Claire feel welcome by keeping her occupied and dancing with her, visiting and showing her around. Pretty much making sure she's never alone... with either of her sons, I gather."

Grady looked across the room and saw Claire spinning across the dance floor with Asher this time. "You know? I haven't talked with my mother all night. I'm going to go tell her what a nice party she throws."

"Your funeral," Lincoln muttered.

Haley caught his eye, releasing Zane from the dance and flashing him a wink. She met Grady at the bar. "Ready?"

"For what?"

"The plan."

Grady grabbed a fresh beer for himself plus another for Patricia, while Haley grabbed one for herself. "Please tell me your plan involves a secret escape out the back door."

"Like yours? I see that flash in your eyes. You're looking for a fight."

He turned toward Haley and saw her matching blue eyes sparked with mischief. "And you're not?"

"Every time I close my eyes at night, I see big tits in a red lace bra, bouncing on top of my husband. The man that spent the last ten years slowly chipping me down to nothing."

"I'm so sorry I wasn't there for you. I should have seen."

"No. I hid it well. From myself, as much as anyone. Sometimes the status quo feels easier in the moment." The corner of her lips turned up in a fishhook grin, but the humor it held was dark.

He glanced to Lincoln. To Ryder and Claire. "I know the feeling. Risks are exactly that. And I haven't taken nearly enough of them."

"Exactly."

He glanced to Patricia and back to Haley. "Ready?"

"It's well past time."

Decked out in a midnight blue gown with a sharply square neckline, she had her arm linked with Bill's and was laughing with her friends at some clever comment. Didn't matter what it was, she knew how to play the game. Grady handed her a beer as they reached her, and she turned to smile at him. "Hello, Grady. Haley," she said, a hint of warmth in her smile.

"Mother." He nodded and took a slow sip, watching her over the rim of his glass. "You have turned what could have been a disastrous evening into a magical event. The atmosphere is somewhere between a glamorous nineteen-forties film and a calm evening in a mountain cabin."

"Thank you." She beamed, the shock evident in her squinty expression. "Are you able to relax after your ordeal?"

"Absolutely," he said, a fire brewing in his gut that had nothing to do with the octane of the IPA.

Bill rubbed a hand over his bearded chin and laughed as he spoke. "We had some excitement around here." He nodded to Grady and flashed him a twinkly eyed grin. "Our Grady is quite the hero."

As only the most loyal, capable, and easygoing of Patricia and Bill's friends had braved the roads to appear, most of the guests actually seemed to be likeable people, which probably said something decent about his mother and step-father. Actively avoiding their social events, Grady couldn't say what his parents were actually like around others.

Grady shrugged, not knowing how to respond without risking Claire's comfort by giving something away. Even armed for battle, he wouldn't risk her.

He didn't have to. Bill laughed every few sentences, de-scribing how the blizzard had turned treacherous. "Sweet girl, but a desert flower through and through. She'd never driven in the snow and had taken a rear-wheel drive out hiking. Well, she called within two hours of the snow hitting, and it was already so thick you couldn't see ten feet in front of you—"

Patricia tensed and added, "And, well, we were all so worried about her. Our boys didn't hesitate."

Mrs. Olsen from the school board asked, her cheeks puffed with a dimply grin. "I thought I heard a rumor she was engaged to Ryder. Did he rescue her?"

Bill shook his head and powered on. "He was about to, but Grady's got a good rig and was on the road in a flash."

All eyes landed on Grady. Mrs. Olsen beamed. "So brave, driving in that storm to rescue your brother's fiancée. I would imagine the visibility made the drive quite dangerous."

Before he could talk, he caught Claire heading over, Ryder at her side. Oh boy. He cringed, imagining the epic awkward-ness if the subject didn't change. Fast.

Bill chortled over his beer and said, "I'll say. But a little danger never stopped Grady. Now, Lenore, I didn't say she was engaged to Ryder. I've heard that rumor as well, but..."

Grady cringed, dreading the next words from his stepfather's mouth.

Patricia's head whipped from Grady to Claire to Ryder. And back to Grady. He closed his eyes and clenched his jaw so tight he risked the integrity of his molars.

Ryder started talking before reaching them, his voice merry and raised as he said, "Mrs. Olsen. It has been too long since I saw you last. Staying out of trouble, I hope?"

"Oh, you know me." She giggled in response, another sucker for Ryder's famous dimples and dashing smile.

"Have you all met Claire yet?" he asked the crowd. "Doc Parson just hired her on."

Pia, an equestrienne friend of Patricia's, equally tall and ramrod postured, marveled with what looked to be a genuine smile. "I heard about that and am so thrilled. Claire, we are regulars. I am sure we'll be seeing you out in the stables often."

"I will look forward to it," Claire said as she shook her hand. "This is such a beautiful area. I'm so lucky to be able to settle here."

Mrs. Olsen introduced herself to Claire and held firm with both hands wrapped around Claire's one. "We are lucky to have you join our community." She shifted one hand to Ryder, so she held both and beamed. "And to have you convince our Ryder to come home."

Awkward didn't begin to describe the cavernous pause. Ryder opened his mouth to speak, but seemed to change his mind and closed it again. Claire's smile suspended on her expression as if she'd frozen in the blizzard after all. Grady feared Patricia would collapse straight over backward if he so much as nudged her.

Still amused with every word he spoke, Bill cleared his throat and chuckled. "I'm not sure anyone could convince

Ryder to give up his career and come home to our little town." Bill glanced to Grady and winked, his smile jolly and eyes lit up.

Haley patted Bill on the shoulder and laughed out loud. "I told Ryder he was going to confuse everyone. It would certainly be an intriguing mystery for those that don't know Ryder very well. Claire and Ryder are roommates down in Phoenix. And, naturally, excellent friends, but nothing more."

Patricia loosened up at his side, a new light in her expression, pouncing on her moment to shine. "When Claire heard about Foothills, she practically begged Ryder to show her around up here. She's always wanted to move up here, haven't you?" She nodded hopefully to Claire who nodded cheerfully back, her smile still petrified. "But, well, I'll tell you. We'd hoped there was something going on between Ryder and Claire. Call me old fashioned, but I'd hoped she'd be the one to bring him home for good. But, as they'd told us all along, they're just roommates."

Gaze turning to Grady, Patricia almost seemed to relax. His brow quirked, his stomach clenched as he tried to read her.

"Bill and I are about the luckiest parents in the world. We'd met Claire as we sat to dinner that first night and were immediately charmed. But when Grady walked in, I could swear the fire in the hearth burned brighter, the sparks between these two were so strong."

Reaching across Grady, Patricia took Claire's hand and pulled her to her other side, examining the simple band on her finger.

Much like the others, Mrs. Olsen glanced at the odd love triangle and said, "That is... quite a story."

Patricia patted Grady's arm, in what seemed to be an affectionate gesture.

Pia's smile widened with the others. "Oh my, I can imagine that storm must have set things in motion. Tell us how the sparks flew when you two met."

Now that the story had set sail, Ryder was on it. In full charmer mode, he said, "It's one for the books, that's for sure. Love at first sight, as they say. Lucky for all of us, both were single and ready to take the next step in life."

Grady bit the edge of his cheek, having no idea how to respond. His family had absolutely lost their marbles.

Haley topped the sundae with hot fudge and a cherry, adding, "While Ryder was ensuring my flight would land safely, Grady drove through the storm because he couldn't bear to lose Claire, having only just found her."

A hint of mist in her eyes, Patricia nodded enthusiastically. "That's my boy. He's always been such a romantic."

After a dozen and a half pats on the back, the others filtered away until it was only the family standing together. Haley shifted so there was no room in the circle for anyone else to come with well wishes or to tease out the latest gossip.

Grady laced his fingers with Claire's, the connection bolstering any hesitation that still hung with him. Now or never.

Patricia cleared her throat and leaned into Bill. As if it were an everyday habit, Bill wrapped an arm around her waist. Grady felt Ryder's breath catch with surprise like his own had, the PDA so unfamiliar. But it didn't seem foreign to their mother and stepfather.

"I *am* proud of you, Grady," she said. "And happy for you. Few would have done what you did." She turned to Ryder and added, "I'm sure you'll find someone soon. Not everyone can make as perfect of a match as Haley and Nate."

Haley cleared her throat and looked to her brothers. She let out a long, controlled breath. "Nate fucked my best friend. In our bed."

Something looked to be choking Patricia right in the craw, her face growing deathly pale.

"I came home for the gala to see my brothers, so I had someone to talk to. I've contacted my attorney about filing for divorce." Head held high, Haley's smile was dripping with confidence.

Total silence. No one breathed except Haley, who took an easy sip of her beer. She studied the brew and nodded. "This is excellent. Well done, Grady."

Heaviness coating his chest, Grady ripped off the last Band-Aid. "I hate being a lawyer," he admitted on a heavy exhale.

"But you are such a talented attorney," Patricia said, her matching ocean blue eyes swimming with question.

"I'm good at a lot of things," he said with a casual shrug. "I quit. I'm going to work at Black Op full time, after I help Lincoln with the transition."

She opened her mouth to speak, but he couldn't help but explain himself after years of dodging her judgment.

"I love the brewery. It's soothing and thrilling. The only expectations of me are my own."

"Well." Patricia paused, then seemed to remember she still held the beer he'd brought her, which, admittedly, he'd delivered out of spite, knowing she wouldn't refuse out of politeness. She took a sip and smiled. "It is a good product. And I could put in a good word at some of my favorite restaurants in Seattle."

"Thank you. I would genuinely appreciate that."

Ryder added, "I don't work for free. But I could make an exception. It'll look good on my resume." He winked and flashed Grady a daring grin. He looked to Haley, and she nodded. They all looked to Patricia. Ryder's smile fell, his dark brow heavy. "Mother, I know you mean well. I know you wanted us to have every opportunity. But we're there. Let us float awhile. We're going to stumble now and again. It's good for us."

Patricia's lips pursed together, and she stiffened.

Grady said, "I know it's not always obvious to you, but you raised good kids into capable adults that know their own minds." He rubbed his thumb over Claire's, and she stood tall at his side. "A few hours ago, I was ready to write you off. If you want your children to stick with you, start acting like it. No more pressure, no judgment."

A relaxed expression softening her smile, Haley looked to be breathing the same sigh of relief Grady had been holding in. "I shouldn't be afraid to tell my mother that I'm getting divorced. You'll never be my shoulder to cry on, but I should know, one hundred percent, that you have my back."

Patricia nodded and sipped at the beer again. Her ocean blues were misty and thick. "I've really blown it, haven't I?"

Bill rubbed his hand over her shoulder and nodded to his stepchildren. "You are some great kids. I have no doubt you're going to give us some sweet grandchildren that we can spoil."

Patricia nodded stiffly, looking almost as if she were about to shed a few tears. "I would really like that. Give me a chance?"

"Fresh start, how does that sound?" Grady asked.

# 21

## S-N-O-W-M-A-N

Wait for it. Almost. In. Range.

Claire gripped the wadded snowball, her fingers freezing as she had ditched her mittens long ago, the clunky things completely useless when it came to a decent snowball fight. Grady hollered a war-whoop as he sprinted in her direction.

Now.

From behind the ice cream scoop shrub, Claire popped out and slung the snowball at her fiancé. The white lobular mass floated and bobbed and caught him square in the chest.

Surprised, he froze and looked down at the icy debris that stuck to his sweatshirt. He glanced up with a laughing grin of horror. Quickly popping down to grab a wad of snow, he took off after her.

Before he could reach her, Haley and Ryder leaped out from behind the snowcapped topiaries and nailed snowball after snowball at Grady.

He let out a roar, unconvincing thanks to the mischievous gleam in his sky-blue eyes, and launched at Claire. Without pause, he scooped her over his shoulder and took off toward the stables.

Still firing away with snowballs built with skill and practice, his siblings hammered him in the back. Head precariously close to the target, Claire gripped her knit cap and yelled, "Watch it. Innocent victim here."

Arm drawn back, Ryder bit his lip wickedly and raised his eyebrows. "Says the woman that nearly blinded me with an icy one the second I stepped outside. This truce is over."

Grady raced into the stables and released Claire before ducking behind the doors. He winked and held his finger over his lips. Claire stood in the middle of the room and folded her arms over her chest, waiting for the onslaught.

But no one came. Claire relaxed her shoulders and shook her head at Grady. "I'm not afraid of a few snowballs."

"That's because they're taking it easy on you. Seriously. Patricia used to hate the snow, knowing the three of us would pretend we were waging war on anyone who dared step outside." Grady tossed the snowball behind him and strolled toward Claire. He peeled off his gloves and traced his freezing fingertips along her numb jawline.

She leaned into his touch and smiled, tugging her lip into her teeth and closing her eyes.

"You're freezing," he murmured. He scooped her hands up and held them in his.

It was too tough to resist. Claire rose to her toes and pressed her lips to his. And slipped her hands under his jacket, digging until she found the skin of his abdomen.

Leaping back, Grady squealed, "Fucking shit that's cold."

"Aw. I thought you wanted to warm me up."

He grinned and stepped close again. "Let's try that again. You took me by surprise, that's all."

Before she could nail him with frozen fingertips to the tummy again, the back door swung open and a barrage of snowballs fired at them. Ryder and Haley were laughing like a couple of idiots, even after they ran out and hadn't done more than hit Grady's boots.

As the laughter eased, Ryder looked at Claire and shook his head. "I don't know why I didn't see it before."

"What?" she asked.

"You are as ornery and sappy as Grady. If I'd had half a brain that night we'd met, I'd have offered to be roomies and sent you to meet my softhearted brother."

She leaned into Grady and snuck her hand under his sweatshirt, his skin blazing hot against her frozen fingertips. This time, he didn't leap away, but held her closer. Grady winked at Ryder and said, "I hope to hell that when I meet the perfect match for you, she'll be willing to tolerate you."

"Smartass," Ryder said with a laugh.

With a shake in her head and a growing sadness in her brow, Haley stuffed her ungloved hands into her pockets and said, "Where was all this relationship-clairvoyance when I married that asshole?"

Grady let out a long sigh and said, "I haven't coldcocked anyone in ages. We can swing by San Francisco on our way back north, and I'll stop and pay Nate a visit."

"Get in line. I get the first punch," Haley snarked. She looked around and finally seemed to settle. "Think Patricia heard us?"

Ryder raised an eyebrow and teased his hands in his dark hair. "I'm done trying to please her. She can spend the next thirty years groveling, or I'm out."

"**H**oly crap, the Grand Canyon looks massive from up here." Grady watched Claire as she grinned as wide as the window she looked out, as giddy as she had building the snowman early that morning.

Grady's hand laced with hers, he leaned close and looked out over her shoulder. "Want to stay there our first night on the road?"

"Have you ever been?"

"I have not."

"Then we shall stay there," she said as she unbuckled and made him switch places. "Your turn. It's so different up here compared to down there."

"The view's better from right here," he whispered.

Blushing and adding a snarky eye-roll, she leaned in and landed a lazy kiss. "Then to San Francisco. You've got a fight to start."

"Maybe on our next visit, we'll make a long road trip and make the national park loop."

"I like it." Claire pulled out the crossword puzzle she'd spent most of the flight down on and glared.

Two blank boxes in the bottom right corner dominated the otherwise full scramble of letters. "So close," he teased.

"Irreparably incomplete. I don't even know where I went wrong. But you know what? I'm okay with it."

Suitcases in opposite hands, they linked hands as they walked down the terminal to passenger pick up. Claire bubbled brighter as they neared the exit, scanning expectantly. Grady's chest rose and fell with the gust of wind that washed over them, the arid, sandy scent soothing compared to the chill moisture they'd left. "The air down here always makes me feel like I'm on vacation."

She took a deep breath and smiled. "I suppose it will always smell like home."

Past security, a twosome waved madly on the sunny sidewalk. "Friends of yours?" he asked.

"I have no idea who those people are," she answered with a wink.

Clearly Claire's parents, arms linked tight. Val's eyes were red and watery already. Big as an ox, Roger beamed, and, as Claire had described, an oversized goofball with tracers following his hand as he waved so fast.

Claire beamed and leaned into Grady. "Hi," she said.

Grinning madly, her dad answered, "Hi."

"Um... this is Grady," she announced. "My fiancée." The thrill of saying it out loud hummed over her skin as the reality of it flooded through her.

Grady released her long enough for introductions and linked back up with her. "Hi," he said, shier than he'd ever felt, not a clue what to say.

"Well," Val said, wiping a juicy drop from the corner of her eye. "Grady, we are so glad you're here. I hope you're hungry. We have a favorite hole-in-the-wall restaurant we only take our favorite people to."

"Sounds amazing. We didn't have time to grab dinner before the flight."

Enveloped in bear hugs and bright chatter, Grady was swept across the terminal and they piled into the back of Claire's parents' car. Her brothers met them at the restaurant and the small but mighty crowd kept the restaurant open late.

That night, they stayed with Claire's family, as both agreed they were too weirded out to stay where Ryder and she had lived together. Feeling relief in the overdue vacation, Grady wholeheartedly agreed to stay a few days. With her family, they hiked up Camelback Mountain, ate out at more favorite restaurants to give him a taste of the Southwest, but he was glad to spend most of the time in her parents' pool relaxing.

On the evening before they planned to leave, Claire's car packed to the gills with her belongings, and Ryder's promise to send the rest of her things along later, they curled up in the hammock to watch the stars come out. Grady took a long pull on the local microbrew and sighed. "It's no Black Op, but pretty good."

Claire snuggled into him and took a sip of her beer. Nodding, she considered and said, "I'll never be able to enjoy another beer after trying yours."

He chuckled and turned to look at her. "Is that code? Symbolism?"

"It wasn't meant to be, but it's true."

An inflating mass filled his chest, flooding his veins and rattling his brain, the words couldn't be contained if he'd tried. If he'd wanted to. Riding it, letting loose, he said, "Claire, I love you so much. Thank you."

Lower lip tucked between her teeth, her smile hardly contained, Claire answered, "What are you thanking me for?"

"For not telling me I was too late, that you were going to marry my brother. For not giving up on me. For letting me... *be*."

"In that case, you're welcome." Claire took both of their beers and leaned over the edge to set the drinks on the side table. Turning toward him, she framed his jaw in her hands and touched her lips to his. "I love you, Grady. Thank you for coming to my rescue."

"Anytime."

Immune to the storm of shooting stars above, he took the kiss further, holding her close. Testing, tasting, his veins filled with heat, headier than the whiskey they'd shared that had led to their first kiss. Making up for lost time, he savored each moment with her.

"Grady?" she asked, breathless and nuzzled close.

"Yeah?"

"Let's get a billiard table in our new place."


**The End**

Carrie Thorne is the author of kick-ass romance novels, specializing in white-hot chemistry, healthy relationships, and a mix of action and dreamily falling in love. Whether it's a sinuous flow down a lazy river or evil bad dudes hot on heels, Carrie's stories will draw you in and ruin your sleep. Happily ever afters are for everyone, and kindness is everything.

She's also an introvert who loves people, travel, fitness, video games, food, and is a true Pacific Northwesterner who lives for rain and outdoors and trees and mountains and ocean, and... she's a total dork. At home, she's lucky to have two creative and confident kids, a witty veteran husband she fell at-first-sight for, and a tiny pup snuggled at her side. In addition to writing romance, Carrie has been a nurse practitioner, a Martian and Earthling geologist, a banker, and she is usually elbow-deep in a DIY project in which she bit off more than she could chew.

Where is she now? Depends on the weather. Cozied up by the fire with a steaming mug of black coffee, or stretched out on the hammock with a frothy IPA in the shade of her forest. Either way, she's working on the next great love story to conquer your TBR list.

*www.CarrieThorne.com*

www.ingramcontent.com/pod-product-compliance
Lightning Source LLC
Chambersburg PA
CBHW021131190726
48288CB00008B/2601